SHORT STORIES
and
ASSORTED NIGHTMARES

MARK A. SNYDER

ISBN 978-1-953223-78-4 (paperback)
ISBN 978-1-953223-77-7 (digital)

Rushmore Press LLC
1 800 460 9188
www.rushmorepress.com

Printed in the United States of America

For Ma, Dad, and Skip

CONTENTS

THE LONG FALL

August 1943, Benghazi, Libya

Falling.

The thunderous sound of the collision, the blinding flash of the explosion, the screams of men on the verge of not sounding human, and now—falling. Edward knows he's still in the plane, knows everything is engulfed in an inferno, yet there is no sound of rushing air. Nor is there any sensation of burning, which he *must* be at this very moment. No, nothing at all. Only the feeling of falling and the guilt of bringing down his own ship and the other one, killing both crews as they all plummet earthward.

"Ed! Christ, get up!" Captain Spinelli yells with a firm backhand to Lieutenant Edward J. Mayfield's shoulder. "Jesus, you're soaking wet!"

Surfacing from fathoms of dark, restless slumber, Mayfield bolts upright in his cot and gasps, a trumpeting emanating from his throat as rushing air fills his aching lungs.

"You okay?" Spinelli asks.

Edward heaves air in and out as the experience fades. Falling. It's the worst. He can't imagine anything more horrific. Not even burning alive would be as bad as a long fall with its pit-of-the-stomach distress, head-spinning disorientation, and tortured anticipation of impact.

His eyes begin to drink in the room and focus on the opposite wall of the barracks, where Jane Russell's pinup peers back. Her ample cleavage is exposed as she brandishes a six-shooter while lying back on a bed of hay. "What?" he asks, vaguely aware that the captain spoke to him.

Spinelli repeats his question, but with more concern, "You okay? You're soaked through with sweat. You sick?"

"No. No, I'm okay."

"You wanna see the doc—"

Ed cuts off the question. "I said I'm all right, Cap."

"You'd better be. I don't want anyone who isn't tiptop. Today's number twenty-two. After this one, three more and we're done."

Still panting but no longer gasping, Edward replies, "I know. I know."

"Stateside."

"Yeah, yeah, bombs away," Edward says without enthusiasm.

"Okay, well, get your ass moving, or you'll be late for the briefing."

The Libyan sun has yet to begin its daily torture of the desert below. In the dark predawn hours, it's still a comfortable seventy-five degrees Fahrenheit, with low humidity, as the airmen find their places in the briefing tent. The slight breeze stirs ripples in the canvas stretched over a wooden frame as dust wafts under the string of incandescent lights. At the front, woolen blankets cover maps for this morning's mission, but rumors about their destination have been circulating for days.

"A-ten-*hut!*" shouts the exec from somewhere near the maps as Colonel Matthew "Mac" MacDonald, the base commander, steps onto the riser. Everyone in the briefing snaps to attention.

"As you were!" barks Mac.

Edward, his captain, and the rest of crew of the *Calamity Jane*, a B-24 Liberator that Spinelli named for his girl back home, take their seats near the back of the tent. Although pretty, *Calamity*'s namesake is no ravishing beauty, so Miss Jane Russell has become the crew's unofficial mascot. Images of the buxom Hollywood star adorn both the interior of the fuselage and the barracks.

This will be the twenty-second such briefing the men of the *Calamity Jane* have faced. The countdown is on. Soon they'll return home, having done their part for God and country.

Spinelli lights a cigarette as Mac and his exec pull aside the blankets covering the maps and turn on the lights. A low thrum fills the tent as the crews get their first glimpse of the flight plans, which are marked off with different-colored strings to represent each bombardment group.

Calamity's captain offers a smoke to his men: his copilot, Edward, who is the bombardier/navigator; radio operator Graves, known on board as Marconi; nose gunner Gibbons; waist gunners Sims and Patterson; ball turret gunners Phillips and Levitt; flight engineer Stevens, always "Stevie"; and tail gunner Rodgers.

Although for the crew it's become something of a tradition to accept a cigarette from Cap, it's actually his way of conducting an evaluation of the men under his command. Looking each of his ten crewmembers in the eye as he extends the pack, he decides everyone seems himself, except Edward. Edward accepts the offering easily enough but is still somehow distant. Spinelli says nothing.

Mac begins the briefing.

"Good morning. Your target this morning is Ploesti, Romania. You will be one of five heavy-bombardment groups—178 B-24s— that will perform a low-level raid against nine oil refineries there. Ploesti alone, it is estimated, supplies as much as thirty percent of the Axis's oil. Radio silence is to be strictly maintained …"

Mac continues with the briefing, but he's just a distant buzzing noise. Edward's mind rings with the destination: Ploesti. There it is. The rumors, as usual, were dead on. After weeks of training for low-level bombing and waiting around two ungodly hot days as the ground crew installed a specialized bombsight in *Calamity*, it is officially being called Operation Tidal Wave. Just the sound of it makes Edward feel as though he's leaped off the world's tallest building.

The twenty-second mission. Or is it the twenty-second thousandth? Why does this morning's sortie feel different? They're all the same. The usual butterflies fluttering around in your gut until someone yells out, "Bogies!" and then that moment of terror—but just a moment—until adrenaline takes over. The *thuddings* from the fifty-caliber machine guns ring in your ears as you train your bombsight on the enemy target.

Edward realizes he's missed most of the briefing, but so what? Hasn't he heard it all 21,999 times before? This merely makes it an even twenty-two thousand.

Mac is wrapping up. "Lastly, ball turret gunners are to stand down for this mission. By not deploying them, the reduced drag will increase range and save on fuel. Happy hunting, and Godspeed, gentlemen. Rain death on the bastards."

As Mac exits, his exec orders the crews to their planes.

As *Calamity*'s crew arrives, the ground personnel finish up readying her for flight.

"All good, Sergeant?" Spinelli asks his crew chief.

"Yes, sir, like she was just delivered from Willow Run," the chief boasts.

Once aboard, the crew make themselves as comfortable as possible until takeoff, only this time without their ball turret gunner, Levitt. For the guys in the back of the plane, it means their usual master of ceremonies won't be there to crack his raunchy jokes and keep the conversation—distraction—going. Levitt is a card. He's never at a loss for words, especially the four-letter variety.

Sometimes, this is the hardest part of the mission: the waiting. At least when you're in a fight, you're doing something. You're not thinking. Waiting means playing out endless scenarios and then trying to force them out of your mind—the single greatest challenge between now and the fight. What if? What if? What if! You know you're going to be shot at, you know your ship will take some hits, you know you're sitting atop ten thousand pounds of high explosives … What if? What if? What if! But if that isn't enough, there's still the matter of getting the plane into the air, pregnant with fuel and ammo. And once aloft, there are the weather, mountains, turbulence, tight formations, and eventually, bandits and ack-ack fire.

What if?

Spinelli and Jones finish the preflight checklist.

"Clear on one!" Spinelli cries out his window.

"Clear on one!" the chief shouts back.

With a loud crack and a puff of black smoke, the three-bladed propeller on engine one begins to whine and turn. With vibrations reverberating throughout the plane, the blades spin and blur into a translucent circle rimmed in safety yellow.

"Clear on two!"

"Clear on two!"

The same process is happening across the airfield, with thirty-nine other B-24s cranking over their four engines. As orders to taxi are given, the airfield becomes increasingly obscured by the clouds of dust blown into the air from the prop wash of the behemoth Liberators.

Spinelli closes his window, but it's little defense against the onslaught of the pinkish-gray menace. Over the headset, he can hear Marconi coughing their orders to follow McKittrick's ship, *Hell's a-Poppin'*, to the runway. Spinelli turns to his copilot and sees wet marks traced down his cheeks—pinkish-gray tears at the end of the streaks.

"You okay, Jonesy?" he asks before realizing his own eyes are watering just as bad. No one onboard is immune from the sting of the dust.

Jones, squinting in his direction, motions okay with his fingers and gestures toward his mouth, indicating that he doesn't want to speak anymore. Spinelli nods in agreement.

The cockpit light has taken on a twilight quality thanks to the mechanized dust storm outside; the windows appear almost opaque.

Below the flight deck, at his navigator's table, Edward shakes out his maps to try to keep the dust from collecting on them but finally decides to wait until airborne to deal with it. The dust is relentless and getting thicker as the line of taxiing planes grows.

From his position in the nose turret, Gibbons shouts into the intercom, "Whoa! Whoa! Whoa! Stop!" Without warning, the wingtip of a wayward 24 becomes visible in the Plexiglas nose gun mere inches away—a ghostly apparition appearing out of the manmade whirlwind of flying sand and dust. Spinelli hits the brakes, and *Calamity* lurches to a halt, her crew all flung forward.

"Son of a bitch! That was close!" Spinelli hollers at the errant bomber in his path, only to regret the mouthful of dust awarded him for his outburst. He spits on the cockpit floor. "Shit."

The ground controllers direct the misguided craft back to its appropriate place in line for taxi and takeoff.

Finally, after a twenty-five-minute eternity, Spinelli turns *Calamity* into the wind and puts on the brakes. *Hell's a-Poppin'* is now out of the way, and he and Jones push *Calamity*'s throttles to full power. She shakes under the strain, and just as soon as maximum RPM is reached, Spinelli releases the brakes and *Calamity* begins to lumber down the dirt strip, kicking up a dust storm to rival any Benghazi has ever seen. The sixty-thousand-pound ship slowly builds speed.

"One twenty … V1 … Rotate," Spinelli orders as he and Jones pull back on the yokes and the nose wheel lifts off the ground. "One thirty," he says as the giant frees herself of her earthly bond. "One forty … flaps up. Gear up."

"Flaps up," Jones replies. "Gear up."

"Okay, let's catch up to the formation," Spinelli hollers over the roar of *Calamity*'s four Pratt & Whitney engines as he cranes his neck to look through the top of the windshield to locate *Hell's a-Poppin'*. "There, let's slide 'er in next to McKittrick." The remaining few bombers of the group join in as they cross the coast, the Mediterranean Sea sparkling below as the planes slowly climb.

"Okay, guys," Spinelli says to the crew, "that was lousy, but they say a bad beginning leads to a good ending, so let's try and get this dust off everything, fly the fuck out of this mission, and get back to base in one piece."

As the bomber climbs, the temperature drop is rapid. As cruising altitude approaches, it's below freezing, so the crewmen don their jackets and gloves. By the time the formation reaches the Pindus Mountains, the climb over will require the crew to use their oxygen masks. But that obstacle is still hours away. The wait begins.

Hours pass as Sims, Patterson, and Rodgers attempt to engage in small talk, but without Levitt, there doesn't seem to be much point. The flight is level and smooth, and without the familiar levity of the absent ball-turret gunner, only the din of the engines fills the back of the plane. Just as Sims is about to make another attempt at starting a conversation, they feel *Calamity* maneuvering—not something that normally happens in formation. In unison they all find the same three words, "What the hell?"

Rodgers keys his microphone. "Tail gunner to pilot: Everything okay up there, Cap?"

"Yeah. Stay off the headset," comes Spinelli's terse reply.

Waist gunner Patterson motions for the others to stay in place. "I'll go check it out," he says.

Making his way through the tightly packed bomb bay across the nine-inch-wide catwalk, Patterson enters the forward part of the fuselage and spots Graves, the radio operator. "Hey, Marconi, what's going on?"

Graves replies, "Not sure. A few ships dropped out of formation, and with radio silence, no one knows why, but Jonesy thinks someone went down. The others may have gone to look for parachutes or Mae Wests."

Edward Mayfield's headset crackles, "Pilot to navigator: Ed, I'm looking at our formation and somehow someone screwed the pooch. I'm not going to trust anyone but you to get us to our waypoint at Pitesti before making the turn to the target at Ploesti. Looks like we're in the lead."

"Roger, Cap," Ed replies.

Patterson makes his way back to the rear of the aircraft. Sims and Rodgers are waiting, faces upturned as he emerges from the bomb bay. Patterson yells above the engine noise and open waist-gunner portals. "We lost a ship. A few others broke formation to search for survivors, and when they did, because there's no radio contact, other planes were caught off guard and had to maneuver, so the formation is all FUBAR, and there's no way to coordinate under radio blackout." There's no further conversation. Every crewman is preoccupied with "What if?"

The ragtag formation is approaching the mountains. As *Calamity*'s group climbs above Bulgaria's peaks, the weather closes in. "Pilot to navigator: We're starting to get socked in, Ed. Can you plot us a course more easterly? I can see more sky off to our port side."

"Affirmative, Captain, but it's going to put us behind the other groups, assuming they stay on course," Edward replies.

"Get me blue sky. Without a proper formation and no radio contact, we need all the visual we can get."

"Roger, come left to three-three-zero. Increase altitude to twelve thousand. We're going to burn a little more fuel, but we're all right."

"Roger, three-three-zero, twelve thousand."

Only the highest peaks have any trace of snow, most of the hills and valleys are lush and green, as the bombardment group plods along behind Calamity Jane.

"Navigator to pilot."

"Go ahead, Ed."

"Cap, the town just ahead is Lukovit. When we reach the river, come right to zero-three-zero to get back on course to our waypoint at Pitesti. I place us about sixty miles behind the other groups."

Descending the opposite side of the mountains, the crew begins removing their jackets. Captain Spinelli is just about to inform the crew to stay sharp and be ready for antiaircraft and bogies, when a frantic voice screeches in his ears. For a moment, he doesn't recognize Marconi's panic-laced voice.

"Radio to pilot! Radio to pilot!"

"What do you have, Marconi?"

"Cap, all hell's breaking loose! Radio silence is broken. The three-seventy-sixth missed its landmark and from what I can tell, ended up near Bucharest! That's HQ for Romania's air defenses! The entire mission is lit up—heavy AA being reported at each target by every group!"

"Have any changes to our orders been issued?"

"Negative!"

"Pilot to navigator: Ed, give me a speed run to target—to Ploesti!"

"Cap, come right to zero-four-five!"

Spinelli keys his radio microphone and intercom. "This is *Calamity Jane* in the lead. As I'm sure you're aware, we've lost the element of surprise. Be prepared for heavy AA at the target. We're headed down to five hundred feet. Course: zero-four-five. All crews stand by. Release on our signal."

"Pilot to crew: man your guns!" Edward's role as navigator now takes a back seat as he readies the bombsight. With no ceremony in handing off one job for the other, Captain Spinelli makes the call into his microphone, "Bombardier ... Ed, stand by to take her on the bomb run!"

"Standing by!"

Before his voice fades in the headsets, the sky is being filled with bursts of ack-ack. At first, it's being shot over the group.

The first round of antiaircraft to hit *Calamity* pierces the fuselage just in front of Sims at the starboard waist gun, blasting clean through her right side and exiting through the ceiling before exploding and shaking the entire ship.

At first, Patterson doesn't hear Sims's screams, drowned out by the explosion and the fifty-caliber eruptions in front of him and from Rodgers in the tail turret.

"Gog, oh, Gog, oh Gog!" Sims is screaming.

Patterson drops to his knees to help Sims, trying to find a comfortable spot on the floor, awash in a sea of spent casings. Sims holds both hands to the left side of what was once his face as blood gushes between his fingers, shrapnel protruding above his cheekbone, his tongue nearly severed.

"Jesus, Sims! Hold on! Here, hold this tight to you face!" Patterson attempts to use the woolen side of the waist gunner's jacket to apply pressure, which causes Sims to scream in louder agony.

The plane shakes as black clouds of AA erupt all around, the shrapnel hitting her aluminum skin like a summer hailstorm. The ground guns have adjusted for the low altitude, and the group is now in the midst of hell.

"Cap, Cap, Sims is hit! Bad!" Patterson yells into his intercom.

"Do what you can for him, but man your gun!"

Sims has stopped screaming, passed out from the pain. Patterson grabs the first-aid kit, unspools a length of gauze and tries to secure the blood-soaked jacket to the side of Sims's face—the gauze grows red and wet immediately.

"Sorry, buddy. I don't know what else to do," Patterson says quietly to his friend and returns to his gun.

"Navigator to pilot: Ready to commence bomb run, Cap! Taking control of the ship."

"The ship is yours, Ed. Do good!"

Spinelli and Jones look at each other as the phantom voice from below the cockpit counts off the distance to the targeted refinery and the cables-and-pulleys ghost moves the controls without their touch.

The captain radios the group, "*Calamity Jane* to bomb group, we're on the target run. Stand by for the drop."

"Bomb bay doors open. Less than a minute to drop," Edward announces.

After a brief eternity, Edward counts aloud to the crew, "Target in three, two, one ... bombs away!" The aircraft bounds upward as the bombs disgorge from her belly, lightening their load. "Munitions clear! Bomb bay doors closed! Ship's control is back to you, Cap! One-niner-zero back to Benghazi!"

The rest of the group drops on *Calamity*'s command. Spinelli begins to turn the ship around and head to the south.

"Captain!" shouts Marconi. "Planes behind us reporting secondary explosions! We hit our mark!"

"Band—"

Before Rodgers can finish his warning from the tail turret, a twenty-millimeter shell hits *Calamity* just below and behind Jones's seat. In an instant, the cockpit fills with smoke and flame. From his position below the flight deck, Edward springs up, seizes a fire extinguisher, and sprays down the copilot's side of the confined space. *Calamity* rolls hard to port, and Spinelli fights for control.

Every fifty caliber aboard is firing at the Romanian and German fighters buzzing what's left of the formation. Even as *Calamity* seems to want to roll over onto her back, the flight engineer leaves his place, making his way through the empty bomb bay to man Sims's guns.

"Jonesy, hard right on the aileron! Feels like one of the control surfaces was hit! Jonesy, hard right!"

Through the acrid haze in the cockpit, Edward can see that Jones is unresponsive, his body and head limp and undulating with the movement of the ship. Edward drops to the floor and pushes the right foot pedal with both hands as hard as he can, helping Spinelli correct the plane's attitude;

"She's fighting me, but she's flying!" Spinelli shouts to Edward. "Okay, I think I've got 'er back. Check on Jones! Is he dead?"

"I don't think so, Cap, but he's bad!"

The sound of bullets ripping through the plane's skin causes everyone to flinch.

Spinelli keys his mic and shouts into his headset, "See what you can do for him! Damage report!"

"Patterson here. Sims is dead. We've got a bunch of holes in us, Cap, but I got the bastard that hit us with the twenty millimeter. I think that other ship off our left can confirm the kill. I can see smoke trailing from number two. Wait! Scratch that! Two's on fire, Cap! Repeat: number two is on fire!"

Spinelli cuts the power to feather the engine and hits the extinguisher. "Is it out?"

"Affirmative."

"Keep an eye on it in case it flares back up. Anything else you can see?"

"Yeah, Cap, tail gunner tells me that we lost the top half of the rudder on the right-side tail, and I can see holes in our starboard wing, but God knows how, nothing appears to be leaking out!"

"Christ, is that all?"

"That's all, Cap."

"Pilot to nose gunner."

"Pilot to nose gunner."

"Pilot to nose gunner. Gibbons?"

Edward, trying to find the source of Jones's bleeding, looks at the captain.

Spinelli motions with his head for Edward to check on Gibbons.

As Edward climbs down from the flight deck and crawls to the nose turret, he can already see Gibbons's blood and what he assumes are his brains splattered on the Plexiglas. He doesn't have to push all the way into the space to see that Gibbons took one to the head. He climbs back to the flight deck and shakes his own head no. Spinelli understands. Edward steps back into the flight-engineer position, where he fights the urge to vomit.

The barrage of fighters is intense but short-lived. The mountains are on the horizon and a little ways after that, the Aegean Sea, the Med, and back to Benghazi.

Keying his mic, Spinelli calls, "Pilot to port waist gunner: Patterson, you read me?"

"I read you, Cap, go ahead."

"Which ship is that off our left flank? Is that McKittrick?"

"Negative, Cap, that's *Screwball* ... Miller's ship."

"Roger."

"Marconi, raise Miller. Have them look at us from below and check us for damage—leaks."

"Roger, Cap!"

The late-afternoon heating of the air is creating turbulence, and *Calamity*'s control-surface damage is making her hard to handle. Spinelli is sweating through his flight suit and cannot take his hands off the yoke.

"Ed, come take the right-hand seat, will ya?" Spinelli hollers behind him, where, under normal circumstances, Stevie would be sitting in the flight-engineer's seat, but he's still manning Sims's gun, just in case.

"Okay, Cap," Edward responds, still reeling from the sight and smell of the nose turret.

"Cap," Marconi reports via headset, "*Screwball*'s moving in under us now. They're banged up too, lots of injuries, but none fatal. Miller says he can confirm Patterson's kill on the Messerschmitt. He also says we lost about a third of the group."

"Jesus wept," Spinelli says to himself. "Roger."

The plane's damage is creating buffeting that makes handing it in turbulence that much more challenging, and Spinelli's arms are beginning to fatigue.

"Ed, take Jonesy's seat, will ya? Hurry up, I need a hand with this beast!"

"I think he's dead, Cap."

"What?"

"Jones. He's dead."

"Damn it. Damn it! All right, well, there isn't anything we can do for him now. We have the rest of the crew to get home. I can't take my hands off the controls, so you're going to have to pull him out of the seat yourself. Drag him back toward the engineer's section and cover him with something but do it fast; I can't hold this by myself much longer."

Edward bends and slides his arms beneath Jones's as he prepares to hoist the dead weight of a full-grown man out of his seat. In his head he counts: one ... two ... three! With all his might, Edward pulls up on the body of his dead shipmate, only to fall backward with only Jones's top half—the twenty millimeter that hit the ship severed him in two just below his chest. Edward stumbles backward, directly into Spinelli. In shock, Edward does not immediately realize that Spinelli has lost control of *Calamity*.

In less time than it took for Ed to process what has happened, *Calamity* inverts, rolling hard to her left, and plummets directly into *Screwball*. The explosion of the two ships is immediate and intense, blowing both to pieces.

Falling.

The thunderous sound of the collision, the blinding flash of the explosion, the screams of men on the verge of not sounding human—and now—falling. Edward knows he's still in the plane, knows everything is engulfed in an inferno, yet there is no sound of rushing air. Nor is there any sensation of burning—which he *must* be at this very moment. No, nothing at all, only the feeling of falling and the guilt of bringing down his own ship and the other one, killing both crews and, in mere seconds—himself, as they all plummet earthward.

"Ed! Christ, get up," Captain Spinelli yells with a firm backhand to Lieutenant Edward J. Mayfield's shoulder. "Jesus, you're soaking wet!"

THE ABANDONED

Friday

Frank thumbs the button on the steering wheel to turn off the satellite radio. Today, even his favorite oldies station is mocking him with Paul Anka singing "Lonely Boy." He's hardly a boy, of course, being in his mid-forties. He has been lonely, though—very lonely—following the divorce and all the typical lifestyle adjustments: furniture, pots, pans, utensils ... and, after eighteen years, learning once again to live alone. He hasn't done that since meeting *her* at his first real job, a few years out of college.

On the way back to the office, he's mulling over a luncheon conversation with Jeff. The remark was meant as a lighthearted joke, but it struck close to home. Jeff had suggested that Frank purchase a myna bird as a companion because it had worked so well for his invalid aunt. I mean, come on. Certainly, the bird talks, but it's only mimicking human speech. Obviously, it's a poor replacement for conversation, and only a real smart-ass like Jeff would have made the suggestion. He hasn't changed at all since college. Well, at least, his can't-go-too-low sense of humor hasn't. But the man wasn't completely predictable. Frank would *never* have imagined a wise guy like Jeff ending up as district attorney. Regardless of Jeff's honorable status, Frank immediately regretted admitting that having too much time alone wasn't easy for him.

"Asshole," Frank mutters as he turns his Caddy into the parking garage, then laughs to himself. "I should have said *that* to your face. But you probably would have laughed." Now feeling fairly certain that his DA buddy hadn't meant to compare him to an eighty-year-old stroke victim, he puts aside the story of the human vegetable and her myna bird, focusing instead on pulling his newly acquired behemoth into his personal parking spot.

Before shutting off the engine, he takes a moment to enjoy the leather- and new-car smell of the ninety-thousand-dollar vehicle. Somehow, a few deep breaths help eradicate the worry associated with the cost of reinventing himself. The settlement was amicable enough, since she's able to provide for herself—no alimony and no kids, so no child support. She got the house but can't afford it alone—neither of them could. While it's on the market, he's paying half the mortgage.

Nonetheless, she'll get the equity when it does sell. Getting rid of that payment would be enough to take the edge off, but, in the meantime, for the first time in many years, Frank is living paycheck to paycheck.

The good news is that he's dropped a few of the pounds he put on since quitting smoking, though that's because his appetite makes only rare appearances these days. Yet, he's happy to cinch his belt a little tighter in the morning while donning his suit pants. And in the same instant, he wonders if the bankroll he put down on the new Cadillac, with its Super Cruise and twin turbos, would have been better spent on a personal trainer, gym membership, hair plugs, and a little cosmetic dental work. He'll ponder that same thought once a month for the next six years.

"All right, back to the grind," he says to himself as he slides out of the driver's seat, swings the door shut, and heads for the elevator. The lights flash and the alarm beeps as he walks away, no need to lock up. It does that on its own.

Making his way to his office, he can't help but notice the women. There are a lot—many of them straight out of college. That's how Marjorie, the editorial director, keeps costs low. Hire them freshly minted, the bright ones, of course, at a minimal salary, then mentor and mold them in your image and style before they can develop one of their own. Frank even thinks about summoning up the courage to ask one of them out now that he's a free man, but he knows there's not one of them within whom the sight of him strikes a lustful chord. In most cases, he's old enough to be their father.

For now, he discreetly admires the occasional down-the-blouse peek of cleavage or a bit of stocking top as he passes through the Cube Farm—a sea of prefab cubicles with built-in desks and shelves that stretch from one end of the large office space to the other, standard issue for editorial assistants. The senior staffers all have real offices along the exterior walls. Looking across the space brings to mind a life-size game of Whack-A-Mole, as assistants pop up when leaving their chairs or sit back down after returning from the printer cubby, toilet, or break room.

Busy drafting a schematic rendering for a new project, a light rap on Frank's office doorjamb pulls him back into the here and now. He turns to find Yolanda Fernandez's petite though curvy frame leaning partway into his office. She's one of the young women Frank often fantasizes about. Standing four-foot-ten, with natural blond hair and large, bright-blue eyes, people are often surprised to learn that she's of full Cuban descent. Her features appear more Aryan than Latin. Despite her stature, her tiny frame supports a voluptuous set of breasts, which she dresses to accentuate, counterbalanced by a derrière that is ample and perfectly heart-shaped. With a tiny waist transitioning between her northern and southern hemispheres, she is the personification of the hourglass figure.

"Knock, knock," says Yolanda.

"Hi, Yoli, what can I do for you?"

"I have a USB thingy from Marjorie with all the materials for the automation project; she said it was too much to attach to an email."

"Oh, okay. I was just working on the schema for that. Here, I'll take it." He spins his chair in her direction and extends his left hand. Instead of entering his office, she grabs the doorjamb with her left hand, leans in, bends down, and offers the thumb drive in her right. This awkward position further opens the top of her blouse, affording Frank an unobstructed view of her capacious bosoms, to the point that he can see them nestled into the cups of a lacy, white bra that barely covers what he imagines are pert, pink nipples.

He can feel his face flush, having made practically no effort to avert his eyes from drinking in her incredible upper torso. "Thanks, Yoli," he stammers, finally making eye contact. She's simply smiling back at him. He feels as if he's about to break into a sweat.

"You're welcome," she says in a cheery voice and pivots to leave his office, her right hand now flexing in a bye-bye wave.

He inhales and sighs audibly. "Wow," says Frank under his breath. He turns back to the computer; momentum has vanished. He stares at the schematic on the monitor—boxes connected by lines, some dashed, some solid in varying colors, arrows indicating information flow, icons showing various databases—but only two thoughts rattle around in his head: the image of Yolanda's amazing rack and another Friday night with nothing to do.

Fuck you, Paul Anka.

Saturday

Despite his best effort to sleep in on Saturday morning, Frank awakens at five. Through the window, the sky is showing just the faintest shades of purple as day begins to break. There's no point in trying to fall back asleep. Since he was a kid, it's always been this way: once he's up, he's *up*.

He slowly walks the short distance from bedroom to kitchenette. It's not much, but then, what does he really need? Right now, it didn't really matter whether he was in a luxury one-bedroom apartment or the Taj Mahal; coffee is the only priority. Without thinking about the process, he fills the paper filter with four generous scoops—that took some getting used to after eighteen years of eight. He grapples with the pot to fill the water to the appropriate line. He may be awake, but sleep hasn't yet left his eyes.

Finally filled with the desired amount of water, he pours the pot contents into the coffeemaker reservoir and flips the switch. For a moment, he allows himself to covet the coffeemaker at *their* house, one that you prep the night before—set it and forget it. He didn't even need an alarm clock in those days; the aroma of the fresh-brewed coffee would have him up long before *she* even stirred.

Now, while the coffee brews, he heads to the shower, where he's sure to encounter Yolanda—in his mind's eye—and this time, when he takes her hand to accept the thumb drive, he won't let go of her, nor will she resist his advances ... or maybe she will—that might be even more gratifying. Either way, however it plays out, the stark fact is that once he's out of the shower, he'll still be the only one drinking coffee at the table.

As he sips his java, he ponders what to do with his day off. It wasn't long ago when setting up a golf date with a few buddies was a Herculean task, between trying to coordinate a day that worked for everyone, dealing with the usual honey-do lists, and for the guys that had kids—well, it almost wasn't worth it. How frustrating! But even more aggravating, now that Frank has all the time in the world to do as he pleases, it most certainly isn't the case for any of the guys. But it becomes doubly irritating when their family obligations prevent them from getting together with him; he detects pity in their voices and they *apologize*. It's gotten to the point that he rarely texts or emails—maybe reply, but not initiate. Everyone has something going on, so why bother? Yes, Frank's weekends are his own.

It's Saturday afternoon and, unbelievably, he is reading. He reads a lot these days, enjoying the latest thrillers to hit the *New York Times* best-seller list and the occasional classic that he'd never had time for, but after a few hours, he needs a break. There's only so much television one can watch, even with a hundred-plus channels.

He thinks about going to the movies, but it's never really been an enjoyable experience for him, even before flying solo. The expense, the endless promos and previews, the sticky floor, then having to sit and listen to the crinkling of candy wrappers and the annoying noises of ill-behaved kids. He shudders at the thought.

Frank decides to head down to the shopping district. "What the hell?" he says to himself as he pockets his key fob, emblazoned with the Cadillac logo.

After parking his Caddy on level four of the garage, being particular to find a corner space to minimize the possibility of having a ding inflicted on his pristine ride, he takes the elevator down to ground level. He strolls toward Sebastian Street, a quaint cobblestone lane only four blocks long, bisected by now-defunct trolley tracks and lined on both sides by two- and three-story buildings with brick-and-wood façades. It's intended to be a step backward in time. The historical society maintains aggressive authority over any outdoor signage or lighting, except during the Christmas season, when stores are allowed to go all out.

For now, he's content to saunter along the west side of the street, passing the various sounds and scents: the candy store's homemade fudge wafts thick and sweet from the open front doors. Passing the toy shop, the G-scale locomotive whistle blows relentlessly as it lugs its tender, boxcar, and caboose in an infinite loop. Ye Olde British Pub, true to its claims of authenticity etched on the windows, smells of stale beer. As he approaches the end of the first block, he peers into the window of a store billing itself as a five-and-dime but is skeptical any such-priced booty could be found there.

Out of the corner of his eye, Frank spies something of interest: a bookstore. Not one of the megasellers, but an honest-to-God independent shop with a Books—New & Used sign, weathered and faded, but still legible on the front window. It's right on the next corner, and the awning over the entrance is absolutely beckoning him to come inside. There's no business name on either the window or awning, only that Books—New & Used sign.

A small brass bell on the interior of the door announces his entry into the dimly lit space. *It's wonderful, exactly what a bookstore should be*, he thinks. He takes two careful steps down from the entryway as the wooden floorboards creak beneath his feet. All the walls are lined with book-filled shelves There's a ladder attached to runners for exploring higher up; in the middle of the room are tables, some piled high with volumes of who-knows-what, others with a semblance of order and organization. Desk lamps glow on each of the tables, allowing patrons to peruse the store's offerings. The shop has a slightly musty, but not at all unpleasant, scent. It reminds Frank of his childhood, when, after a long winter, his family would open up their seashore summerhouse.

"Good afternoon. May I help you find something?" says a voice from his right. He turns to see a young woman behind the counter, leaning against the windowed wall, staring down at her phone. She is backlit by the sunshine pouring in, but he can make out short, black hair with blue highlights, an exposed midriff with a belly button ring, large holes in her earlobes, and tattoos on her shoulder. "No, thank you. I'm just browsing," Frank explains.

Her gaze never leaving her phone, she replies, "All right, please feel free to let me know if I may be of any assistance."

Her proper grammar is a bit stilted and not what he'd expect from this very attractive but distracted young woman apparently hellbent on punishing her parents.

He makes his way down the left-hand side of the bookstore, opposite the counter, where the shopgirl remains transfixed by her cell. He approaches the far corner of the space, his gaze fixed on a wide spine with gold-leaf lettering that bears a single word, "Alchemy." *Ah, that sounds interesting*, he thinks. As he passes a table on his right piled high with books and reaches up for the literary curiosity, there is a barely detectable movement in his peripheral vision accompanied by a sort of clicking sound.

Momentarily forgetting the book, his arm still extended in midreach, he turns to discover a large, gray parrot making short, side-to-side movements on a perch atop a large metal cage. The top of the cage is wide open like the metal doors in a sidewalk standing upright in anticipation of a delivery into a building's basement.

"Well, hello there," says Frank.

The bird stills itself, cocks its head, and studies Frank with the golden eye on the left side of its head. The right eye is not visible from his vantage point.

"Hello," he repeats, but the bird continues to stare, remaining motionless.

"Pretty bird. Pretty bird," he squawks, remembering something a childhood friend once taught a parakeet—he called it a budgie—to say, but this much larger bird merely continues to observe him.

"Okay, have it your way. I tried. Be antisocial. See if I care," Frank says to the gray bird as he turns to once again locate the book with the one-word title. Before he can resume his search, a small voice with the slow, cracked but articulate quality of a frail old woman says, "Take me home, Frankie."

Startled, he spins toward the bird, but it doesn't move or relax its piercing glare.

"What did you say?" Franks asks.

With a nearly imperceptible movement of its black beak, its golden eye laser-focused and the pupil slightly dilated, in the same voice, the bird tells Frank, "Do not go 'round the milk wagon."

"What? ... What?" He pauses for a moment to look around, thinking perhaps it's a gag—*Candid Camera* or the like—but the shopgirl is still glued to her phone, its screen illuminating her delicate facial features in the shadows. There's no one pulling his leg.

With a shake of its head and body, the parrot recommences its original pattern of sidestepping and bobbing.

"Hello? Pretty bird." He wants to hear the bird speak again. "Polly wanna' cracker?" But the bird pauses only long enough to wipe its beak on the perch before again moving back and forth.

He spends a few minutes more watching the bird, but it says nothing more and continues its routine, never removing its gaze from Frank.

Approaching the shopgirl, Frank can see that her head is bent; her glazed-over eyes are still scanning whatever social media site or text app she'd been on when he first entered. He interrupts, "Excuse me, miss, what can you tell me about that bird in the far corner—the parrot?"

Without physical acknowledgement of any sort, her eyes never leaving her device, but still polite as can be, she replies, "It's an African grey parrot, we don't know his name. He belonged to one of the shop owner's relatives, who passed away several months ago. Mrs. McElroy, the owner, has been taking care of him but instructed me to tell anyone interested that he's for sale."

"Does it talk a lot? Is it trained?"

"I'm here with him most of the day, and I often hear his nails on the metal bars when he climbs around the cage. He occasionally makes clicking and whistling sounds, but I haven't heard him talk. To be honest, I'm a little frightened of him, which is why I asked Mrs. McElroy to keep him in the back. It's nothing against the parrot. I get freaked, um, I mean become uneasy around large birds, even seagulls unsettle me when I'm at the beach."

"I see."

"If you're interested, I believe she is asking fifteen-hundred dollars, including the cage. Oh, and I can tell you that she recently took him to the vet. He's in good health, and his nails and wings have been trimmed, so he won't scratch if you hold him, and he can't fly away."

"Oh, uh, no, no, thanks. I was just curious. I appreciate the information, though. Thanks," Frank replies, wondering if she ever even looked at him. *I could rob the shop, and she'd never be able to describe her assailant*, he thinks. "Well, thank you again," he offers, making his way to the door.

"Thank you for coming in, and please be sure to visit us again," the shopgirl says, eyes steadfastly locked on her device.

He walks along the rest of the west side of Sebastian Street and halfway back down the east side without much conscious thought about the shops and boutiques. Even though he doesn't have much of an appetite these days, the scent of garlic always makes his stomach rumble and his mouth water. The aromas wafting out of Pica's Pizza are too much to resist, and he stops in for a slice and a beer.

It only killed a few hours, but not a bad way to burn part of a Saturday, he thinks as he steps off the elevator onto parking level four. "Maybe I'll come back tomorrow for that book."

He gets into his car and pushes the start button—no need for keys. So long as the key fob is in the proximity, it's unnecessary to reach into one's pocket to unlock a door, pop the trunk, or start the engine.

Frank descends the garage levels, moving slowly and steadily around corners barely wide enough for a car, but when he gets to level two, there's a traffic jam. After a solid five minutes, he hasn't moved, and cars are now stacked up behind him.

A half-level down, he sees a woman approaching the passenger door of a car several hundred feet ahead of him in line. He steps out and hollers down to her, "Pardon me, miss, do you know what's going on?"

She looks around, unable to discern the direction of the question in the echoing cement structure.

"Up here!" Frank waves an arm.

She spots him and says, "There's been a power outage, and the electronic arms and payment kiosks won't work. They're supposedly sending someone over to open the gate manually!"

He flashes her an OK, which he transitions into a thumbs up. "Thank you!" Before slipping back into his Caddy, he relays the message to folks behind him, reminiscent of the way covered wagons communicated as they traveled in long trains to tame the West. *A few minutes without power, and we're helpless*, he thinks. He thumbs the satellite-radio button, but the parking structure blocks the signal. "Shit," he complains to the dashboard and fumbles to figure out how to get good old-fashioned commercial radio.

Twenty-two minutes later, he's finally moving again. The garage manager has the electronic arm up and is letting everyone out without paying until, with just three cars to go, the arm comes down. He sees the manager and the driver of the car at the gate briefly exchanging words, before the manager shrugs and walks away. The driver slips a credit card into the parking kiosk; the gate lifts; and he's gone—back to normal operation. Now, Frank is fuming as he yells in frustration, "I may not have anything to do, but I don't want to sit and wait to not do it!—or whateverthefuck!"

When it's his turn at the gate, the first two attempts to swipe his card fail. After realizing he's inserting it backward, as he turns it around and it falls from his hand. "Uh, shit!" he says, opening the door, but there isn't much room between the car and the kiosk. His hand squeezes down past the rocker panel, and as his fingertips scrape the cement floor, he touches the edge of the card but can't get a grip. It feels as if the seat belt is going to slice through his left ear, before he finally gets a fingernail under the edge of the card and grabs it. He sits back up, closes the door, and checks the mirror, only to see the guy behind him laughing and shaking his head. "Fuck you," he says into the rearview mirror, hoping the window tint is dark enough so the guy can't read his lips.

The gate lifts, and he steps hard on the gas, rear tires sluing and smoking, the squeals echoing throughout the garage. "Easy, easy," he says to himself, but no sooner does he turn down the narrow, two-block, one-way street that leads to the main avenue than he finds himself stuck behind a small box truck. "Ugh! C'mon!" he gripes.

On the next block, the street widens to two lanes, so he just needs to keep his cool until then, but the truck is slower than molasses in January. As they approach the next block, the truck is veering toward the right, but at a snail's pace. As soon as there's enough room, Frank again punches the accelerator to get around it, just as a cyclist bolts out from a blind spot created by the larger vehicle. The cyclist has his arm extended to indicate a left-hand turn, but there isn't time to react. The Caddy's auto-braking sensors clamp the brakes down hard, and a collision light flashes in the heads-up display on the windshield, but Frank's car just has too much momentum to stop in time.

The cyclist's helmeted head bounces off the hood, then the windshield, and his rag-doll body slides off, coming to rest beside the driver's side door, with the bike laying in the street a few yards away.

Frank hits the OnStar emergency button as he watches the truck driver climb down and approach the cyclist. The biker is moving—a good sign—and Frank yells to the truck driver not to move the cyclist until paramedics arrive. As he's rolling down the window to repeat his warning, OnStar's advisor comes on and asks the nature of the emergency.

As he explains the circumstances, a passerby flags down a patrol cop. Help is on the scene, so Frank ends the call and goes out to talk to the policeman, cyclist—now on his feet—and truck driver.

Getting out of the car, Frank sees the side of the truck for the first time, and a chill runs through him. Staring back at him is an illustration of an oversize, green cartoon cow—the mascot of Organic Dairy Farms. He hears the parrot's voice in his head, "Do not go 'round the milk wagon."

At home that evening, sipping a Scotch, he plays the day's events over in his mind, trying to find some logical explanation. He must have misunderstood the bird. It's just not possible to believe otherwise.

"Do not go 'round the milk wagon."

It's a relief that the cyclist wasn't badly hurt and equally so that the cop ticketed him for making a left turn from the right lane. Frank initially had doubts about the trucker, who seemed angry at him, but once the policeman explained that bicyclists have to follow the rules of the road, the guy's attitude seemed to shift from supporting the biker to supporting him.

"Do not go 'round the milk wagon."

Frank pours himself a double, this time not bothering with ice.

"Do not go 'round the milk wagon."

Sunday

The bell over the shop door tinkles as Frank enters. In his head, however, it's as if a church-bell clapper has gone amok, thanks to his unabashed imbibing the previous evening. A small, backlit figure to his right turns toward him and in a relic voice says, "Good morning, may I help you?"

Frank, expecting the shopgirl from his previous visit, is greeted by a tiny and withered old woman. "Oh, uh, good morning. I … uh, I just thought I'd browse a bit, if that's all right?"

"Oh, certainly, certainly. If there is any way I may be of assistance, please don't hesitate to ask. We're a bit old-fashioned here—no computer machines to catalogue everything. We rely more on the Dewey decimal system, though to be completely honest, I go more by memory to know where things are."

In his best attempt at cordiality, through the pounding behind his dried-out eyes, Frank replies, "That's most impressive, considering the size of your inventory."

In appreciation, she nods her head toward him, a wrinkled grin illuminating one side of her face, the other in shadow. He returns the gesture with a smile of his own, as warm as he can muster without too much head motion, in an effort to prevent his brain from sloshing around anymore than it already is.

He heads toward the left-rear corner of the store, pretending to slowly scan the titles on the shelves, not wanting to appear too obvious in his purpose. At first, as he makes his way to the back, he doesn't see the cage, but as he passes the overstacked table of books, he spies it. It's been moved a couple feet, and the top doors that support the perch are now closed. The bird within is sidestepping left to right, right to left, while bobbing its head, but already its brilliant amber eye is fixed on Frank.

"Hello again," Frank says in a hushed tone. "Remember me?"

The bird continues its dance and gaze.

Frank steps closer to the cage, but once again seeing the creature, he begins to doubt his earlier experience. He wonders what kind of trick his mind played on him, though the very real damage to his car offers some evidence of sanity. "Nothing you'd care to say to me?" he asks.

Side to side, bobbing its head, the parrot keeps watch on Frank.

He thinks for a moment. *Perhaps it was something I said? Maybe the cadence of my speech got the bird to react ...* He sighs, crouches, and places his hands on his knees to study his subject a bit more closely.

The bird stops, cocks its head, and its left eye riveted on Frank, says, "Take me home, Frankie."

Frank bolts upright, stifling a gasp with his right hand, his eyes wide open. The bird doesn't move, with the exception of its eye, which continues to home in on his eyes, never breaking contact. He peers around the stack of books on the table, but the old woman doesn't seem to have noticed anything.

He takes a breath and asks the bird, "Are you fuckin' with m ... are you for rea ...

Can you understand me? Bird, can you understand me?"

The parrot, motionless, only stares.

"Say it again, birdie, say it again," he commands softly. "How do you know my name? Damn it, say something."

Stoic silence.

He is leaning forward to again get a glimpse of the elderly owner, who is still going about her business, when he hears the parrot speak. "I can help you get that girl Yo-lan-da."

He snaps his head around to stare at the bird, which resumes its now-familiar dance and bob.

"What?" he hollers within a whisper. "Say that again. What did you say? Bird, talk to me! What did you say?"

Frank's heart races within his chest; he consciously concentrates on slowing his breathing and pulse, and feeling somewhat under control, proceeds to the counter.

"Did we find something we like?" inquires the old woman.

"No, oh, well, yes, actually. I thought you were talking about books ..." Noting the perplexed expression on her road-mapped face, Frank clarifies, "What I mean is, you have a wonderful selection of books, and I could spend hours just perusing, but I'm actually quite fascinated by your parrot. Might you be interested in selling him?"

"Oh, I see. Um, yes, yes, he's for sale, but are you familiar with what it takes to care for such an animal?"

Drawing on his childhood pal once again and the earlier conversation with the shopgirl, Frank fabricates a reply. "Yes. I had a budgie as a boy—even taught him a few phrases. Oh, I know this is a much larger and more exotic creature, but I would think the routine would be similar—regular vet visits, keep the talons manicured and the wings trimmed." Frank smiles at her.

"And the diet, of course. You cannot just feed him anything, there are certain seeds and fruits that could sicken or kill him," she counters. "He needs—"

"Of course, he'll have nothing but the best of care," Frank politely interrupts. "Say, what can you tell me about the bird—his origins, age, any details?"

"Oh, little, I'm afraid. I can tell you that he's an African grey and a boy. Beyond that, I really don't know much; we don't even know his name. The veterinarian says he's healthy and could live to be anywhere from sixty to a hundred years old, though he can't be sure of his current age, other than he's a full-grown."

"I see. May I ask how you acquired him?"

The old woman's eyes soften. "He belonged to a friend of my older sister in Colorado, who commit ... passed away unexpectedly. None of her family—I believe they were estranged—wanted the poor thing, and my sister, as a final act of friendship, volunteered to take the bird, but my sister, Dina, suffered a massive stroke only a week later. She was a heavy smoker and drinker. I often tried to tell her that unfiltered cigarettes and bourbon would take their toll, but me being the baby, she would say that I had no right telling her how to live her life. Well, it had been a while since we had exchanged letters, and, as I say, we tend to be old-fashioned, but Dina had never written me anything about the parrot. It wasn't until I went to her funeral that her landlady—Dina lived alone; her husband passed nearly a decade ago—insisted I take him. Well, I assured her I hadn't the wherewithal to care for such an animal, but she was insistent—were I not a proper lady, I might even say pushy. I don't mind telling you it wasn't easy to get him back here on the train, and I had to wait for a special van to meet me at the station to transport the cage. He lives here in the bookstore because there's simply no room for him in my apartment. How about you, young man, have you plenty of room?

"Not to worry, I have more than enough," Frank lies.

"I just couldn't let him go unless I knew he'd have the absolute best of care and quarters, you see. I owe that to the memory of my sister."

"I understand perfectly, ma'am. Now, tell me, I assume he can speak? What sorts of phrases or words does he know? What sorts of things have you heard him say?"

With a dismissive wave of her hand, she says, "I've never heard him utter an articulate sound. Squawks and screeches on occasion, but that's all. When I first brought him home, I tried to bribe him with treats, but to no avail. After trying to coax something out of him for a fortnight, I'd had my fill. So if it's of great import to you that he be a well-versed chatterbox with a grand vocabulary, then I'm afraid you'd be wasting your money."

"Hmmm, I see. No, it isn't that important, though I imagine it would increase his worth if he were a chatterbox, would it not?"

"I suppose that is true. I was thinking of asking fifteen hundred dollars for him, which includes the cage and the supplies I have on hand, but in light of your observation, I would be willing to take, say fourteen hundred."

"Well, I do have to arrange to have him moved. I certainly cannot fit the cage in my car, so there is that expense to think of as well. What would you say to eleven hundred?"

"Shall we split the difference and agree on twelve hundred fifty?"

"Would you be willing to accept a personal check, ma'am?"

Monday

Frank arrives at work, pours a cup of joe, and appreciates his good fortune—no one else yet at the coffee station. Java in hand, he hurries to his office and shuts the door behind him. The first order of business this morning: wake up the computer and search for a service to haul the bird and cage to his place. After forty minutes of typing in various search terms, he finds a link that offers comparison pricing of local moving companies.

Despite being alone, he reads aloud as he scans the web page, "Okay, your search has returned nine companies fitting your criteria—same day, within ten miles. Sort by rating, best-to-worst and voilà—hello, Gold Star Moving. Four-and-a-half out of five stars, eighty-three reviews, seventy-five five-stars, and only eight four-stars. We have a winner."

The movers are surprisingly agreeable to meeting Frank's timetable, but there is a snag: they'll only move the empty cage and are unwilling to take responsibility for the bird.

"Okay, in that case, I work until five and will have to stop and get a pet carrier. How late can you guys work?"

"We go nine to nine daily," comes the reply.

"All right, let's meet at the bookstore at six. I'll see if they can accommodate me. If not, I'll call back; otherwise, let's plan on meeting there at six, okay?"

"Six o'clock at 300 Sebastian Street. Got it."

"Great, thanks."

"See you then."

Turning back to the computer, he initiates a new search but this time looks up the bookstore's number. He picks up the phone and makes the call.

It's answered on the second ring. "McElroy Book Emporium." The voice's youthful tone immediately conjures up an image of the shopgirl, her bare midriff and that taut, flat stomach with the belly button ring.

"Uh, hi. I was in the store the other day and arranged to purchase the parrot."

"Oh, yes, Mrs. McElroy said you'd be calling to arrange moving him. How may I help you?"

"I've secured a mover, but I won't be able to get over there until close to six. I'm hoping that won't be a problem."

"The store closes at five-thirty, but I don't mind waiting to let you and the movers in."

"Hey, that's wonderful. Thank you so much. I'll make the inconvenience worth your while."

With a lilt in her voice, the shopgirl, with the blue-black hair, replies, "It's no trouble. I'm happy to help."

Not wanting to risk being late, Frank departs the office early and stops at the pet store in the mall. It's one of those megastores with every conceivable pet-related item in multiples stacked floor to ceiling.

Making his way to the pet carriers, he mumbles to himself, "They certainly have everything in abundance, except *help*." He scans the inventory selection, which starts with small cases and gradually increases in size to cages that look as if they'd accommodate a small horse. He rules out the bare-metal type and vacillates between the molded plastic and soft-sided vinyl ones, before finally selecting the soft version in blue with a zippered front and built-in perch. Although he was able to find what he wanted without assistance, he makes note of the fact that aside from the cashier, he's seen no other employees during the entire visit. He shakes his head.

He finds a (hopefully) ding-proof parking spot on the second level of the garage—no problem after regular business hours—and walks toward the bookstore. It's quarter to six, but the store's front door is locked. He switches the carrying case to his left hand and, to cut down the glare, shades his eyes with the right, putting it up to the glass to peer inside. He sees the shopgirl coming toward him.

She opens the door, and he conceals his disappointment that her stomach and belly button ring aren't exposed this evening. He says, "Thanks, and thanks again for waiting for me. I really appreciate it."

"You're very welcome," she replies and turns to walk back to the counter, where she set down her phone.

What her long blouse covers is made up for by the shortness of her skirt, and Frank's eyes are mesmerized, watching her plaid pleats dance near the tops of her thighs as she walks back to the counter. Though he generally prefers broader hips, he cannot help but appreciate her locomotion.

The shop-door bell dings, and Frank turns to see two large, black men in beige uniforms. The first one coming through the door asks, "Are you Mr. Tou ... Tro ..."

"Yeah, that's me, just call me Frank."

"Okay, Frank. You've got a cage we're moving?"

Frank hoists the pet carrier for the men to see. "That's correct. Let me just collect my bird, and you can take it from there." He turns back to the shopgirl and asks, "He's still in the back corner?"

"He is," she confirms. "I'm so glad you're taking him out of here."

"Ah, right. I remember, you're not a big fan of birds." Frank smiles at her.

"I'm not a fan of *big* birds. Little ones are okay." She returns his smile. "Mrs. McElroy put some supplies for you in a bag on top of the cage."

Frank makes a beeline for the back, and as expected, the bird is doing its favorite dance: the side step, bobbing its head to a rhythm only it can hear. Frank unzips the front of the case, opens the door to the cage, and reaches in. As his hand moves toward the bird, it stops dancing, extends a leg toward Frank's hand, grabs his index finger with its claw, and pulls itself up. Frank is surprised by the weight of the creature but also at the ease with which it climbed onto his hand. After a careful extraction, he eases it into its temporary abode. As if rehearsed, the bird steps onto the carrier perch and resumes its dance.

Frank zips the case and moves toward the front of the store, taking a roundabout path that bypasses the movers. He pauses to set the carrier down on a table and pulls a fifty-dollar bill from his wallet.

As he leaves, he extends his hand to the shopgirl. "Thank you again so much for accommodating me."

She shakes, surprised by the palmed portrait of Ulysses S. Grant. She looks at the folded bill. "Wow, thank you. That's more than generous!"

"Well, I hope that makes up for inconveniencing you this evening.

"It was really no trouble. Thank you again."

Returning to his car, he wonders if he should have slipped her his phone number, maybe even writing it on the bill. On the walk, he allows himself a few minutes to let his mind muse over the idea of dating someone so much younger—well, screwing someone so much younger. After all, it could happen. She clearly must have some daddy issues to account for her risqué wardrobe, ink, hair color, and piercings. "Huh, yeah, right," he says aloud and sighs.

He opens the Caddy's passenger-side door, noting the scratches and dents on the hood, places the carrier on the seat, and secures it with the seat belt. Peering inside, he queries, "Doing okay, big fella?

Ready to see your new home? Oh, and hey, remind me to call my insurance guy tomorrow, eh?"

The bird rubs its beak on the perch.

Frank thanks and tips the movers, closing the door behind them. After flipping the deadbolt, he crosses the living room toward the cage, retrieves the bag Mrs. McElroy secured to it, opens the top, and places the perch in position.

"Okay, birdie, are you ready to check out your new place?" Frank asks calmly, making slow and deliberate movements to unzip the front of the carrier. Despite the car ride and a stint in the smallish blue case, the bird seems none the worse for wear and eagerly accepts Frank's hand.

He extends his arm, and the parrot steps onto the perch atop the cage. It makes several turns, inspecting its new surroundings, and then begins to step and bob. It watches as Frank walks past the snack bar, which separates the living room from the kitchenette, and opens the fridge.

Frank returns with apple slices, places a few on the cage, and hands one to the bird, which it takes by one end in its beak. Its right claw grips the other end, and it begins to eat. After filling the water bowl, Frank pours a Scotch, falls into his overstuffed, black leather recliner and swivels it away from the wall-mounted flat-screen toward his new roommate.

"Okay, my friend, what do you have to say to me now?" he asks, feeling that the question might be rhetorical at best. And, as expected, the bird keeps grabbing, ripping, and crunching apple slices.

He observes the bird through another pour of his good stuff—a bottle of fifteen-year-old Johnnie Walker Green Label. "If you don't tell me your name, we're going to have to come up with one for you, aren't we? How about it, birdie, what's your name?"

The only sound is the tearing and eating of apple flesh.

"Well, if you're not going to talk to me, we may as well watch a little TV, okay?"

Crunching.

Frank awakens in his recliner as the eleven o'clock news wraps up. He glances over at the parrot, finding it atop its perch, head turned backward and nestled between the shoulders of its wings. Frank walks into the kitchenette, rinses out the rocks glass, fills it with tap water, and drinks it down.

"Sorry to wake you, but it's time for bed," Frank says, gently stroking the grey's chest. The bird's eyes slowly open as it turns its head toward him and reaches out with a foot to climb onto his hand. He gingerly places the bird on its perch, removes the one from the top, and closes the roof panels. The parrot has already resumed its sleeping posture, as Frank partially pulls a cover over the cage.

"Good night, birdie," he says.

Frank isn't sure, but believes he hears a reply, "Night."

Tuesday

Morning arrives too quickly, and Frank wills himself into the kitchenette to start the coffee maker. He squints in the direction of the cage and can see that the parrot is awake and doing its usual side step and bob. With the coffee brewing, he walks over and uncovers the cage.

"Good morning, my little feathered friend," he says to the bird. "Will you be all right if I set you up on your top perch? I suppose you can always climb back down to play with your toys and get your food and water," Frank prattles, opening the top panels.

He goes about what he assumes will become his regular morning routine: as coffee drips, he washes and cuts up the recommended fruits and veggies. He chats to the bird while chopping and realizes that having another living creature in the room makes it okay to talk to himself. That was something he would never have allowed himself to do before. "See that, birdie? Because I'm talking *to you*, I'm not some lonely, post-middle-age guy."

He places fresh water and food in the cage, crosses back to fill his coffee cup—one sugar—moves into the living room, picks up the remote, and turns on the TV. Casting a glance at the parrot gnawing on an apple slice, he says, "Let's see what happened overnight, eh?"

After enduring a story on the safety of local school busses and a piece on a blind woman knitting scarves for the homeless, the newscasters go to break with the promise of a weather forecast on their return. Frank uses the opportunity for a quick pee and a coffee refill. The forecast is about as interesting as the rest of the programming: some sunshine with partly cloudy skies and the chance of an afternoon shower. "Could they get any more vague?" he asks the bird.

"Well," he says, "I think I have time enough for another half cup." Lifting himself from his recliner, he realizes the bird has stopped moving and is staring directly at him.

"Leave early. At least ten minutes," the bird advises.

"What? Why? Tell me why. Bird, tell me why!"

Dancing. Bobbing.

Frank realizes he won't get any more out of the parrot, not once it returns to its routine. He decides to do as the bird suggests, forgoes the remainder of the coffee, and heads for the shower.

When he purchased his Caddy, Frank was given a ninety-day trial period for satellite radio, but between the parking garages and downtown buildings, the dead spots had become too annoying.

Since the cyclist incident, he's been tuned to regular commercial radio and hasn't really given it a second thought until just now. He's had so much on his mind that the twenty-four-speaker sound system has been relegated to background noise.

Waiting for the left-turn signal to enter the company's parking garage, the familiar five-note sequence preceding a breaking news story catches his attention, and he increases the volume.

The voice is familiar: the hotshot, part-time weatherman. When not subbing on forecasts, he generally mans the traffic dungeon on the network's local affiliate. "From your Channel Six News Leader, this is Dylan Stryker with breaking news. At seven-fifteen this morning, a southbound Metroliner collided with a gasoline tanker at the Cypress Road crossing in Meadowbrook. While details are still sketchy, it has been reported that the tanker truck was stuck in rush-hour traffic and failed to completely clear the railroad crossing. The Metroliner clipped the rear end of the tanker, derailing several cars of the four-car passenger train and causing the tanker to erupt in a fireball, which engulfed several nearby vehicles. The explosion was felt for blocks, and there are reports of broken windows up to a half-mile away. First responders are on the scene, but there is no word yet on any casualties. All rail service has been halted at this time, and the entire section of Cypress Road from the interstate to Route 661 is completely blocked off to allow emergency crews to work the scene. On the interstate, drivers are being routed to International Boulevard from the north and Westfield Park Boulevard from the south. We have a news crew en route and will be bringing you updates as they come in. For Channel Six, I'm Dylan Stryker. We now rejoin regular programming."

A song comes on somewhere in the middle, a quasirecognizable tune from the nineties—maybe Hootie, maybe a soundalike—everybody sounded like Hootie back then. Frank turns down the volume to white-noise level once more.

"Leave early. At least ten minutes."

Frank's blood runs icy cold. On any given business day, he's usually stopped by the southbound Metroliner at *that* crossing. As the light-rail commuter passes by, he always uses those few minutes to check the day planner on his phone.

"Leave early. At least ten minutes."

A horn blares behind him. The light is green.

Throughout the morning, the office is quiet as staff gradually trickles in. Seemingly, no one's commute is spared by the incident. Text messages have been the first order of business, everyone reaching out to friends and coworkers to check on whereabouts and status.

Frank's phone buzzes—a text message from *her*: "Plz let me know u r ok."

He debates not sending a reply but can't sink to that depth. He responds simply, "I'm OK."

Sipping his coffee, Frank is watching the live news feed online. By ten o'clock, seven are confirmed dead in the vehicles closest to the explosion, including the tanker truck driver. No fatalities are reported from the Metroliner passengers, though more than two dozen are injured. Damage from the blast and ensuing inferno is expected to keep that section of road closed for up to three weeks.

Frank decides to freshen his coffee and visit the restroom. He takes the long way around, scanning the Cube Farm and outer offices for any absences. He's relieved to see a full complement, though the day's productivity will clearly be impacted. He passes Yolanda's cubicle. It's vacant, but he can see her in Marjorie's office, their backs toward him, as they focus on the boss's computer screen.

He spends the remainder of the morning entering search terms such as "clairvoyant" and "parrot" into the browser, but the searches produce nothing meaningful. In fact, one result is practically an insult—a cheesy, little-heard-of 1977 movie called *The Psychic Parrot*.

Periodically he checks the live news feed—the death toll remains the same. Authorities are working on removing the

Metroliner cars that didn't derail, but that section of track will be closed for days, interrupting commuter as well as freight service.

As he contemplates lunch options—traffic is going to be a nightmare—an internal email blast from Yoli is delivered to the inbox: *Pizza in the conference room! Come and get it!* Anticipating the entire staff's lunch-hour dilemma, Marjorie ordered enough pies for the entire second floor. Frank grins and shakes his head. "Oh, people," he says to himself, "she did the math ... cheaper to feed you than have everyone coming back late. I'll bet they were still counting bodies when she placed the fucking order."

The afternoon, while largely routine, includes a call to his insurance guy. Good news/bad news: he's fully covered and his rates won't increase since the cyclist was cited for the accident, but the soonest date the body shop can take the car is three weeks away. He confirms the appointment, not knowing he has less than seventy-two hours to live.

The day behind him and forty minutes late due to detours, Frank enters his apartment to the smell of burned coffee. "Ah, fuck," he says as he drops his laptop bag and heads to the kitchenette. The auto-off worked; the power light is unlit; but the pot was on long enough for the remainder of the morning coffee to be baked into a bubbled, hardened lava.

He squirts a shot of dish soap into the pot and runs the tap until the water is hot. He fills the pot a third of the way and swishes the foamy solution around, then sets it down on the counter. Turning toward the parrot, he says, "You know, this is all your fault, right?"

Dancing. Bobbing.

For several minutes, Frank regards the bird in silence as it performs its routine. He pulls a rocks glass from the cabinet, bumps the ice dispenser in the freezer door until three cubes—Are they still cubes if they're semicircular?—drop in with a clink. He adds a short shot of water and a long pour of Scotch.

Walking toward the bird, drink in his right hand, he points at it with his right index finger. "You and I need to have a serious talk, pal of mine." He sips the Johnnie Walker.

The bird halts and scrutinizes Frank. After a moment, a small, creaky voice asks, "Are you certain that is what you want?"

Frank is frozen. He stares at the parrot and it stares back. After the better part of a minute passes, he takes a deep breath and says, "You *can* understand me."

"Yes," replies the bird.

"That could have been me this morning ... at the rail crossing." Frank's voice is hushed, his nerves making the words shaky.

"That *would* have been you," the grey corrects.

"Oh. My. God," escapes Frank in an audible whisper.

"Let us not drag Him into it."

"Who, God? So what ... you're ... you're the devil?"

"No, of course not."

Without taking his eyes off the bird, Frank takes two swallows of whiskey and asks, "Who are you then?"

"We are known by many names."

"We?"

"We have many talents upon which to draw."

"Do you have a name? What should I call you?"

"Perditus."

"I see. And just what is it you want from me, Perditus?" asks Frank.

"Why, to fulfill your heart's desire, of course."

"Of course. And what, steal my soul? Possess me like in some movie?"

"We cannot *steal* your soul or take possession of you. This ornithological vessel is nothing near as complex or willful as that of a man."

"This isn't happening. I'm losing my mind. I'm, I'm, I'm David-fucking-Berkowitz. Hey, don't mind me … just doin' what my parrot told me to … Oh, Christ, this is too fucking much. I need to sit down. No, I need another belt!"

Frank leans hard against the kitchenette counter and refills his glass, his hand shaking and dribbling good whiskey onto the white Italian marble countertop.

The bird, motionless on its perch, does not withdraw its gaze from Frank's back.

He pours another, still hacking from gulping the last one with an uncomfortable quantity of air. He rubs his forehead with his left hand.

"I know your desire," comes the slow, cracked voice.

Frank turns to face the parrot, preternaturally aware of his labored breathing and racing heart. "Wha—" He takes a deep breath. "What do I desire?"

As before in the bookshop, the reply comes in a gravel-throated whisper, each syllable exaggerated, "Yo-lan-da."

"Uh … this can't be. I've gone insane. Can I be dreaming?" His head swims because, despite his overindulgence, he knows it's not a dream, leaving only two possibilities: madness or *reality*.

"Yo-lan-da," the bird whispers again.

"Okay, okay." Scotch in hand, once again Frank points his right index finger at the parrot. "Let's say this is really happening. I'm having a lucid conversation with my fucking African grey parrot, who is being controlled by—what? A demon? Is that what you are?

"Think of us as angels."

"Oooooooh, good. Yeah, that's good. Angels." He sips the Johnnie Walker, takes a deep breath and lets out a long exhalation. "Okay, angels. I'll go along because yes, I do *desire* Yolanda. I haven't been laid in like seven months, and I'm so horny that right now your ornithological vessel is starting to look good to me. So tell me, angel, how do I go about scoring Yoli?"

The bird closes its eyes and lowers its head. Several moments pass, and just as Frank begins to once more question his grip on reality, the bird's eyes open, the left one staring at him. "Shaker's this time tomorrow."

"Shaker's? The bar on Bay Street?"

"Yes."

He checks his watch. "You want me to be at Shaker's at eight-thirty tomorrow night. Is that right?"

"Yes."

"And then what?"

"Be honest with her."

"Be honest. With Yolanda, you mean?"

"Yes."

"I don't get it. I'm not understanding how ..."

Before Frank can find the words to finish his thought, the bird says, "Timing. The right place. The right time."

"Okay, so I'll be there. Then what?"

The parrot wipes its beak on the perch and recommences its bobbing and sidestepping.

"That's it?" Frank protests, but the bird only dances. He pours another whiskey, a big one.

Wednesday

The new morning ritual is complete, without any sort of interaction with the angels. The parrot happily munches on fresh fruit, while Frank drains an extra cup of coffee. After a few more drinks, he'd gone to bed and passed out. He vaguely remembers rationalizing that, after the extended conversation with the parrot, stupor would have to substitute for sleep. He's paying for that decision now, saddled with a headache and what feels like a fur-covered tongue. A couple of aspirin accompany the next sip of coffee. He's running late, but it's of little concern. The roads are going to be nightmarish again today without the commuter rail and with a large section of Cypress Road closed.

Finally dressed and laptop case in hand just before exiting the apartment, he looks at the bird and says, "Okay, Perditus, don't forget, I'll be home late. Wish me luck with Yoli." The bird, without paying him any notice, continues ripping into a slice of apple.

By ten o'clock, after a couple more cups of joe, he's feeling plugged in, and his day is humming. He decides to do a little reconnaissance to help prepare him for the evening at Shaker's and strolls to Marjorie's office, just outside of which Yoli sits. He grabs the USB thumb drive that Yoli had delivered to him a few days ago. It'll serve as his excuse for visiting the other side of the floor.

As he approaches Marjorie's office, he notices her vacant chair. Yolanda, seeing him in her vicinity, turns and says, "Hi, Frank. She's downstairs for a meeting. Anything I can help you with?"

"Ah. I just wanted to return her USB. It's been sitting on my desk, and I didn't want her to think I pilfered it," he says with a smile.

"Oh, um, just put it on her desk."

"Okay. Do you have a Post-it, so I can leave a note?" Yoli is wearing a white button-down blouse—rather conservatively fastened, unfortunately—tucked into a form-fitting navy-blue skirt that stops short of her knees. He sees her kicked-off heels under her desk. If standing, without her shoes, she'd barely come up to his chest.

She spins her chair in the opposite direction and reaches to retrieve a pad from the prefab credenza behind her. His eyes trace the contour of her waist and the flare of her hips as her bottom comes off the seat. *If she turns around right now, I'm caught . . . again*, he thinks. As she reseats herself, he quickly looks away, as if scanning the hall in search of Marjorie.

"Here you go," she says in a singsong voice, handing him the pad.

He scribbles "Here's your USB back. Thanks, Frank," peels off the top sheet, adheres it to the USB, and hands the pad back.

"Thanks," he says and steps into Marjorie's office to deposit it next to her mouse. On his way out, he mouths "thank you" as she's now on a call. She smiles and waves.

By six-thirty, the office is quiet. Frank closes out the project he's working on and opens Netflix. He's feeling too anxious to stay focused and decides that a distraction is in order. Looking at his My Shows menu, he vacillates between *Arrested Development* and the original *Star Trek* series. The latter wins out. He launches an episode entitled "Amok Time," in which Spock apparently—but, of course, not actually—kills Kirk in a fight over a woman the Vulcan is pledged to marry. It isn't until Spock explains that he is suffering from an uncontrollable lust, known as pon farr, that Frank realizes the irony of the selection. He wonders if he'll have the courage to face the consequences of his own inner drives.

Having watched a second episode, in which Scotty is accused of murder, it's now time to head to Shaker's. He's anxious, and his hands are trembling. "Appropriate for a place called Shaker's," he observes.

Pulling up in front of the bar, he allows a valet to take his Caddy. Never something he would do under normal circumstances, but until the grille and hood are repaired, he'll afford himself the luxury of not having to find a safe parking spot.

As expected, the music is loud and the lights are low, except those pulsing to the rhythm over the dance floor. Moving toward the bar, he can feel the bass reverberating in his chest. The bartender nods to him. Frank places his order, "Johnnie Red, double, neat." The barman wastes no time filling it, and Franks asks him to start a tab. The barkeep makes a swiping motion. Frank gets it and pulls out a credit card. He decides to kill one drink to settle his nerves before venturing away from the bar.

Refill in hand, it doesn't take him long to spot Yolanda sitting with a younger guy at a small table. She's no longer wearing her office attire. Her dress is a plain, beige, but skintight, and she's

wearing gold pumps—what his ex used to call fuck-me pumps.
In her usual style, the dress is low-cut, providing an ample display
of cleavage. The kid's hairstyle is trendy, and he's wearing skinny
jeans, which Frank thinks makes guys look bowlegged and
awkward. Seeing her sitting with Mr. Hipster, Frank begins to
doubt whether he should even be here, let alone trying to pick up
a girl more than a decade and a half his junior. He scans the room,
noting that he's a little out of his peer group. He decides to leave.
Turning, he heads back toward the bar to settle up and get the
hell out. Taking one last look, he sees Yolanda waving to get his
attention.

He smiles and waves back, but now she's gesturing for him to
come over. "What the hell?" he says aloud, barely audible with the
din of the music and crowd noise. He approaches the table and says,
"Hi Yoli. I don't want to interrupt your date or anything."

"Hi, Frank." She smiles. "Oh, we're not on a date. We just
met." Leaning forward to be heard over the driving music, she says
to the hipster, "This is Frank from my office." A brief pause and she
continues, "I'm sorry, I've forgotten your name."

Mr. Hipster is noticeably annoyed. Rising from his seat, he
gripes, "Obviously I'm wasting my time here." He turns to Frank,
extends his hand, and as they shake, says, "Nice to meet you, Frank,
I'm Frank as well. Have a nice life." Frank As Well then huffs off in
the direction of the dance floor.

Yoli's eyes grow large as she places her right hand over her
mouth to hide a mischievous smile.

"Sorry, I didn't mean to—"

Before he can finish, she cuts him off, "Don't apologize. His
sort is not my type."

"Really, why? Nice-looking guy, good physique, looks affluent
enough …"

"Immature millennial."

Frank motions. "Looking around, I don't think you're going to
find much else in a place like this."

"I'm sure you're right," she replies, "but I didn't even plan on
going out tonight. I'm angry with someone and was just looking to

have a little fun. Speaking of which, what brings you to a place like this on a school night?"

He laughs. "To be honest, desperation. I don't know what I was thinking. In fact, I'd only been here for five minutes before deciding to leave. That was right when you waved me over, and I spoiled the revenge thing you had going with Mr. Hipster."

Yoli also laughs. "Stop saying that. You didn't spoil anything. I told you that guy was not my type. At all."

"May I ask who you're angry at? If it's not too personal."

She sighs. "I've been in a sort of long-term relationship, and I've wanted out forev … for quite some time. He's too controlling. Always has been, and I'm to the point where I need out. I only recently moved into my own place, and he won't leave me alone, calling, showing up unannounced, and tonight he was there, sitting in his car when I got home. So I threatened to call the police. We had a big fight, and after he left, I just didn't want to stay home alone."

"Wow. I'm sorry. I had no idea you were going through something like that. You're always so bright and pleasant at the office. No one would ever know you've had such a rough time.

"You're sweet," she exclaims.

"What are you drinking? I'll get us another round."

"Cosmo."

In the few minutes it takes him to retrieve their drinks, Frank observes Yoli shoot down four different guys who approached as she sat alone. He returns to the table and hands her the Cosmo. "Here you go."

He considers commenting on the traffic she drew in his absence, but before he can think of how to phrase it, she says, "The guys here are relentless."

"Can't say I blame them, Yoli. You look amazing, but then you always do—for as long as I've known you."

Frank is surprised to see color rise in her cheeks. There seems to be a disconnect between her modesty and provocative fashion style.

"Oh, please," she protests.

Frank hears the parrot's voice, "Be honest with her." He continues, "Seriously, I've been crazy about you since the day you started working for us. You're the stuff *fantasies* are made of." As soon as he hears his own words, he regrets them. "I, I, I'm sorry. I shouldn't have said that. Blame it on the Scotch ..."

"Don't apologize. Honestly, that was a very nice compliment. I don't believe it's true, but it's nice to hear nevertheless." After an awkward gap in the conversation, she says, "I think I'd like to get out of here; it's so noisy."

"I understand," he replies, feeling embarrassed and dejected. "I'll go settle up at the bar. Would you mind waiting, and I'll walk you to your car?"

"Sure. What's your address, so I can put it into my phone's GPS in case we get separated?"

"Uh ... what?"

"You don't mind if we go to your place, do you? I'd offer to go to mine, but I'm afraid *he* might be waiting for me again."

"No!" he says a little too loudly. "Of course not. Thirty twenty-two Breyer. I'm in three-o-seven; my guest spot is right next to mine, so just follow me."

He places his hand on the small of her back, while guiding her into the parking garage elevator. It's the first time he's ever touched her in a deliberate manner, and he's relieved that she doesn't react negatively. He then reaches across and pushes the button for the third floor. It dutifully illuminates.

"Nice building," she observes.

"Thanks. It is, but my place is pretty small. I had to find something in a hurry. After eighteen years, my wife decided—right out of the blue—that she wanted something different out of life and dumped me. She got the house because her family helped us with the down payment. Now I'm stuck with a twelve-month lease. As soon as it's up, I'll find something a little bigger."

A chime sounds, and the elevator doors open. They make their way down the hall to his apartment and, as he's unlocking the door, he says, "Ah, you know, I don't think I have the ingredients for a Cosmo. In fact, I know I don't. Would a vodka martini suffice?"

"That sounds fine," comes her reply.

Upon entering, the bird cage dominates the setting. "You see why I need a bigger place?" He nods toward the parrot while closing the door behind them.

"Oh, it's beautiful!" Yoli exclaims. "Male of female?"

"Male."

"His name?"

"Perditus," says Frank as he commences making the drinks.

"Oh, Latin."

"Is it?"

"You don't know what you named your own bird?" she asks.

"Oh, uh, no. He sort of came with that name. Do you speak Latin? Do you know what it means?"

"A little, from college days. There are several definitions, but 'abandoned' is the one I'm most familiar with. It can also mean 'reckless.'"

"Interesting. His owner, well, technically the owner before last, passed away, so it fits … abandoned." He pauses, thinking, *I guess it fits my circumstances too.*

He hands her a martini; she sips, her bright-blue eyes fixed on his. Towering over her, he sips a Scotch. She places her glass on the end table and moves in toward him. Standing on tiptoes, she reaches her arms up. He bends down, and their lips meet. Hers are full and soft. He feels her mouth open and touches the tip of his tongue to her upper lip, and with that, she reciprocates. The kiss is long and deep. Frank is unaware that his glass has fallen onto the carpet as his right hand traces the curve of her hip and cups her left cheek. His left hand moves from her ribs upward to her breast; he can feel her nipple harden beneath her dress in response to his firm touch.

She pushes him toward his black leather recliner; he falls backward into it, pulling her on top of him. His hands continue to explore her compact frame; her dress rides up as she straddles him. She begins kissing his neck and biting his left earlobe.

"Oh my God, that feels good."

Her voice—soft, warm, and breathy—moans, "You like that?"

"Oh, yeah, I like that."

"Tell me about your fantasies. I want to make them real for you," she whispers, her lips skimming the outer edge of his ear.

Frank moans.

"Tell me, Daddy, what turns you on?"

He slides the spaghetti straps off her shoulders and the dress drops, exposing her breasts. She loops her arms through the straps, presenting her upturned palms to him as if helplessly bound, a wry smile on her face. He returns her gaze, moving his hands upward from her waist until each is cradling her bust. With the index and middle fingers of her right hand, she gently takes his necktie and wraps it around her left wrist. "Tie me up, Daddy," she says softly, grinding against him.

He moves his right arm around her waist, pushes the recliner upright, and stands. Her legs are wrapped around him, and they kiss again. He moves them into the bedroom, then bends to set her onto the bed. He pulls off his tie as she slithers out of the beige dress; she sits back on the bed in a flesh-colored thong, lace-topped nude thigh-high stockings, and those gold high heels.

Having thrown his shirt to the floor, he moves over her; she lies back, extending her arms above her head. He knots one end of the tie around a headboard post; the other he ties around her wrists. "My ankles," she says, "don't forget my ankles."

Another deep kiss, tongues mingling. He arises and says, "Stay right there." He disappears into the small walk-in closet for only a moment and reemerges with several ties in hand.

As he places a hand on her left ankle, she makes a point of waving her freed hands in front of him, as if she's a magician finishing up a magic trick. "Uh-oh," she chides, her voice sultry and soft. "You were never a Boy Scout, were you? Daddy needs to make better knots."

Determined to prevent a repeat, he secures one ankle to the left-bottom bedpost, the other on the opposite side. He reties the knot around her wrists, this time making it tight and wrapping the tie around each wrist before binding both together. He adds some length by using another tie. She's so tiny that a single tie is too short to reach the center post of the headboard now that her legs are bound. He takes a moment to drink in her beauty and to get his head around the vision of this blonde goddess before him, bound and vulnerable.

He stands and removes his pants and boxers. As they drop, Yoli smiles at the sight of his erect phallus. He lies next to her, brushing aside a few errant strands of long, golden hair that has fallen across her face. She feels the rigidity of his manhood against her thigh. He places his mouth on hers as he fondles her body; his hand moving from her breasts down across her stomach to her panties, where he gently massages her through the delicate material. Their tongues entwined, he moves his hand beneath her underwear and explores. She moans; her hips undulate. His left hand squeezes her breast as he works his tongue over her nipple; her breathing comes in gasps. He continues working his way down her torso with his mouth, biting and French-kissing her stomach and belly button. Reaching her panties, he tears them off, moves to the end of the bed, slides his arms beneath her bound legs and buries his face in her. As his mouth caresses her, she pushes herself up to force his tongue deeper. Her gasps are louder and quicker until she unleashes a sound halfway between a squeal and a moan, and he can feel her entire body shudder with release.

"Oh my God," she groans. "That was amazing."

He positions himself over her, and as he begins to penetrate, she winces and makes a throat-clearing sound. "Are you all right? Do you want me to stop?" he asks.

"No, don't stop. It's just that I've only been with one guy, and you're considerably larger than him."

That makes Frank smile. He enters her further; her face contorts, reflecting some discomfort but mostly unbridled pleasure.

She tosses back her head with each forward motion until he's fully inside her. "You okay?"

"Yes."

He moves slowly outward and then back in. "You still okay?"

Her bright-blue eyes lock onto his, and she tells him, "Fuck me, Daddy."

Seven months of pent-up frustration drive him like a machine. Head back and eyes tightly closed, Yoli moans, groans, and grunts, moving in unison with his thrusts, all the while exhorting him, "Oh, fuck me, fuck me!" He watches as with each thrust, her breasts bounce up and down, her long blond hair splayed out in every direction, as he obeys her commands.

"Choke me!" she shouts.

"Choke you?"

"Yes! Now!"

His right hand appears huge against her petite, slender throat. He squeezes and feels her thrusting up against him, her movements still in rhythm with his own. He can take no more and releases with a force unknown since his college days.

Despite the intense orgasm, he remains rock hard. "Oh, I'm not done with you, little girl," he says, his words coming out in pants.

"Wait," she says.

"Something wrong? Am I hurting you?" He releases his grip.

"No. Untie my ankles."

Frank complies, finding that the knots have tightened as a result of Yoli's thrashing. It takes several minutes, but he undoes them without resorting to scissors. "Do you want me to untie your wrists?" he asks.

"Noooooo," she replies in her sultry tone, "I don't." She then turns over onto her stomach, draws her knees upward, and hoists her bottom.

"Oh ..." says Frank. "I may need a minute."

She looks over her shoulder to see that his erection is now a semi. She motions with her head. "Bring that here."

He's on his knees next to her. He brushes her hair back from her face. She takes him into her mouth. Her lips are soft, her mouth wet and warm. He places his hand on the back of her head; her hair is soft as satin. Though she can't accommodate much more than the head, she has him rigid again in no time. "Okay, Daddy, I think you're ready for me. Just hope I'm ready for you."

He first caresses her derrière and then, overcome with desire, delivers a playful yet forbidding bite to her right cheek.

"Ow!" she hollers. Laughing, she scolds, "Hey, that hurt. Do it again."

He straddles her and slides his tool between her cheeks several times. Then with one hand, he guides it in. She's tight. He uses some saliva as lubrication and begins once again to penetrate. She pushes back against him, and, once again, with each fraction of progress, she grunts. Her eyes closed and face red, he asks, "Are you sure you want to do this?"

Her reply comes in two parts with the next two thrusts, "Don't. Stop."

He drives deeper.

Her voice is labored, but her intent is clear. "Do me, oh Daddy, fuck my ass!"

He cannot contain himself; she's making him wild, and he uses all his might to comply with her demand. Her face is scarlet; with each lunge into her, she grunts—the sound so rhythmic it's almost melodic. He cannot hold back much longer when she cries, "Cum for me, Daddy!" He does so immediately and collapses onto her back. He's breathing as hard as her when he rolls off. He lets his arms drop to his sides and exhales hard.

"Oh my God, Yoli. That was the best ever! I would never have guessed you could be so wild—I've never had a woman say things like that to me. Oh my God, you can't be real; this must be a fantasy."

She turns her head toward him, her hair covering most of her face; she puffs upward to rearrange some stray strands. "I'll get better; you're pretty big compared to what I'm used to." She smiles.

"Better? Christ, you'd probably kill me."

"You can untie my hands now."

Frank returns to the bedroom, having fixed fresh cocktails. "Sorry I don't have a martini glass. It's on my list of stuff to get someday, once I settle in."

"Where do you think that'll be? Is there a particular place you have in mind? You think you'll stay around here or maybe look for something closer to the water?"

"Oh, I don't know. Lately, I've been toying with the idea of moving someplace far away, Wyoming or Maine. There are just so many memories here, not to mention that since the divorce, I feel like such an outcast. We have all these mutual friends, couples, you know, and somehow now they're just *her* friends. The isolation has been tough. I feel like maybe I should just move elsewhere, completely new, you know? Start fresh."

"I understand about wanting to get away," she says.

"Well, true. We're sort of in the same boat. You said you just left a long-term relationship. How long were the two of you together?"

"I don't want to talk about that … *him*. Let's talk about the future. There are so many possibilities. We can go anywhere—do anything."

"We?"

"Of course. I'll go anywhere you want to."

"Yoli, don't you think it's a little too soon to be making plans together? I mean, my divorce isn't even a year behind me, and you just got out of a relationship. Hell, your ex is still stalking you."

"But you said you've been crazy about me since we met—that's a couple of years now," she says, voice slightly raised.

"Well, yes, but that was meant as a compliment to your physical beauty and a handful of interactions we've had—you always seem so sweet and—"

"You son of a bitch!"

"Wait! I'm only saying we don't really know each other yet. We should take some time to learn about …"

In a fury, Yoli gets out of bed and starts gathering her belongings.

"Yoli, please, wait!" Frank pleads. "I don't think you understand what I'm saying!"

Her face crimson, her eyes tearing, she screams, "I understand you got what you wanted from me! You lied to me and manipulated me!" She dresses on the fly, making her way through the bedroom into the living room.

"Yoli, please, don't go! Stay and talk to me!"

Her dress askew and her hair a bird's nest, she heads for the front door. Frank approaches quickly and grabs her right bicep, but she twists out of his grasp and stumbles headfirst into the door.

"Are you okay?" Franks asks.

She hisses, "Don't you fucking touch me! I gave myself to you! I humiliated myself for you! You're no different than my fucking father!" She scrambles out the door, slamming it behind her.

He can hear her yelling at the top of her lungs in Spanish as she runs to the elevator.

Once again, Frank finds his head spinning in a surreal whirlpool of adrenaline and confusion. Her *father*, she said. What the fuck? He looks over at the bird; it's asleep on the perch.

Thursday

Frank makes several trips past Yoli's cubicle, but she apparently took the day off. He contemplates asking Marjorie for Yoli's home phone but decides to avoid the inevitable awkward conversation that would follow.

Back in his office, the phone rings. He doesn't recognize the caller ID. He picks up the receiver and says, "Frank here."

The voice on the other end says, "It's me. Do not say my name, but do you know who this is?"

Frank recognizes his friend Jeff instantly. "Yeah, sure. What's—"

"Can you meet me someplace where we can talk? It needs to be private, and it needs to be now."

"Sounds serious," Frank replies.

"Very, but not over the phone and not anyplace public. Can we meet at your apartment?" Jeff asks.

"Sure. When?"

"As soon as humanly possible. You're at thirty twenty-two Breyer, right?"

"Yeah. Three-o-seven. Half an hour?"

"See you then." Jeff ends the call.

Jeff arrives ten minutes after Frank and knocks. Before Frank can fully open the door, Jeff slides in and closes it.

"What's with the cloak-and-dagger routine, old buddy?" Frank inquires.

"Listen to me," Jeff says gravely. "I could not only lose my job and be disbarred, but I could face jail time for obstruction of justice just for being here right now. That's why I called you from a pay phone and told you not to say my name."

"What in God's name are you talking about, Jeff?"

Jeff inhales deeply and exhales with an audible huff. "When I first saw the name, I thought it was a funny coincidence. I didn't recognize the address, but then I saw the place of business and realized that I'd forgotten you moved out after the divorce."

"You've lost me, Jeff."

"Frank, do you know a woman by the name of Yolanda Maria Fernandez?"

"Yes. I, uh, I work with her."

"Frank, I don't know how to tell you this other than to just say it. I have the application for an arrest warrant on my desk charging you with the rape of Ms. Fernandez."

"*What?*"

But before Frank can say more, Jeff holds up a hand to silence him and continues, "More than rape, Frank—*aggravated* rape, also kidnapping, false imprisonment, and aggravated assault. But that's not all. There's photographic evidence. She has bruises and marks on her wrists and ankles consistent with being forcibly restrained as well as a handprint on her throat."

"Oh, Jesus!" Frank rasps.

"Let me finish," Jeff admonishes. "Marks on her hips, particularly the left, consistent with her undergarments having been torn off. Contusions on her right arm—again in the form of a handprint—a significant bruise on her right buttock due to a bite—definitely human—and a bruise above her left eye extending to her left temple."

"Oh my God! Oh my God! This can't be." Frank's voice is cracked and high-pitched.

"Frank, let me finish," Jeff scolds again. "In addition, the medical report states there are tears to her vaginal area consistent with rough penetration. DNA in the form of semen was collected from her vagina as well as rectum. She's alleging forcible sodomy."

"Oh my God! No!" Frank has his hands to his head.

"Frank, how in hell did this happen?"

"Jeff, you've got to believe me; this woman is nuts. We bumped into each other at a bar last night and came back here. She was just getting out of some relationship, and you know my deal. Well, one thing led to another, but, Jeff, she's crazy. She insisted I tie her up—that's why she has those marks. She told me to choke her! She's the one that initiated the anal stuff, Jeff—I swear to God! I did bite her on the ass, but if it left a bruise, it's only because she made things so intense! Oh, God! How can this be?"

"What about her arm and face?" Jeff asks.

"When we, uh, well, when we were done, we started talking, and she was saying how she wanted to move somewhere with me, and I said it was too soon. I don't know, she got all freaked out and started yelling that I manipulated her. I tried to calm her down, and as she was trying to leave, I grabbed her by the arm—only to stop her, not to hurt her. She pulled away and fell face-first into the door. Jesus, Jeff, I swear to God …"

"Look, buddy, I have to tell you that I've seen guys put away for a long time for a lot less. How do you account for the vaginal injuries she sustained? Did you use sex toys or some other object?"

"No. She was really tight; in fact, it was uncomfortable for her at first. She told me the guy she'd been with—only one, she said—was a lot smaller than me. Or maybe she did something to herself afterward? I don't know, Jeff. She's fucking insane!"

"Okay, okay, calm down. I have to ask—did you have a camera set up or take any cell phone video that might corroborate your version of the story?"

Frank shakes his head. "No, nothing like that."

"Frank, the building's surveillance cameras show her entering the apartment with you. It looks completely voluntary, but a couple hours later, the tapes show her running out disheveled and hysterical."

"How can that be? It was just hours ago!"

"It's the age of the internet—doesn't take much to email an mp4 file, Frank. Do you have a good attorney? Believe me, you don't want a public defender on this."

"No, but I can ask the guy who handled my divorce. Maybe he knows someone."

"Okay, Frank, now listen to me very carefully. Because of the overwhelming physical evidence accompanying this report, I don't have a choice in the matter; I have to issue the arrest warrant."

Frank's breathing is a series of interrupted gasps.

Jeff continues, "We're going to keep it low-key. You stay right here. I'll send plainclothes guys in an unmarked unit, so there'll be no commotion. As long as I have your word that you'll go with them quietly, I'll tell them to keep the cuffs holstered, and you can walk out like you're headed to a business lunch. Okay?"

"Jesus, Jeff, there's no other way?"

"I'm sorry, but no. Not from where I'm standing. Look, I know you. *I believe you.* You say this chick has issues; they're out there, man. You just need a lawyer who can take that and run with—"

Before Jeff finishes, a high-pitch scream fills the living room. Both men whip their heads in the direction of the bird cage. From the top of its perch, the parrot, mimicking a woman's voice, begins to scream, "Frank! Let go of me! No, Frank, no! Stop, Frank, please stop! You're hurting me!"

Jeff looks at Frank, his eyes wide. Frank looks back; the color has drained from Jeff's face.

Jeff says, "I'd better go."

"No, you don't understand! That bird ..." Frank attempts to explain.

Jeff cuts him off, his voice now without compassion, "Just wait here and don't resist, Frank. Don't resist, and you'd better pray that a parrot can't be called as a material witness."

Frank closes the door behind Jeff, falls back against it, and slides to the floor, crying into his palms. He sobs uncontrollably for several minutes. Looking up, he sees the parrot staring at him.

"You did this to me. I knew you were no angel."

The bird replies, "We are angels, but there are many *types* of angels, Frankie. We are of the *fallen* variety."

"What's going to happen to me, do you know?"

Jeff's office line rings. "DA's office, Jeff Cohen," he answers.

"Lieutenant John Tomlinson, plainclothes unit dispatched to serve a warrant on a rape charge for one Fran—"

"Right, Lieutenant, problem?" Jeff asks.

"Well, yes, sir. We arrived at the premises, but there was no answer."

Jeff thinks, *Jesus Christ, Frank, don't let them tell me you fled.*

"We gained entry forcibly and found the suspect hanged by a belt in the bedroom."

"Ah, shit," says Jeff under his breath, then, "Is the suspect alive?"

"Negative, sir."

"Okay, thank you, Lieutenant. Go ahead and process the scene."

"Yes, sir."

Lieutenant John Tomlinson turns to his partner and says, "Bill, call in the meat wagon and ghouls."

"Copy that," says Bill. "Hey, ya get a load of that bird in the other room?"

John walks over to get a closer look. The bird's yellow eye is staring directly at him, and a soft, creaky voice says, "Take me home, Johnny."

TO BE WITH GOD

Thursday, March 5, 2048

T-plus 6 hours, 30 minutes

On the display, Earth and its moon are shrinking as Specialist J. Murphy Cameron hurtles through the vacuum of space toward Mars. From his current vantage point, the moon appears much larger than the blue marble it orbits. He's close enough to see the Colonies and can even pick out the maglev lines connecting them. Just beyond the terminator, where night is permanent, the structures glow with artificial light.

There was a time when it took as long as three days just to reach the moon from Earth, but much has changed in the nearly eight decades since the Apollo program moon landings. In the realm of change, though, nothing could possibly compare to the world-altering events of 2019, a year so transformative that the US government was compelled to tell the truth.

Though the sole occupant of the craft, Murphy is neither the pilot nor an astronaut. He is a passenger. No flight crew is required; the saucer-shaped vehicle is completely automated. Murphy prefers to call himself a digger, or if formality is required, an archaeologist. He also has a new skill. In the hold of the craft is a highly specialized piece of equipment. He had spent eighteen months learning to operate it while stationed on the moon at Blue Rocks—a facility named for its bright-bluish surface rocks, discovered in 2013 by the Chinese probe Chang'e-3. Later, research revealed the rocks to be fragments of a massive shattered ancient dome.

After learning to live off planet and going through all the simulations and scenarios thrown at him by his instructors, there was a brief trip back to Earth. That was when the final improvements to the biointegrated excavating suit, or BES, were installed. Then it and he were loaded into this shuttle and launched into the void.

In less than two weeks, he'll arrive at Cydonia to relieve a team member who will ride the shuttle back home with newly discovered artifacts. Then he can begin his part in the excavation of the pyramids and other archaic structures. He is at the threshold of realizing his life's ambition: digging on Mars. But in the meantime, he enjoys a view of the moon as it fills the 3D retinal display— imaging so true-to-life that space- and aircraft manufacturers no longer install windows. He knows that in a few short hours, only distant stars will fill the array.

A notification appears in the upper right-hand corner of the display: "Incoming Message. Blue Rocks." Although there is no physical surface to the retinal display, the haptic feedback gives him the sensation of having touched the notification to accept the incoming message. Within a small, rectangular area, one of his moon-stationed colleagues appears to him in three dimensions, as if he's peering through an opening, in sharp contrast to the old two-dimensional, flat, silicon-based screens. He cannot help but smile when he sees her icy blue eyes looking back at him and her long, auburn tresses draping over her shoulders.

"Murph!" barks Adriana Simms, another digger slated for the next Mars rotation in September. "I miss you, big guy. How's the ride so far?"

"Hey, beautiful, I miss you too," he replies. "The ride? Not bad, had a great view of the Colonies as I went by. Feels a little odd to be passing by instead of putting down."

"Yeah, well, in six months, I'll get to know exactly how that feels. I just keep telling myself that everyone's made it safely without incident." She smiles. "You doing okay with the zero grav? I know you had some issues in the microgravity back here at Blue."

"So far, I'm fine; though I do prefer to stay strapped in as opposed to floating. I've got two weeks; maybe I'll get used to it. In the meantime, I've got plenty of nausea meds on hand and an ample supply of barf bags."

At this, Adriana laughs aloud and advises, "Until you're steady, keep a couple on your person. You don't want to accidentally let loose and have *that* floating all over the cabin."

"There's a pleasant image," he retorts, thankful he never yakked in front of her. Even so, there were plenty of witnesses to the one time he *had*, solidifying his reputation for having a weak stomach.

"I just wanted to check in before you reach Blue's com-gap threshold to let you know that the last packet from Dr. Spencer had some pretty interesting imagery."

"Has she correlated any of the hieroglyphs she's found with those from Earth?"

"No, not a perfect match. The Egyptian symbols appear to be, at best, a derivative of what she's finding in Cydonia. But she is certain that the newest hieroglyphs depict a Martian end-times scenario. They picture a small planet with an estimated diameter of about fifteen hundred miles in orbit between Mars and Jupiter. They show that several thousand years ago, Mars's orbit was considerably more elliptical than it is today. The smaller planet's orbit at one point brought it so close that Martian gravity ripped it apart, pulling tens of thousands of gigantic pieces of debris— some the size of our moon—onto its surface. Tens of thousands in a matter of minutes! The resulting impacts were cataclysmic. The Martian poles shifted several degrees, the atmosphere was decimated, the oceans boiled off, and its orbit completely changed."

"And there were survivors left to record those events? Good God!"

"Apparently, however, she cannot yet determine how long after the event the glyphs were made, but the timing of the catastrophe, based on her dating methods, aligns with ancient Earth texts that include the biblical flood."

"Wow, isn't that interesting! But, uh, still nothing matching Egyptian symbols …"

"Not a one, which further supports the hypothesis that the Egyptians merely overlaid their culture atop what a much earlier race built."

"Oh, I can't wait to dig!" exclaims Murph. "It's going to be a long ride; I wish they still did suspended animation for these trips, and I could just wake up and be there."

"When it took five months to a year to get to Mars, then, yeah, I agree, but for a couple of weeks, nah. You'd spend more time recovering from a hibernation hangover than it takes to get there."

"I know, I know. Hey, once you process Spence's packet, will you forward it to me? I'll have plenty of time to—"

"Of course!" Adriana assures him. "Spence. I'd love to hear you call Dr. Spencer *Spence* to her face. She'd pound you into dust."

"If anyone could, it'd be her, I hear."

"Okay, we'd better finish up here, or we're going to experience time lag between transmissions, and I just hate that. Don't solve all the Martian mysteries before I get there, okay?"

"No promises," he replies, smiling. "I'll be looking forward to seeing you."

"Until then, I'll be keeping you in my prayers."

"Oh, you beautiful nutjob, you. Okay, well, thank you, but we've been down this road. As a man of science, faith has no room where empirical evidence is available. You're a scientist …"

"Funny to hear that coming from such a nemesis of mainstream Egyptology. You're the one blasting them for refusing to consider evidence *they* claim is a leap *at best*."

"My science is sound; my methods and conclusions are solid. They just don't want to let go of what they've convinced themselves is true."

"Nevertheless, you'll be in my prayers, Mr. Empirical." Murph's smile as he shakes his head ever so slightly only endears him to her even more.

"Waste your time however you see fit, so long as it doesn't involve another guy."

"Try to enjoy the ride!" she says, blowing him a kiss.

The features of the moon's surface fade as Murphy's craft enters the Blue Rocks com-gap—the point at which transmissions can no longer take place in real time. Even with the advent of superluminal electromagnetic field/wave propagation, known in layman's terms as faster than light radio or FTL radio for short, the distance still requires between two and eight minutes to complete—a marked improvement over the twenty-plus minutes using conventional radio.

Much has changed in Murph's thirty-two years of existence, beginning with the Day of Disclosure, when he was only three and a half. On an August day in 2019, a dozen high-ranking United States Air Force officers absconded with a pair of highly classified craft and landed them in New York City's Central Park. Effects were immediate and dramatic.

The craft, initially thought by many to be alien in origin, descended in broad daylight, hovering over the expansive grassy area adjacent to the Jacqueline Kennedy Onassis Reservoir before finally setting down amid the ballfields. There were initial attempts by the US government to lock down the area, but within minutes, tens of thousands of posts to what was then known as social media captured the world's attention. The theft of the giant black triangular craft had been so flawlessly and secretly executed that the news media was aware of the event long before the military even knew they were missing. The nation's secret space program, propagated by the deep state, had been exposed.

In the following hours and days, chaos ensued, and the stock market plummeted. In Washington, DC, fingers of blame were pointing in every direction; wild accusations were made against any and all incumbent politicians. Anyone with a history in DC was suspect.

In 1960, the Brookings Report had predicted this sort of turmoil if evidence of extraterrestrial life was presented to the general public. But these spaceships were of terrestrial origin, manned and piloted by United States military personnel—all born right here on Earth.

As is the nature of things, the ships, known in conspiracy theory circles as TR-3Bs, were just the tip of a conspiratorial iceberg. The cloak of national security no longer protected black programs; the voice of the people was now the will of the nation, not that of the deeply entrenched career politicians.

An avalanche of long-held governmental secrets was made public; the most notorious event was first reported July 8, 1947. Headlines had heralded: "RAAF [Roswell Army Air Field] Captures Flying Saucer on Ranch in Roswell Region." The army air forces—later renamed the United States Air Force (USAF)—issued an immediate retraction and a cover story that a weather balloon had been mistaken for debris from a crashed flying disc. Decades of speculation swirled around what happened in New Mexico, but the weather-balloon farce remained largely unquestioned until the 1970s, when UFOlogists began to take a closer look, picking apart the cover story.

Following the Day of Disclosure, it was learned that the army air forces did possess flying saucers—eleven of them. The craft, however, did not come from outer space but were the spoils of the Allied victory over Germany in World War II. Nine of the saucers were captured Nazi Wunderwaffen—Miracle or Wonder Weapons—that had been under development in the waning months of the war. The other two had been reverse engineered by the US military. These American-made prototypes were the smashed remnants discovered on the Foster ranch.

The Nazis had produced saucers in several sizes and configurations. For years, the UFO phenomenon provided an excellent distraction for the general public while the well-funded black programs refined these gravity-mitigating technologies.

The disclosure of the self-acting engine, Nikola Tesla's machine that could gather heat—solar energy—from the ambient air, sent petroleum stocks into a tailspin. Industry giants' days were numbered as free-energy technology was released from the confines of top secret classification.

In the months to follow, the nation's churches and synagogues experienced a resurgence in attendance. Ironically, it wasn't God in whom people lost faith, as predicted, but rather their elected leaders and the high priests at the altar of finance.

It took years to sort out. So many investigations were launched that a number of people being investigated never lived to see the outcomes. Disclosure was the catalyst for the greatest changes in US governing policy since the Bill of Rights. No incumbent politician with more than a couple of terms served survived subsequent elections, and term limits for every seat were enacted. But those politicians remaining through the fray in Washington, DC, were steadfast in establishing a nationwide power distribution grid based on Tesla's principles, even naming the first functioning transmission spire Wardenclyffe Tower in his honor.

As the gas, coal, and oil industries died, new ones arose. The search for more powerful and durable electric motors raced forward at breakneck speed; development of new alloys and composite materials for extended space travel went from boutique to mainstream seemingly overnight. Car makers spent billions retooling assembly lines for the production of non-fossil fuel powered automobiles, and aerospace companies introduced their top secret extraterrestrial navigation systems into the mundane realm of public transportation. Power to propel vehicles of every type was abundant, renewable, clean, free, and literally in the air.

The piecemeal efforts of space tourism entrepreneurs—still struggling achieve low-earth orbit—replaced their multistage, fuel-burning liquid and solid rockets with circular plasma-filled accelerators called magnetic field disrupters or MFDs. These devices gave the military's TR-3Bs and private sector spacecraft the ability to defy Earth's and just about any other planet's gravitational forces.

Returning Americans to the moon became a high priority at the beginning of the new millennium's second decade. This time, however, the remnants of an ancient civilization and its long-dormant mining operation were not airbrushed out of photos or edited from film segments. During the Apollo program years, the general populace saw other photographs from NASA's lunar rovers that clearly depicted images of statues, pyramids, and other anomalous structures, which NASA explained away as: "Just rocks. Coincidence." For those who believed NASA had faked the moon landings, they could now be assured that astronauts *did* go there, but despite their amazing accomplishments, much was withheld from their worldwide audience to prevent the disruptions predicted by the Brooking's Report.

Children born after 2026—the beginning of Mars colonization—never knew a life without interplanetary travel. The first manned mission there returned high-definition video of structures that looked as if they'd been relocated from the deserts of Earth's Middle East, but these had been subjected to unimaginable bombardment with no protective atmosphere and eons of exposure to solar radiation.

Within the next few years, an effort was put forth to terraform the red planet. Transmission towers pulling energy from the Martian magnetic field powered autonomous reactors at the poles, melting the ice caps for water and pumping hydrogen and oxygen into the atmosphere to reconstitute a habitable environment.

Those same transmission towers also powered a scientific research colony. Beginning in 2029, designs were produced to establish a habitat in the Cydonia region. By 2035, reactors at the poles were in full operation, and unmanned cargo craft began ferrying modules for the new outpost. In addition to living quarters, farming units were sent; greenhouses were built with the assistance of robots; and apparatuses for remotely digging wells and others to process and filter groundwater were systematically installed.

In 2042, despite several setbacks, the initial six-person astronaut team arrived in Cydonia. They finally completed residential construction, tested the various systems, and prepared the habitat for occupancy. Three team members rotated home after nine months—the standard Mars mission tour of duty was later extended to eighteen—and three others arrived to replace them. The team of six had principal responsibility for the maintenance and expansion of the infrastructure that eventually supported a colony of thirty to fifty scientists and researchers who served eighteen-month, overlapping tours.

The total transformation of the planet took decades, but in July 2047, the one hundredth anniversary of the Roswell incident, the first naturally occurring, measurable precipitation was recorded in Mars's Tempe region.

Thursday, March 12, 2048

T-plus 174 hours, 30 minutes

It's been three days since Murphy experienced any sort of nausea, and for that he's grateful. It's much easier to work out when not fighting back the urge to expel one's lunch. And work out he must. The battle to stave off muscle atrophy and bone loss is daily, especially in zero gravity. Once on Mars, the microgravity makes exercising feel more normal, though a daily routine is still mandatory. In the shuttle, he circuit trains between the treadmill, stationary bike, and resistance bands. He stays focused on his stats, trying to improve a little each day. Not that fitness is of any particular interest to him; although it is a good distraction from the thought that at this point in the flight, if his shuttle departed from its programmed course, it would take several minutes for a distress call to reach either Blue Rocks or Mars. In turn, it would take several more minutes for corrective measures to make their way to the ship's nav computers, and at the current speed, well … he conjures up Adriana's words: "I just keep telling myself that everyone's made it safely without incident." For a moment, he contemplates saying a prayer. "Wouldn't even know how!" he mutters to himself.

The shuttle, while a relatively small craft, offers room enough for up to four passengers to move around and not feel crowded.

There are multiple compartments: lounging area, sleeping berths, kitchenette, commode, gymnasium, workstation, and zero-g shower—an enclosed chamber where one grapples with floating blobs of water with a small vacuum serving as a drain. There are also multiple cargo holds and supply cabinets. Most everything in the interior is molded as part of the ship or, if not, is secured to the floor or a bulkhead. Great care was taken in designing interior structures with rounded corners and edges and, where possible, padded surfaces. Weightlessness causes more than its fair share of contusions, regardless of one's training.

Murphy is finishing up an extra set on the resistance bands when he hears the alert from the com panel indicating a packet arrival. Despite the inability to reply in real time, he still experiences a sense of urgency to see what's coming in and scrambles to free himself from the apparatus, leaving the straps to float like the limp arms of a drunken octopus.

The notification is in the top right-hand corner of the display: "Incoming Message. Mars Science One." He taps the alert.

"Specialist Cameron," says Dr. Spencer, "I'm told you go by Murphy. Well, Murphy, we're looking forward to your arrival next week. I've been meaning to contact you, and I must apologize for taking so long to do so. We've been incredibly busy, and it seems as though for every answer we think we've found, two new questions arise—extraordinary times. I should also apologize for pulling you into rotation early, but when our only specialist with expertise in the taphonomy subdiscipline had to leave, your name was at the top of every list. We can really use your analytical skills, particularly in establishing rate of decay in our recent findings. You should have received the last data set we transmitted to Blue Rocks, and I hope it's enough to keep you from being bored during your trip. Rarely does a shuttle fly with only a single occupant, but we are in a bind. Hopefully, when you arrive, you'll find the inconvenience well worthwhile. I look forward to buying you a beer. See you soon."

Murphy replays the message and definitely sees what he thought he'd noticed during the first playback: a slight raising of one mannishly thick eyebrow when she said "recent findings."

Could they have found something organic? They must have; it would be the only explanation for needing a specialist in the study of organism decay and fossilization. He wants to reply to Spencer's message but first needs to take a few deep breaths and organize his thoughts.

He taps the reply icon. "Record in three," he commands the console. Better to record his message before sending so he has the chance to redo it if he screws up.

Three beeps and the recording indicator glows.

"Dr. Spencer, I received your message. No apologies necessary. I couldn't be more thrilled to be joining the team, though I am sorry it is at the expense of losing Specialist Danby. I hope things work out for her. I'm most intrigued and looking forward to putting on my taphonomist hat and getting my hands dirty. I have reviewed the latest packet from Blue. I've also been developing an algorithm that might prove interesting if applied to some of the partial glyphs—using existing data and extrapolating the missing portions on a 3D printer. I'll be curious as to your opinion when I'm able to share this. In the interim, if there's anything I can do remotely, don't hesitate to reach out. Murphy out." He taps the control to stop recording, then hits Transmit.

He checks his appearance in a mirror. "Not bad, considering," he mumbles, referring to his somewhat disheveled hair and his ill-fitting flight suit, both casualties of the weightless environment. Then he commands, "New message to Adriana. Record in three."

Again, the three beeps.

"Hi, beautiful. I'm halfway there. I've been replaying your messages to keep me company when I'm not focused on Spencer's stuff. Oh, in fact, I just heard from her. Seems nice enough. She didn't come out and say so, but I think they may have uncovered something big—as in significance, not size. She only spoke in generalities, but my guess is whatever they found is organic. How incredible would that be? Guess I'll find out next week. In the meantime, I'm trying to keep myself busy. I've probably talked to my folks more in the past seven days than I have since I left home. I've watched a lot of movies; turns out I'm a fan of John Wayne.

They called him the Duke—old, old movie star from the mid-twentieth century. I wish I had more to share, but I won't complain that the trip has been uneventful. I miss you and can't wait until I see you again in September. It'll be nice to actually interact, but until then, I'll just keep looking forward to receiving your messages. Hey, maybe you'll forget to put on clothes in the next one?"

He stops recording and sends the transmission. Though she wasn't the least bit prudish in their time together at Blue Rocks, he wonders how she'll react to his suggestion. It was flippant enough to blow off as a joke if it doesn't go over with her; otherwise, he's hoping that she'll comply.

Ninety minutes pass before the com panel chimes with an incoming message.

Adriana's smile greets him, and she says, "I'm sending you an encrypted packet. 'For your eyes only,' Murph, so I hope your retinal scanner is in working order." She winks, pleased with her pun, and signs off.

A moment later, the com panel chimes again, alerting: "Incoming Message. Blue Rocks. Encrypted—Retinal Scan for Access."

Thursday, March 19, 2048—0700

Murph is awakened by the alarm clock. It's o-seven-hundred hours Cydonia time, and he's about three hours away from landing on the new world that he will call home for the next year and a half. Since leaving Earth, he's adjusted his wake-up time a little more than half an hour a day, as a Martian day is thirty-nine minutes, thirty-five seconds longer than Earth's. Back home, it's sixteen hundred hours. His strategy is working, sort of. It'll still be a while before he completely adapts to the nine-hour difference.

Checking the monitor, Mars fills most of the field of view. The atmospheric moisture content makes the sky appear in hues of blue—deeper toward the poles—but at the equator, much of Mars's reddish surface is still visible. Clouds envelop portions of the sky near the poles as well. Though still referred to as the red planet, in a matter of just a few years, the phrase will be a misnomer. Though not yet visible from his vantage point, a series of lakes have formed in low-lying areas. Some bodies of water in the area once called the Gami crater have natural salinity and are now considered inland seas. Geologists and surveyors continually map out areas that are natural basins as Martian oceans are slowly reestablished.

He spends his morning in a brief fight with the zero-gravity shower, then enjoys a packet of strong Colombian coffee—he's too excited to eat—and reviews his notes in preparation for his first face-to-face with Dr. Spencer.

The com panel chimes: "Incoming Message. Mars Science One." Murph taps to accept the transmission. Facing him is a cleanly shaven young man with short, cropped hair. Murphy can make out a uniform—obviously not part of the scientific contingent but rather a member of the United States Space Command. The USSC is the successor to NASA, but no longer under Department of Defense oversight. Just like NASA, USSC is government funded and dedicated to space exploration; unlike the old agency, the new one is a truly civilian organization. But make no mistake about it, USSC still operates with military precision.

"Specialist J. Murphy Cameron, good morning, sir. This is Mars Science One shuttle port," the young man declares.

Murph awaits his next words.

"Specialist Cameron, do you read me, sir?" the young man queries.

"Oh, yes! I read you," Murph responds. "My apologies, I've become so used to transmission packets from Earth and Blue Rocks that I forgot that I'm within range of real-time Mars transmissions. Good morning to you as well. Go ahead."

"No problem, sir. I have some instructions for you. I'm sure you've heard these before, but it's SOP as you approach the Martian atmosphere to be given a refresher. One: check about the cabin for any free-floating items and securely stow them. Two: change out of your flight suit and put on your pressure suit. Three: strap into a seat. Four: remain in your seat until we come into the shuttle to get you. Do you understand these instructions, sir?"

"Yeah, gotcha," says Murph. "Secure loose items, put on my pressure suit, strap in, and stay there until your team comes aboard."

"Very good, sir. You have thirty minutes from the time this transmission was initiated until you're in the upper atmosphere. The craft will descend to an altitude of one hundred feet in the following half-second, then set down. The shuttle's MFD will give you a smooth ride all the way to the surface and will power down within two minutes after touchdown. This is done in order to ease your body into microgravity. The gravitational pull here is more than double what you experienced at Blue Rocks but only about a third of Earth's. Again, stay seated until we come to assist you. On my mark, you'll have twenty-six minutes." The young man's eyes dart toward an unseen clock. "Mark," barks the USSC man. "Mars Science One out."

Murph had been told all this information during his orientation but appreciates the refresher. At Blue Rocks, the BES that he trained in had to be artificially weighted to duplicate Martian gravity. All those hours spent in the simulators and the practice BES are now about to be put to practical use. He's almost giddy but finds focus to prepare for landing. Things now seem surreal, especially after two weeks in relative isolation. The thought that in mere minutes he will be walking on the Martian surface feels incredible.

As promised, his touchdown is smooth. As the mercury-based plasma in the MFD slows from its operational rate of fifty thousand rpm, Murph begins to experience gravity for the first time in two weeks. Strapped into a seat, it feels as though he is sinking into the cushion, a strange sensation. He can hear the spaceport crew making its way to him.

"Specialist Cameron, don't get up just yet, sir. We'll get your straps undone and assist you," says a young man entering the compartment. He appears to be in his late twenties or early thirties, with three chevrons on his sleeve. A much younger woman—attractive, olive skin, raven hair, and a single chevron—accompanies him. She seems so young; Murph guesses it's her first deployment.

His straps removed, each takes a shoulder and sit Murphy upright. "We'll give it a ten count and then try standing, unless you need more time, sir?" the sergeant says.

Murph, again noting the young woman, replies, "I'm good. Let's do this."

"Yes, sir," responds the sergeant. As they help him to his feet, Murph immediately regrets his machismo. His head spins, and he feels the contents of his stomach defying the planet's gravitational pull and seeking an exit. He raises a hand to cover his mouth, but he's too late; his coffee is liberated. Streams of dark-brown fluid bounce and splash in slow motion before finding the floor.

Crimson-faced, Murph exclaims, "Shit! I'm so sorry!"

The sergeant puts a towel in Murph's hand before he finishes his apology. It's obvious to him that the sergeant has seen it all before. He can also tell by the look on the private's face that he hasn't made his hoped-for impression on her. In fact, her complexion has turned ashen as she averts her gaze from the scene.

"Happens to a lot of people," offers the sergeant. "Do you need a few minutes?"

"I'm so sorry," Murph repeats. "I think I'll be okay. Everything feels heavier than I expected."

After cleaning off his chin and hands, Murph attempts to toss the towel over his regurgitated java, but in Martian microgravity, it's a painfully slow descent to the floor, making even more of a spectacle.

"Sir, don't worry about that. The ship will be processed. It happens all the time," the sergeant reassures him. "We'll assist you out of the ship. Your gear and materials will be sent to your quarters in Complex Seven."

Exiting the shuttle, Murph follows the sergeant's every instruction to the letter.

Though occasionally distracted by queasiness, Murph's orientation to Mars Science One feels good in the figurative sense. He is still in partial disbelief over the opportunity to walk on Mars; he knows it'll be hard to sleep tonight. The experience of taking those first steps on the planet's surface and seeing with his own eyes the Martian sky, landscapes, and structures will be exhilarating. Although images transmitted through the retinal display are as good as a view through a glass window, they're still only fabrications. To be able to see and touch *real* things—the more exotic, the better—has preoccupied his dreams since childhood.

Introductions are made to the scientists in the lab. Dr. Spencer, along with most of the other diggers, is absent; all are at various excavation sites. Murphy will head out with them in the morning. For now, he spends some time getting up to speed, though everyone is tight-lipped about the recent findings.

His introduction to Dr. Spencer is scheduled for eighteen hundred Cydonia time. That allows ample opportunity for him to inspect his quarters. As promised, everything has been delivered and stowed. He opens the closet to check on his BES—everything looks good. In the distance, he sees one of the many sites he hopes to dig, the D&M Pyramid. It is named for DiPietro and Molenaar, whose imaging work helped discover structures in early Viking space probe images. He's overcome by a feeling: *eighteen months isn't long enough!*

On the table next to his workstation, he spots a terrarium featuring Martian soil types that Dr. Spencer left as a welcome gift. A card touts: We're glad you're here! It's signed by some fellow diggers he has yet to meet.

Thursday, March 19, 2048—1800

Science Module Eight

"Happy to have you here," says Dr. Roberta Spencer, extending her hand to Murph as she enters the room at precisely eighteen hundred hours.

"Happy to be here, Doctor," he replies, impressed by her strong grip, making her salutation all the more genuine. He notes that although she would never be considered beautiful in the classic sense, there is something very pleasant about her appearance, which he hadn't picked up in her message. *It just goes to show, no matter how refined retinal displays may be, there's no substitute for the real thing*, he thinks to himself.

"Well, where shall we begin?" she asks.

"I have to know. Your recent findings—are we talking organic?"

"Better," she says, smiling. "Walk with me."

Murph follows her into an adjacent room that illuminates upon entry, revealing a laboratory. In the center stands an imaging workstation similar to the one he trained on but newer and more complex in appearance. The machine powers up with a low hum as they approach. Through a window in the apparatus, he can see an object, but his view is partially obstructed as Dr. Spencer begins opening images on the device's retinal display.

"Take a look," she offers.

Murphy's eyes grow wide at the sight of a skeletal hand—three long, slender fingers with an opposable thumb—embedded within what appears to be rock. "You found that here, on Mars?"

"We did, in what we now believe is the base of a giant sphinx in front of the D&M. Initially, we thought we were working with rock, but then this piece broke off—a happy accident, I guess. As soon as we saw the interior of the rock, we knew it had petrified from an organic source. Imagine our shock when imaging showed a biologic within!"

"This is incredible; we could have DNA, Martian DNA ..." Murph interjects.

"Most assuredly we do; we have reason to believe that this creature's skeletal structure is intact, entombed in the petrified material—"

"Possibly a form of mummification?" Murph interrupts.

"We think perhaps a procedure ancient Egyptians carried over into their culture. You're going to help us make that determination," says Dr. Spencer. "Before you start the lab work, I'd like you to come out to the dig in the morning and take a look for yourself."

His eyes still wide, Murph enthusiastically responds, "Try and stop me!"

The remainder of the evening is spent discussing methods for removing the petrified plant material from the bone. The implications of the discovery and speculation as to why other Martian corpses hadn't been found are also batted around. Murph and Spencer easily feed off each other's excitement; it isn't until Murph apologizes for being unable to stifle a yawn that the pair take note of the late hour and part company.

◦◦◦

Friday, March 20, 2048—0600

Complex Seven, Crew Quarters

Murph awakens, surprised he was able to sleep after the previous evening's stimulating and wide-ranging conversation. He reaches for a coffee packet. Pulling the tab, it heats instantly. Once again, he's too keyed up to eat. His java is just the way he likes it— strong, hot, and black. He opts to shower before donning his BES. Because of the long hours spent in the suit, common sense dictates being as clean as possible.

The microgravity shower is considerably more enjoyable than the zero-grav one, plus with ample well water supplying Mars Science One, he can enjoy a long, luxurious wash.

Before donning the BES, Murph puts on a regular pressure suit. He imagines the large, cumbersome suits once worn by Apollo astronauts, which required a dressing team, and wonders if he could have tolerated wearing what amounted to a personal spaceship. In comparison, his pressure suit is akin to a leotard. The combination of highly sophisticated composite materials and the terraforming of the Martian atmosphere have eliminated the need for anything more elaborate. Several regions currently have sufficient barometric pressure to make protective suits unnecessary; however, for the time being, they are mandatory. The suit also protects from cold and exposure to solar radiation, though the latter is a remote threat since terraforming.

Slipping into the BES is no worse than some of the ski suits he's worn on vacation in Aspen or Tahoe—two places that, at the moment, could not be further from his thoughts. In his last few days on Earth, the BES had been fine-tuned to interact with several nanochips that had been injected just beneath the dermis on his wrists. This configuration is designed to project information, which flows between the sensors integrated into the suit's fabric to the retinal display that he'll peer through while working the site. The display requires no surface for projection and, though similar, is far superior to the antiquated technology called heads-up display or HUD.

The first message relayed through the display is his rapid heartbeat. "No shit, sweetheart, I'm about to step onto Mars!" he tells the suit, adjusting his headset.

The rover for the six-person team sits just outside the airlock. The exit light changes to green, the door opens, and Murph takes his first step. The surface reminds him of the dirt road that ran by his uncle's dairy farm near Springfield, Missouri. The soil appears to be more like reddish dirt than the talc-like gray dust covering the moon's surface. As he walks toward the rover, he takes a moment to turn around and look at his footprints. Though preceded by many others, his are now truly and officially part of the Martian landscape. He allows himself the fantasy of stopping briefly to cast a plaster mold, which, in the far-off future, he'll set on his professor's desk, allowing him to wax eloquent to his poor, unsuspecting students with accounts of today's events.

The rover seats are heavily padded because the rocky surface—leftover rubble from the day Mars died—even in microgravity, is still full of bone-rattling ups and downs. The team arrives at the sphinx just before o-eight hundred, and as the others unload equipment, Murph cannot help but stare at his surroundings. The other scientists go about their business, not wanting to interrupt this moment, all understanding his awe. Murph is completely enraptured. However, he becomes increasingly aware that his coffee is betraying him once again. He lifts his visor in the nick of time to expel his liquid breakfast—a reflex that only a few years ago might have cost him his life. But now pressures, temperatures, and atmosphere in the Cydonia region are within human tolerance for short periods.

Cleaning himself off, he checks to see if he'll again be the butt of jokes. But it appears that fortunately the other diggers are far more interested in getting the equipment hauled into the sphinx.

Murph pulls himself together and proceeds toward the immense stone base that once supported a sphinx. This mammoth is more than three times the size of the Great Sphinx of Giza. Unlike Giza, though, where the sphinx was carved out of the limestone bedrock, the this one is granite—an unexpected find on Mars. It was discovered in late 2013 by NASA's Mars Reconnaissance Orbiter using spectral imaging.

Dr. Spencer is several steps ahead of Murph as they descend a staircase taking them beneath the base. Over his headset, he hears her issuing instructions concerning where to set up the new equipment brought along for more detailed imaging of what the scientific team has dubbed "The Mummy." The steps are awkwardly spaced, obviously a design for much taller beings. As the team members in the lead move into the hallways, they trigger the illumination—laser diodes powered by the solar radiation in the ambient atmosphere—to reveal long, polished, albeit dusty, corridors that, unlike the outside of the structure, have remained intact. The passageways are wide enough for team members to walk four abreast beneath ceilings that tower twenty feet above them. There are hieroglyphs carved into the smooth façade at each intersection, placed like street signs though literal translation is not yet possible. Dr. Spencer, who speaks several languages and holds an advanced degree in cryptography, is charged with making that breakthrough.

The team enters a large chamber. Murph's display shows the dimensions as sixty feet long, wide, and high. The farthest wall has a deep indentation. A phrase springs into Murph's head: an open garage. He quickly realizes that, despite his earthling-brain interpretation, the area measures twenty feet high, wide, and deep. To the left of the garage, a portion of a wall has given way. It is the only part of the space that is not square and flush. The contents of what had been either behind or within the wall are spilled onto the cavernous surface. Around this landslide-like mound, the scientists are setting up the imaging equipment.

Once the imager is placed and calibrated, the team forms a semicircle around the Mummy to afford them views from a variety of angles.

He doesn't notice Dr. Spencer at his side until she lays a hand on his shoulder and whispers, "Feeling better, Murph?"

A brief flash of embarrassment reddens his cheeks, realizing his upchuck had not gone completely undetected. "I'm fine, Doctor. It was just …"

"Don't worry about it. Glad you're okay," she says. Then, keying her mic, she addresses the team. "Stand by. Okay, power up."

A brief, low hum follows, and suddenly each team member is looking through the petrified material at the entirety of the skeletal remains. By simply focusing their eyes on small thumbnail images in their periphery, teammates can view one another's perspective, either zooming in or switching spectral mode without disrupting anybody else's image.

"Big fellow, isn't he?" Murph observes.

"Well, we assumed that from the dismembered hand, but of course we couldn't know for certain until now," Specialist Bond chimes in. "Based on the hand size and using human anatomical proportions as a guide, we estimated his height at around nine feet.

"Actual height, nine-eleven and a half," says Dr. Spencer.

"Concur," respond a couple overlapping voices.

"Murphy, what are your initial thoughts?" Dr. Spencer inquires.

"Based on our conversation last evening and what we saw in the lab, I believe we have an excellent chance of removing the petrified material," says Murph. "The lack of atmosphere worked in our favor, preserving the bones. That'll also go a long way in helping us to exhume him and get his bones into a better preservation vessel. I'm hoping those femurs have well-preserved material. We should learn a lot."

Making a sweeping motion, Dr. Spencer directs Murphy's attention to a series of hieroglyphs on some large sections of the broken wall that have been righted and placed carefully to the side of the slide area. "We've combed through what you see here," she says. "But anything else containing glyphs must have been pulverized. These are the partial sections we scanned and forwarded to Blue Rocks via packet. You mentioned an algorithm ..."

"Yes, Doctor. With your permission, I'd like to scan these fragments using an old technology, 3D-SAR Ground Penetrating Radar, apply my algorithm, and produce a solid 3D model," Murph explains. "The resulting output should give us a replication of what these pieces looked like as a whole."

"Murph, you have my full authorization in whatever needs to be done to explain this creature's presence and get a handle on the symbology. Everyone hear that?" she shouts.

"Copy that!" comes the unanimous team reply.

Saturday, April 19, 2048—2330

Complex Eight, Lab Module

After determining the fossilization rate of the organic material encasing the Mummy, Murph estimated the age of the bones as being on the order of 76,000 years. No other specimens have been uncovered, despite the various teams' use of the new calibrated settings on their imaging equipment.

The dating of the skeleton has once again sent the remaining handful of old-school Egyptologists back on Earth into a frenzy. Many years ago, most mainstream archaeologists accepted the proposition that the pyramids, Great Sphinx, and other structures on the Giza plateau were tens of thousands of years older than previously imagined.

Since confirming and cross-checking his dating methods two weeks ago, Murphy has focused on assisting Dr. Spencer in deciphering the baffling symbols.

The revelation hits Murphy like a bolt of lightning—it's not the same! Its depth is different! "How could I have missed something so obvious?" Murph blurts out. The few others working late turn their heads in time to see him depart the lab at top speed.

As a child, Murph had a recurring nightmare of being chased through the darkness by a monster, and no matter how rapidly he churned his legs, they failed him, allowing only slow-motion movement. Though no monster is chasing him, the sensation is still vivid, with Martian gravity restricting his mobility to little more than bouncing in the general direction of his destination. "Shit! I should have just called her," Murph says, reprimanding himself as he heads toward Dr. Spencer's quarters.

On arrival, he is far more winded than expected and tries not to sound like a lunatic when Spencer's voice comes over the com panel. "Who is it, please?" she asks.

"Mur … Mur … Murph … Murphy," he gasps.

"Oh! Just a minute," she replies.

Moments later, the door opens and a disheveled Roberta Spencer with a bad case of bedhead—on the right side—beckons him. "Come in, Murphy. What's got you so agitated at this hour?"

"They're not the same! The depths vary. It's got to be the key!" His eyes are luminous with excitement despite the burlap bags under them, the result of long hours at the dig followed by even longer hours in the lab.

"Come again? And slower this time, please. Take a breath, collect your thoughts, and give it to me intelligibly," she orders, her own pulse beginning to race in anticipation.

Murph inhales deeply. "The double characters; they're not double. The shape is the same, but the depths are different—consistently! They're not double characters at all. I didn't realize it until I took our 3D recreation based on our extrapolations and scanned it using the architectural team's real-time resonance modeler. Once I turned the image ninety degrees and started slicing through, I could see certain characters cut deeper than others. Heavy-handed carving, right? Wrong! There is a difference of ninety microns in the depth of the characters, even though they look identical to one another—totally imperceptible to the human eye. There could be others! We need to start at the beginning and measure the depth of each symbol in addition to considering its shape."

Spencer blinks a few times, staring into his wild eyes as she processes what he just said.

"It's going to take months, but Murph, if you're right ..." Dr. Spencer is now clutching both of his hands in hers, shaking them simultaneously. "Listen," she says, "you look as tired as I feel. This is an order: get back to your quarters, take a good hit of straight oxygen, swallow a six-hour capsule, and meet me for breakfast at o-seven-thirty. Got it?"

"Got it," he replies.

Initially, upon arriving back at his room, he fears being too excited to sleep but suddenly finds himself completely drained. He notices the semiweekly packet from Adriana waiting for him.

"Tomorrow, beautiful, tomorrow," he says and lies on his bunk. In mere moments he's fast asleep.

Monday, September 7, 2048—0845

Complex Seven, Crew Quarters

Murph sits in the corner of Adriana's quarters while she arranges her belongings. He studies how enticingly the pressure suit contours her physique as she recounts the highlights of the two-week shuttle trip with her three traveling companions: a geologist and two USSC replacements. In the mirror, she glimpses his eyes focused intently on her backside and realizes he's not following her story at all. She stops and queries, "Okay, Murph, what were the last two sentences I just said?"

"Huh? Oh, uh ..." he stammers.

"Uh-huh! About what I expected," she chides. "Okay, where is that man of science, Mr. Intellect, Mister Empirical, excavator on a new world with the latest technology? Any idea? Honestly, you're still a Neanderthal!"

"Hey, be glad it's your ass I'm staring at and not one of those USSC grunts," he replies, laughing. "Besides, it's not just your derrière that has me distracted."

"Oh?" Adriana feigns insult.

"Well, what I mean is that *is* a lovely distraction! But there's a lot I have to tell you, although I want to wait until you're settled in. You are absolutely *not* going to believe it."

"Is this about the skeletal remains?"

"Yes and no. I mean, we went all out on the Mummy and published just about every ..."

"Buuuuut ..." she says, drawing out her interjection.

"*But* we focused on its age, condition, composition, DNA—every finding that will keep the eggheads back at Blue and on Earth occupied for years. What we *didn't* elaborate on was: Why were there no others? What was this guy doing sealed into a huge, empty chamber?

"And?" she asks.

"Most of this is in the preliminary stages, and we're still working on significant parts of the cipher, but it appears that our friend stayed behind intentionally, acting as a gatekeeper. He recorded events and—just guessing—when things became unbearable, he encased himself in his tomb, took something to bring about his demise, and drifted off—job done."

"He recorded events for who?" Adriana asks, puzzled.

Murph raises his eyebrows, leans in, and answers, "*Us*, darling, for *us*. Somehow the chamber we found was used as a portal to another place—maybe even a different time. Of course, our best bet is that they relocated to somewhere in Orion Nebula; the references are obvious. At more than thirteen hundred light years away, these ancients were capable of interstellar space travel still well beyond even our most cutting-edge technologies."

"But I thought you found the key to the glyphs."

"We did, sort of. Determining the three-dimensionality of their written words *was* significant; however, this race was not as forthcoming in leaving written records as others …"

"Like the Egyptians?" Adriana interjects.

"Well, for one, but you have to keep in mind that Egyptian hieroglyphs postdate the race that built the pyramids, temples, and monuments. Egyptian hieroglyphs are akin to graffiti found in inner cities. Those grand downtown buildings may have been constructed a hundred or two hundred years ago by the rich during prosperous periods. But over time the decay of American cities brought in less affluent residents, who moved in as the well-to-do left. The ethnic gangs who flourished in these neighborhoods marked their territory, but they were not the builders," Murph explains. "They just overlaid their own version of the English language and symbology on the extant walls."

"No wonder you're so loathed in Egyptology circles, comparing one of the cradles of civilization to street gangs."

SHORT STORIES AND ASSORTED NIGHTMARES

"Hey, there are fewer than a handful left who refuse to accept recent findings and still cling to the politics and practices of old," says Murph. "There are those who seem willing to die out with their outdated ideas, which have been proven inaccurate, at best, or lies—to cover up those inaccuracies—at worst."

"All right, so I have a question for you: If this race was so advanced, why are all the structures and monuments empty? No abandoned computers, displays, or desks. Where's all their equipment?"

"You, my dear, are thinking like an earthling," he scolds, smiling at her as he shakes his head.

"Wha—"

"Back home, we have artificial mountains comprised of rubbish—trash of all sorts, but particularly plastics. Until legislation was enacted to enforce costly recycling laws, as a species, we were running out of places to dump discarded materials that took eons to decompose. My theory is that our friend's people either had materials superior to plastics that posed no such issues, or they found a way to make biodegradable plastics, glass, and the like."

"Incredible. Is that possible?"

"You tell me. We're sitting on Mars with a mummified biologic who died while our ancestors were living in caves," says Murph.

"So what's next?" Adriana inquires.

"Spencer's letting me focus on the portal. I think these structures, much like the ones on Earth, were used as a form of energy similar to our transmission towers, pulling power from the magnetic field. At least, she's letting me run with that theory for now. I'm planning on doing some more exploration with ground-penetrating lasers. It just isn't adding up. There is this cavernous space under what would have been the belly of the sphinx, but no adjacent chambers, and there should be—possibly one with a power source."

Murph rises to his feet, positions himself behind Adriana, presses close, and pushes her long auburn hair to the side, exposing her slender neck, which he begins to kiss just below her left earlobe.

"Mmmm," Adriana moans. "Oh, that feels nice. I've missed you. I wish you were going to be with my team at the D&M dig."

"You tackle the pyramid, baby. I have my hands full of sphinx," Murph says. Quickly changing subjects, he quietly whispers, "Hey, you know, pressure suits are only required when passing through airlocks. You don't have to wear it in your quarters." She laughs; he smiles and begins to gingerly slide down her zipper.

❦

Wednesday, September 9, 2048—1320

Sphinx Dig

After hours of exploration, Murphy begins to see what he'd hoped for from the ground-penetration equipment—returns consistent with a cavity. This one is beneath what had been the paws of the huge structure. The team projects the beam at an angle to estimate where the suspected void begins and ends.

"I can't be certain, but I think we're seeing some symmetry here," Bonds says into his mic. "Looking at about sixty feet in length—wouldn't be surprised to see the same for depth and width."

"If so, we should start looking for the passage into the chamber somewhere around here," Murphy says, pointing toward the center of the newly measured space. "About centered, just like the stairs that lead to the Mummy's lair. Can we get that equipment over here, please?"

After a few more hours of testing, the ground proves too hardpacked for the GPL to discern whether a staircase similar to the one in the Mummy chamber exists. "I'm making the call," announces Murphy. "Let's dig!"

The team, using an old-fashioned, time-honored technique, begins to mark off a grid, the suspected location of the buried staircase. They start removing material in a systematic fashion, sifting through excavated soil, all the while looking for any indication of artificial elements.

After only a few hours of digging, "Jackpot!" comes over the com from Bonds. "You called it, Murph, I've uncovered what can only be a riser—we've got steps!"

Wednesday, September 16, 2048—1010

Sphinx Dig

Dr. Roberta Spencer arrives at the site, having been summoned by Murph. "We've got an opening," he says as she approaches after exiting the rover.

"Thanks for waiting," Spencer says, smiling. "Not sure I could have exercised the same the self-control for you. I probably would have been in there no matter what!"

"Well, to be honest, we did look—just a little peek—but not with any artificial light."

"And?" she asks.

"Pitch black," Murph replies, laughing. "Our displays definitely picked up objects—nothing organic or biologic—but there are artifacts of some sort, and I insisted we save the honor of getting the first real look for the boss."

Once again, Murph can see in Spencer's face the enthusiasm that makes her so genuine and gives her that attractive quality he can't quite articulate.

"Shall we do this?" Spencer asks.

"Let's go," Murph answers.

Illumination pods in hand, Spencer, Murphy, and Bonds make their way down the newly excavated staircase. They find the same large steps as the other location, near the opening that leads to the chamber. The open doorway has not been completely cleared of debris, requiring the threesome to climb over the remaining mound of Martian soil. As the artificial light fills the space, the three scientists stand rigid, eyes locked on the far end of the room.

"That ... those are ..." Murph loudly whispers, his voice throttled by the sight before him.

"That's what I'm seeing," agrees Spencer.

After the passage of several moments, Bonds chimes in, "Of course, we're only speculating without a complete syllabary, but I have to admit to you that it's my first hypothesis as well."

Against the back wall stand two tablets—squared bases with rounded tops— towering the nearly sixty-foot height of the space. On each tablet are five sets of hieroglyphs.

"Oh my God," Murph blurts out.

"You said it," agrees Spencer. "The theologians back home are going to have a collective brain aneurism when we tell them we've discovered the Ten Commandments written in the original Martian.

Murph looks at her and asks, "Who says the Martians wrote them? Moses claimed it was the finger of God on Mount Sinai; perhaps He created more than one set? Perhaps stones like these are all throughout the universe?" Murph can't believe the words are his. It's as if his brain has disengaged from his mouth; he cannot stop his speculation that God may exist.

Bonds begins to openly weep.

Tuesday, September 29, 2048—2430

Murphy's Quarters

Murph lies awake in his bunk, recalling the events of the previous two weeks. The discovery of the tablets served as the primer needed to translate the Martian hieroglyphs. One by one, the secrets of the red planet have been giving up the ghost, but there is one that Murph cannot let go of. A fragment from a broken tablet, recovered near the Mummy's final resting place, held only one decipherable passage: "To be with God." Unfortunately, it is one of several pieces too broken to give context to the passage, making it impossible for his algorithm to extrapolate.

He stares at an image of the Mummy on his display and asks, "Is that where your people went—*to be with God?* Does God live in Orion Nebula? Did you actually know a living God, or did you act on faith?"

Wednesday, September 30, 2048—0630

Adriana's Quarters
Adriana awakens to her alarm and sees the communication icon flashing on her display—a message from Murphy. She pulls a tea pouch from the cupboard, pulls the tab, adds a packet of sweetener, falls into a chair, and taps the icon. "This better be good, Murph. I haven't even had my frigging tea yet," she says, sipping.

"Good morning, beautiful. First, I want you to understand how difficult my decision is," Murphy begins.

Hearing those words and seeing his serious demeanor, she sits up straight and sets down her tea.

"I've often thought about a future for us, a future together, but regrettably I am obsessed with finding answers. I've been toying with the portal in the Mummy chamber, and I think I can replicate the power needed to activate—"

"Nooo!" she screams.

"The gateway. I've kept no notes on this, as I don't want anyone else attempting to follow me. If this turns out to be a mistake, I don't want to be responsible for other lives."

Her eyes wide, tearing, she screams again, "No!"

"I've left a similar message for Dr. Spencer," he says with a wry smile, "but in hers, I didn't say 'I love you' because I want you to know, Adriana, I really *do* love you. This is something I have to do—I'm going to try to be with God. If I do, maybe He'll arrange for us to be together again. In the interim, please, please, be happy."

The playback ends. Adriana scrambles to her feet, grabs her robe, and tries to run toward the door that opens to the hallway, only to feel the quagmire of Martian light gravity. She gets as far as her com panel and slams it and hollers a command, "Dr. Roberta Spencer. *Now!*"

Spencer appears, and it's obvious to Adriana that the doctor has received her version of Murph's message.

"I'm sorry, dear," Dr. Spencer says. "I did *not* see this coming."

Adriana is crying. She nods her head in agreement. Her nose is beginning to run. She grabs a tissue and through it responds, "Neither did I. Oh, Murph." She softly sobs. Abruptly, she pauses and then with a small smile says, "If he does find God, I hope he doesn't throw up in front of Him."

Spencer returns Adriana's sad smile.

THE DAY EARTH DIED

V-Day

Scientists tell us it will be instantaneous. Vaporized in the blink of an eye. Vaporization Day. V-Day, some are calling it. The asteroid hurtling toward Earth is more than half the size of our planet's moon, nearly 1,100 miles in diameter, moving at 88,000 miles per hour. Between the moment it first touches Earth's magnetic field and the moment it touches the outer atmosphere, every living thing on the planet—without exception—will perish from the shock wave. The ensuing collision will take place between two galactic bodies, both devoid of life.

There is some speculation that the moon will not survive; that it'll be torn apart by the magnitude of the blast and resulting gravitational forces. There is another theory that since the moon will be on the opposite side of the impact, it may be jettisoned into deep space to travel on as its liberator had once done, gliding through the cosmos, or perhaps ending up trapped in the orbit of some unknown, distant planet.

In the past two weeks, since its unanticipated discovery, astrophysicists have run the gamut of explanations as to how such an enormous object had gone undetected for so long. Despite the chorus of outcries, from citing the lack of funding to monitor the universe to the excuse that it had been hidden from sight by its angle of approach, all answers provide only cold comfort.

There are those who call the rock "Nibiru"; some call it "Planet X." The internet pseudoscience behind the names refers to a hypothetical or—more likely—mythical planet, which makes it presence known once every twenty-five million years. The bottom line, however, is that it is *not* a planet. It's a planet *killer*. In its passage through the solar system, this lifeless ball of rock and dust has been steered by the sun's gravity into a path that will cross Earth's orbit. The same invigorative fiery ball of gases that warms the Earth in that delicate balance that allows life to flourish is now about to be responsible for its demise.

If one must refer to the space rock by name, then it is 2038FG22, discovered two weeks ago, on the seventh day of March in the final year of Our Lord 2038, the twenty-second asteroid to be found this year. Within hours of the panicked announcement, the worldwide scientific community had calculated the day and time of cataclysm. The astronomer who discovered it, therefore having naming privileges, opted—for obvious reasons—not to associate himself with the Earth annihilator.

Just days ago, there was a poorly coordinated multinational effort to deflect the asteroid from its path. The nuclear-armed nations launched hundreds of missiles toward the rock. Bloom after bloom were observed by telescopes throughout the world as the superweapons, so dreaded for decades with their unimaginable capacity for utter destruction, proved impotent against this inexorable force. Even the handful that successfully detonated failed to significantly alter either its mass or course. Earth's fate was sealed when the glow of the last nuke faded, revealing that the rock had prevailed.

But these actions almost superseded the planet's obliteration by the asteroid. The unprecedented number of launchings triggered American autonomous systems—often called doomsday devices— that nearly plunged the globe into World War III. Launch detection systems, in place for decades, had automatically attempted to intercept what they were perceiving as incoming hostile targets, while launching counterstrikes. These weapons were designed to be a deterrent to any foe seeking to execute a surprise nuclear attack on the United States, guaranteeing MAD, mutually assured destruction. Other nations with similar defense schemes faced the same scenario, scrambling to convince their supercomputers that they were *not* under attack and redirecting the machines instead to launch nuclear warheads at a target in space.

The president made her public pronouncement, pulling no punches. She urged restraint and compassion by the citizenry in the remaining few days to come. There would be no evacuations, no relocations to hardened bunkers, no ark of any sort—it all would be pointless.

For several days, chaos has reigned in the major cities, skyscraper fires burning out of control, stores being looted of any and all merchandise, the streets becoming a free-for-all bloodbath, gunfire heard around the clock. There were initial attempts by authorities to maintain order, but the police presence soon dwindled as, overwhelmed by the madness surrounding them, the men and women in blue returned to their homes to huddle with their loved ones and await the end.

There are still a few broadcasts, but those presenting themselves as journalists are actually unknowns; perhaps just craving whatever fame and notoriety they can amass before the airwaves go silent forever. Most of the coverage is appalling carnage taking place in the streets.

NASA and the other space agencies have telescopic cameras trained on the rock, providing live-streaming feeds. Even up close, though, the asteroid appears as an unassuming white dot—perhaps, slightly brighter than the rest.

A church pastor in New York had commandeered what used to be The Prayer Channel and has been broadcasting continuously for the past three days. His eyes wild, his complexion waxy and pale, he preaches nonstop, not even pausing for a drink of water, his pants stained with urine, and his shirt soaked through with sweat. He is the personification of a madman. He'll likely drop dead before the rock hits.

In one report, a large passenger jet crashed into another on a JFK runway. Both pilots, attempting to ferry family and friends to a remote area—wherever they thought that might be—were in the process of taking off without air traffic control when their paths intersected, resulting in a massive fireball and the incineration of two planeloads of would-be refugees. The reporter claims similar events are taking place in cities around the world.

There's no real communication possible, other than the previously mentioned lunacy at a handful of television stations. With few exceptions, people have gone to find a familiar place to die. Utilities and other automated public services remain in operation, while any functions requiring human initiative have largely been abandoned.

My team has picked out a spot atop a high ridge that will give us a spectacular vantage point to observe the end. Isn't it ironic that even as Earth is about to be destroyed, we still can't quite accept …

"Whatcha workin' on there?" queries Danielle's sweet voice in my headset.

"Oh, hey. Uh, just recording some notes—for posterity, I guess," I reply.

"Not to be morbid, but *whose* posterity, exactly?"

"Your guess is as good as mine, but someone was here once—long ago—and maybe someone will come back again. Perhaps whoever built these pyramids will return. I think they'd like to know about us, that the third planet was once home to a reasonably intelligent species of being who ventured to other worlds."

"It could be eons before another creature comes across our site, and, even then, do you think your computer could survive? I mean solar radiation …"

"Yeah, I thought of that. Once I have my thoughts written down, I plan on using the 3D printer to output these pages as tablets, providing our alphabet, numbers, etc., as a primer, hoping they can figure it out."

"Guys, I think it's happening. No transmissions at all now," Sig reports, "only static."

"Man your scopes, folks!" I say as the four of us peer into our viewers, each one trained on the Earth.

"Oh my God," says Lindsay. "Look at that!"

No other words are spoken as a small, brilliant streak appears from the blackness and Earth explodes, its magma core pushed through its crust on the opposite side of the impact. The heat from the collision creates a spectacular light show of reds, oranges, and yellows—the sight juxtaposed with absolute silence. The only sonic disturbance is the excited breathing of my colleagues in my headset. No matter how many times you try to process the scientific reality that sound cannot exist in a vacuum, the total destruction of a world—an entire planet with billions of souls inhabiting it—shouldn't happen without a sound. And yet, it just has.

For hours we watch in silence as the nebulous cloud-like mass that had been our home darkens, until it is no longer discernible from the space in which it drifts. The moon is no longer visible—either destroyed or on its way to God knows where. Regardless, the science station there was surely obliterated.

"Well," I say to the other three, "shall we make our way back down to base?"

"Show's over," says Danielle, her voice choked.

We start back down the side of the ridge toward our encampment and spacecraft, leaving our scopes trained on what had been our home world.

Breaking the silence, I say, "Here's a thought—just throwing it out there—we are scheduled to lift off in nine days, but now that we're officially a doomed Mars expedition, would anyone be interested in doing some sightseeing? Leaving early and navigating—setting down on another part of Mars or paying a visit to Phobos before our supplies run out and we join our brethren in the hereafter?"

"Sure. It's not like we have anywhere else to go," says Danielle.

MOONSHOT

Glossary:

RETRO   **Retrofire Officer**—Responsible for abort procedures and trans-earth injection, or TEI, retrofire burns.

FIDO   **Flight Dynamics Officer**—Responsible for the space vehicle flight path.

GUIDANCE   **Guidance Officer**—Monitors onboard navigational systems and onboard guidance computer software.

SURGEON   **Flight Surgeon**—Directs all operational medical activities.

EECOM   **Electrical, Environmental, and Consumables Management**—Monitor cryogenic levels, cabin cooling/pressure systems, and electrical distribution systems.

GNC   **Guidance, Navigation, and Control Systems Engineer**—Responsible for the reaction-control system and main engine.

TELMU   **Telemetry, Electrical, and EVA Mobility Unit Officer**— Monitors the electrical and environmental systems, plus astronaut spacesuits.

CONTROL	**Flight Controller**—Has overall responsibility for success and safety.
PROCEDURES	**Procedures, or Organization and Procedures Officer**—Monitors and enforces mission policy and rules.
INCO	**Integrated Communications Officer**—Monitors in-flight communications and instrumentation systems.
FAO	**Flight Activities Officer**—Checklists, procedures, etc.
NETWORK	**Network**—Supervises ground-station communications.
RECOVERY	**Recovery Supervisor**—Coordinates spacecraft recovery.
CAPCOM	**Capsule Communicator**—Communicates with astronauts.

October 10
Business World Network, Studio A—New York, New York

"Welcome back to *Net Worth*. I'm your host, Steve Kardon. As promised before the break, joining me in the studio today is one of the nation's growing number of high-tech multibillionaires. She is *rocketing* to success since developing a hot, must-have app. And, not unlike a few other intrepid entrepreneurs, she is launching her own space endeavor, more specifically, an American return to the moon. Join me in welcoming Tori Navarro." An enthusiastic round of applause from the studio staff. "Thanks for being with us today, Tori."

"Thank you for having me, Steve."

"Tori, before we get into space exploration, tell us a little about your latest app. I understand it's something new in voice recognition, correct?"

"I'd be happy to. Let me start by saying that voice recognition is only a small part—albeit an integral one—of what the app offers, particularly in regard to app security. However, *speech* recognition is what gives the app its fluid integration between human and device. We have developed proprietary software in computational linguistics, a quantum leap beyond traditional speech-pattern recognition—"

"Sorry to interrupt, but I'm not sure I follow. Is there a difference between voice and speech recognition?"

"Most definitely. Using *voice* recognition, your device, let's say your smartphone, hears your voice and recognizes it as you. It's the same way you unlock your phone with a fingerprint. All those ridges, whorls, and valley patterns on your fingertip are unlike anyone else's, making your print unique. Well, your voice has measurable pitch points, cadences, and a number of other measurable factors that make your voice singular, hence *voice* recognition. Now, *speech* recognition is the ability of the software to process what you say and *understand* what was said, so you can launch the app. Here, I'll demonstrate on my phone." Tori produces an iPhone and places her finger on the home button. The fingerprint icon appears but fails to fill in. "Hmmm, let me try it again," she says with a nervous chuckle, but again, it fails. "Third time's the charm?" There's an audible chuckle from the show's crew, but this time the phone unlocks. "Whew! That could have been embarrassing," she jokes. More laughter.

"So what makes this thing tick?" asks Steve.

"Many of the app capabilities are closely guarded for security reasons. What I can share with you and your international viewers is that we're using digital, artificial, neural integration, or DANI for short."

"Ah! Hence the app name," Steve points out.

"Correct, we call her Dani. Now, for those of you with iPhones, to launch the Apple AI assistant, you use the command:

'Hey Siri.' In order to open DANI, simply use the command, 'Dani Dani.'" Steve gestures to his guest to demonstrate.

Tori holds her phone a little closer and says, "Dani Dani."

A clear and sultry female voice replies, "Hi, Tori, how may I help you?"

"Open my credit-union app and move three hundred dollars from savings to checking."

"All right." After a momentary pause, the voice resumes, "Your last credit-union session has timed out, and its app would like you to reenter your password; may I do that for you?"

"Yes," Tori replies with a slight smirk.

"I now have access. Please confirm, transferring three hundred dollars and no cents from your savings account to your checking account. Is this correct?"

"Yes," Tori replies.

"Transaction complete. The credit-union app is asking if you'd like another transaction."

"No, but open my Universal Cellular app and pay my bill," Tori says.

"All right. The amount is forty-five dollars and sixty cents and is due on the sixteenth of the month. Would you like to pay that amount on that date?

"Pay that amount on the *fifteenth*," Tori replies.

"Authorization complete. Payment to Universal Cellular will post October fifteenth in the amount of forty-five dollars and sixty cents. Is there anything else with which I may help?"

"No," Tori says, and with that, the stage personnel erupt in spontaneous applause. Tori smiles and nods in acknowledgement.

"Wow," says Steve. "So you just transferred money and paid your phone bill in less time than I could by typing the commands on my phone, and you did it without a single hiccup. Impressive. Now, what if I tried that with your phone?"

"Here," she says, handing it to him. "Give it your best shot."

Steve holds up the phone so the camera can get a clear view of the screen. "Dani Dani," he commands. The screen turns red with a terse error message: *Voice not recognized*, accompanied by Dani's announcement: "Voice not recognized." "Okay," says Steve, "but I'm a guy; so sure, my voice isn't going to be hard to distinguish from yours. Would you mind if we experimented a little?"

"Go right ahead," Tori assents confidently.

"Mandy, Barbara, would you ladies join us on set, please? For you folks at home, two of our producers, Mandy Lepidus and Barbara Barnes."

The women step onto the stage and shake Tori's hand before sitting either side of her on the white sofa.

Barbara goes first, "Dani Dani," but without success.

Then Mandy takes a turn, "Dani Dani," but cannot fool the app.

"What if the app is already open? Could someone rip your phone from your hand and start issuing commands?" Steve asks.

"Well, let's try it," Tori says. Mandy is still holding the phone, and Tori commands, "Dani Dani."

Once again, the sexy voice replies, "Hi, Tori, how may I help you?"

Tori nods to Mandy.

Mandy says, "Open my—"

Before she can finish the bogus command, the screen turns red, the phone locks, and Dani replies, "Sorry. Voice not recognized."

"Wow, Dani cut her right off," Steve exclaims.

"Yes, and not only that, she locked the phone as well. And you can set preferences. For example, after five unsuccessful attempts, you can have Dani wipe the phone clean or lock your apps so that any of them that require passwords will logout and require a new login. There are a number of ways to customize it for security," says Tori, "including creating secret pass phrases that only you and Dani know."

"Not to be a wise guy, but what about impersonation? I can remember as a youngster watching Rich Little on *The Tonight Show* with Johnny Carson. He sounded more like Johnny than Johnny did! What's to prevent a scenario where your voice is imitated?" Steve asks.

Tori replies, shrugging, "That must be a little bit before my time. Sorry, I don't know who you're talking about." Again the stagehands laugh. "But in terms of someone imitating a voice, it's just not possible with that degree of accuracy. What we can hear is only part of what is being measured. If you were to make it analogous to a fingerprint, you'd have to slice off the other person's skin and overlay it on yours. Even then, you'd have to make certain there was a large enough sample to match all the measured points."

"What if you had a bad cold or laryngitis—or just had your tonsils out?" The stage crew laughs at Steve's antics.

Smiling, Tori replies, "Of course, there are limits, but I think you'd be surprised at just how broad the range is for Dani's recognition capabilities."

"What about languages other than English?"

Tori replies, "Yes, she's fluent in a number of languages and even dialects, with more coming online steadily."

"Well, what if *you* were to speak to her in a foreign language, would she still recognize you?"

"She would, because my voice is my voice, and Dani is programmed to auto-detect language. I lived in Florida, where much of the Cuban immigrant population speaks a mixture of English and Spanish, what we jokingly call 'Spanglish.' Dani can even understand this dual-language dialect."

"We've got to take another commercial break, but when we return, Tori Navarro is going to fly us to the moon, and if her rocket is anything like her app, I have no doubt that it will be a successful mission. We'll be right back."

"Once again, welcome back to *Net Worth* here on BWN. I'm Steve Kardon, and with us today is Tori Navarro, creator of the wildly popular Dani app. For those rejoining us, during the break, we did our absolute best to trick the Dani app, and every attempt was thwarted. Pretty impressive stuff, Tori. It's easy to see why your program was snatched up by the Silicon Valley giant AdapTech.

Speaking of which, I know they do a lot of work for NASA, and with you having your own space endeavor, do you think you may end up in competition with another enterprise employing your creation?"

"That's entirely possible, Steve," Tori replies with a good-natured smile. "NASA is the only one currently talking about the moon. Musk's group, Space-X, wants to go to Mars. Virgin Galactic is struggling just to get to low-Earth orbit. So, yeah, in the future, we may be up against one or more of them. But I think we have the edge. Aside from the fact that NASA's a bureaucratic quagmire, they'll be depending on vendors to equip them with AI. Much of the technology we created for Dani has been integrated into our space access system, or SAS. Although I cannot go into too much detail, our components literally talk to one another and even problem solve."

"Tell us about your plans; how confident are you about getting to the moon?"

"To be blunt, we wouldn't be doing it if we weren't one hundred percent certain, and Dani has afforded us a ten-figure budget to make it happen."

"Money is one matter, and not to downplay how substantial an investment we're talking about, the technical and physical demands of such an undertaking are staggering. I'm assuming you didn't just wake up one morning and decide, 'Hey, if my app sells, I'm going into space ...'" Chuckles from the studio hands.

Laughing, Tori replies, "No, no, it wasn't like that at all. Growing up, I listened to my father talk about the space race with the Soviets and the moon missions of the late sixties and early seventies. How disappointed Dad was that NASA finally settled for unmanned probes to other worlds and confined humankind to low-Earth orbit with the space shuttle program ..."

"Your father worked for NASA, did he not?" Steve interjects.

"He did, he did. He started out at JPL in California; he headed part of the team that created what eventually became the Cassini Space Probe, though at the time he didn't know it. Our space agencies kept their people so compartmentalized—and still do—that sometimes they didn't even know what they were working on. Anyway, shortly after my mother passed away, he was offered a position with NASA working on the space shuttle program. He thought the change would be good for us, so we moved to Florida. He loved his work; though he never got over 'abandoning the moon,' as he put it. All the while, he was constantly upgrading the electronics in the various orbiters as well as designing and overseeing the upgrades. When they retired the shuttle fleet, he was offered a position on the new Orion project but never got the chance, due to a distracted driver, a young man on his smartphone … a painful irony."

"I'm sorry," says Steve.

"Me too. Thanks. He was a great talent."

"And I'm guessing a great inspiration?"

"Oh, yeah. He also taught me quite a bit about managing a team. I have to credit Dad with instilling in me the ability to spot and recruit 'the half dollars in an industry full of steel pennies'—one of *his* father's expressions."

"And about your team …"

"Well, going back a few years, after receiving my PhD from the University of California, Santa Cruz, I was happy to be back in California and decided to stick around for a while, much to Dad's chagrin. But he was so accustomed to seventy-hour workweeks that he didn't give me too much grief for not coming home. So between acquaintances, old friends of my father, and some classmates, I started assembling a group of like-minded individuals. Several of my key people came from Scaled Composites, Burt Rutan's company. When Northrop Grumman bought Scaled, working there lost much of its appeal to a whole lotta folks. We have people from Boeing and test pilots from Lockheed, and I have several of Dad's JPL coworkers. Basically, everyone who knew Dad was happy to offer their consultative services, even if they didn't come with us. All we lacked was funding. It wouldn't have been difficult to find venture capitalists anxious to throw money at us. Our team's pedigrees and willingness to kick in personal investments—more than a few 401ks and second mortgages—made us appealing. The potential investors, however, only saw the commercial potential. But we wanted to stick to science, so instead, about half-a-dozen years ago, we created a small software development company—raising the funds on our own while burning the candle at both ends—and now we're a month away from our first unmanned test flight."

"That's incredible," says Steve. "Tell us more about your ship and facility. How does anyone even go about getting through all that governmental red tape?"

"We have an excellent legal team; they've squared us away with the FAA. However, there were a couple of other 'agencies,'" Tori emphasizes, making air quotes, "whom I won't name that were very interested in all of our personal backgrounds, politics, and religious beliefs." Chuckles from the crew. "As I say, the pedigrees of these scientists speak for themselves, so the vetting wasn't as bad as it could have been. As far as our ship design, SAS, it is a single-stage, two-burn, modularly constructed system. Those big, beautiful Saturn Vs that took us to the moon fifty years ago were their own worst enemy. There was such a delicate balance between power and diminishing returns. More power means more fuel, which means more weight, and more weight requires more power, which requires more fuel and so on. Those ships stood over three-hundred-sixty feet tall, measured thirty-three feet in diameter, and weighed six-and-a-half-million pounds—all to carry three people."

"Well, to be fair, Tori, it was state of the art at that time," Steve points out.

"Not meaning to denigrate this technological accomplishment in any way, merely drawing a contrast. SAS-One is smaller than a lot of yachts sailing on the Hudson. It's eighty-four feet tall and twenty-two feet in diameter. The first-stage ascent motor will take the ship and crew into the thermosphere, where the shuttle orbiter used to fly, about three hundred and fifty miles up. The reusable motor capsule will dislodge, rotate one hundred eighty degrees, facing its heat shield downward, and fall back to Earth. Its landing will be softened using small retrorockets and parachutes. The outer walls of the engine compartment will slide into place over the exterior of the crew compartment—the way a sliding door works on a minivan." Tori gestures in an outward, then upward motion. "This additional shielding will get our crew safely through the Van Allen radiation belt and any solar flares."

"Doesn't sound like they'll have much of a view …"

"Ah, no, there's no view. There are no windows, but they'll have plenty to see from cameras and sensors. The cockpit is pretty amazing in terms of how much information is displayed."

"Your crew, Tori, consists of only two astronauts; is that correct?"

"It is. SAS-Two will set down on the moon as a single unit, no need for a command module to orbit; so our pilots fly there and get to do all the EVA stuff themselves. They don't have to feel bad for someone stuck in orbit who only gets to watch, like Michael Collins during Apollo 11." Tori gestures, as if looking out a porthole, and gets snickers from the stagehands.

"How long will they be able to stay on the moon?" Steve inquires.

"Well, our first flight is unmanned. It will orbit the moon and then come home after four days. Apollo 8, which was manned, took seven days for the same mission. Again, that's how much more efficient our boost-to-weight ratio is, and the lightness and strength of our composite construction is far superior to any of the alloys used during Apollo missions. Our engine design is also much more efficient, and, of course, our computers are light years ahead of those from five decades ago. We're hopeful that a successful mission will put us on course for the first manned return to the moon within six months. Once we send a team, it will be up to their discretion when to return, but they'll have a maximum of eight, maybe nine days."

"Where are you planning to land?" queries Steve.

"We sorta have an internal lottery going to determine that. Some of us want to set down in Mare Tranquilitatis—the Sea of Tranquility—and explore the Apollo 11 landing site. I do want to point out that under no circumstances will our crew do anything other than record and capture images. We consider the site sacred—not to be disturbed, not even a footprint. Others want to land where Apollo did not tread, and still others want the dark side of the moon. So, as yet, we haven't made a decision."

"How about the trip home?" asks Steve.

"After lifting off the lunar surface, they'll pilot SAS-Two into Earth's atmosphere, but before entering, the minivan doors open outward to serve as a heatshield, and the ship is oriented to have those shields facing downward. Once SAS-Two approaches the troposphere, parachutes are deployed, and the booster engine is employed to soft land, hopefully right back at our facility in Willow Springs."

"Willow Springs?"

"Just outside Mojave, California, not far from Scaled's spaceport facility and Edwards Air Force Base."

"Sounds like a prime spot ..." Steve places a hand to his ear and fumbles with his earpiece. "Tori, I'm sorry, but I'm being told we're running long, and I still have so many questions for you. Will you come back after your flight next month and speak with us some more?"

"I'd be happy to; thanks for having me on today."

"It's been a pleasure."

November 16—8:37 a.m.
Willow Springs, California—Launch Day

At SAS Control, the vibe surrounding the first unmanned flight is electric. Today, 140 technicians, scientists, and other experts—less than a third of the complement needed to launch a shuttle—are on hand. The last moon launch of a human-rated rocket occurred December 7, 1972, before a majority of folks in the flight control center were even born.

From her vantage point, Tori watches the entire room, her headset crackling with conversations between various launch teams and the flight director. The countdown clock has stopped at T-minus ten minutes, a predetermined hold to allow for the resolution of any last-minute issues.

Though an unmanned test, all teams, including flight personnel, are participating. Those not involved in the actual launch are stationed in simulators that will communicate commands remotely to SAS-One. Tori's aim is to make this test as real as possible.

"Launch teams, I need a go/no-go to resume." It's the voice of flight director, Vincent D'Angelo, a former colleague of Tori's father and close family friend. "RETRO?"

"Go, Flight!"

"FIDO?"

"Go, Flight!"

"Guidance?"

"Go, Flight!"

"Surgeon?"

"Go, Flight!"

"EECOM?"

"Go, Flight!"

"GNC?"

"Go, Flight!"

"TELMU?"

"Go, Flight!"

"Control?"

"Go, Flight!"

"Procedures?"

"Go, Flight!"

"INCO?"

For the first time in the human history of space flight, a familiar, synthetic female voice, serving as the integrated communications officer, replies, "Go, Flight!"

"FAO?"

"Go, Flight!"

"Network?"

"Go, Flight!"

"Recovery?"

"Go, Flight!"

"CAPCOM?"

"Go, Flight!"

"We are at T-minus nine minutes and counting. We are go for the launch of SAS-One," Vincent announces. A spontaneous cheer erupts throughout the facility.

With the resumption of the countdown, the cheering is short-lived as technicians man their displays and the teams prepare for launch.

Vincent's voice comes over the headsets: "T-minus five minutes and counting. Transferring all power to SAS-One internal fuel cells."

"Check! Fuel cells are go," comes the reply.

Vince announces, "SAS-One is now on internal power. Retract access arm. Perform auxiliary power unit prestart."

"We are go," comes the reply from the pilot in the simulator.

"Go for APU start."

The teams proceed with their respective checklists as the countdown continues. Despite having rehearsed this routine dozens of times, Tori can detect an edge in most everyone's voices. She allows herself the momentary distraction of considering Dani's capacity for evaluating stress, perhaps even lie detection.

"T-minus two minutes," Vincent announces.

Within the simulator, the voice of Commander Wilson follows Vincent's: "Flight crew, close and lock visors."

"Check, closed, and locked," replies Specialist Manning.

"T-minus thirty seconds. We have auto-sequence start. SAS-One's computers now have primary control," says Vincent. "There will be no aborting the launch from this point forward to zero. Eleven. Ten. Nine. Eight. Seven. Six. Go for main engine start ... we have main engine start ... two ... one ... and liftoff! SAS-One is en route to the moon!"

Cheers and applause shatter the quiet of the control room.

"Three-and-one-half miles in altitude, speed now Mach 1.6. Everything's looking good," Vincent confirms.

All eyes not riveted on system monitors are fixed on the large HD display—a split screen, one side showing a view of the ground from an external camera, the other providing a view of SAS-One from the ground. A bright blueish-white plume of flame obscures the bottom of the rocket. The SAS engine is so efficient that there is minimal vapor.

"T-plus two minutes. SAS-One is twenty-nine miles in altitude, traveling at Mach 3. Main engine running at ninety percent, go for throttle up."

"Go for throttle up," replies Commander Wilson from the simulator. He advances the T-shaped handle into the full upright position. SAS-One responds immediately.

"Power now at one hundred percent," Vince confirms.

SAS-One continues to climb and increase speed; all the while, Vincent calls out velocity and altitude. Every station within the control room is reporting the latest levels and tolerances, fortunately all well within expected limits.

For the first time since waking at 2:00 a.m., Tori is beginning to relax as she listens to overlapping voices crisscross the room. It is starting to take on the perfunctory feel of an exercise, and her team no longer sounds on edge.

"T-plus seven minutes, altitude approaching three hundred and thirty nautical miles. Stand by for throttle back to seventy-two percent," Vincent instructs the flight crew.

"Copy. Standing by for throttle back to seven-two percent," Wilson confirms.

"Go with throttle back."

"Copy. Throttle back."

"Main engine cutoff in one minute. Stand by for main engine cutoff and module ejection," Vincent says.

"Copy. Standing by for MECO and ME," replies Wilson.

"MECO in nine. Eight. Sev—"

The control room goes silent as stunned team members stare at monitors and consoles no longer displaying data. The split screen on the large HD display is black on one side, with blue text indicating: No Signal. The other, the view from the ground to the heavens, where SAS-One should be, displays only a distant ring of blue fire, high up. It has the appearance of a doughnut composed of bright-blue flame, swirling, growing wider as it slowly dissipates. There is no sound in the room except for the ping of hardware trying to reestablish a connection.

A rumble of what sounds like distant thunder.

An eternity of a moment passes in dead silence, interrupted only when a synthetic voice comes over the intercom: "Flight, INCO. I have lost all contact with SAS-One, including all secondary and tertiary systems. No telemetry is incoming from primary or backup systems. It appears the mission has experienced a catastrophic failure." The words hang in the air.

"Flight, copy INCO?"

"Copy," says Vincent in a whisper. "All stations, Flight. We're in lockdown. Secure all data; back up all systems immediately." Vincent turns toward Tori's post. Mouth agape, she stares at the blank monitor above his head.

Her wide eyes slowly descend and fix on Vincent's. She silently mouths, "What?" All Vincent can do is shake his head and shrug.

The team goes quietly about its business, all focused on preserving data for the upcoming postmortem. Each has put hours, days, months, years into this project, to the exclusion of all else—friends, family; some relationships didn't survive. Without saying the words, each knows that this could be the end of a dream, one that mere moments ago appeared to be within reach. The moon has never felt as far away as it does right now.

The vibrations are felt just before the low thrum of the four-bladed, twin-engine Blackhawks can be heard. Three ships in formation make a swift descent into the Willow Spring Launch Facility compound, stirring up clouds of the desert sand that surrounds the paved parking area. Techs, who had been observing the launch outdoors, shield their faces as the choppers touch down.

Brian Lane, who had earlier been at the launch pad, now bolts for the doors to enter the launch control building.

No sooner does the landing gear touch the asphalt when the helicopters' doors open, and several armed men scramble out of each bird, establishing a perimeter. None raise their weapons in a threatening manner; yet, the blood of each person observing the scene runs cold.

Spotting Tori, still locked in a staring contest with Vincent, Brian shouts, "Tori!" It's the first sound above a whisper since the loss of SAS-One. Every head snaps in Brian's direction. "Tori, we've got company—choppers! They must be from Edwards. They got here so fast; they couldn't have come from anywhere else, could they? They're all black, no markings, with dark window glass! They don't look military."

Still trying to wrap her head around what just happened, Tori hadn't been aware of the helicopters. But now she notices a cadre of men in dark suits entering the control room behind Brian. They're all wearing glasses, not exactly sunglasses and not mirrored, but dark and reflective enough to obscure their eyes. Each has an earpiece, not unlike the one worn by the television host. Each man moves intently toward the various workstations. Two men from the rear of the group move in Tori's direction.

Moving to intercept them before they can reach her, she asks, "Who the hell are you, and what do you think you're doing?"

Vincent rises from his console and positions himself between Tori and the two men. He then places a hand on Tori's elbow to both calm and reassure her.

The men produce their credential wallets and then flip the covers to reveal identification cards and badges. The slightly taller man's card bears the name Stephen Smith, Special Agent, United States Central Intelligence Agency. The other, Thomas Walker, is with the Federal Aviation Administration. "We're sorry to see you've run into some trouble," says Walker.

"What are you doing here?" Tori demands.

Walker responds in an even tone, "We are concerned about the airworthiness of your—"

Tori cuts him off, "Bullshit! NTSB investigates accidents, and this wouldn't even fall under—"

"Nevertheless," Walker says, speaking over her, "this is a joint investigation, and I suggest you and your associates cooperate fully."

"We don't even know what happened yet—" Tori begins to protest, but again Walker interrupts her.

"We'll help you determine that," says Walker.

As quickly as they appeared, the suited men are leaving the control room. Tori and Vincent watch in stunned silence. The other agent, identified as Smith, has already turned and is following the group.

Walker says to Tori and Vincent, "We'll be in touch." He then turns and follows Smith.

Tori takes a step to pursue, but Vincent grabs her arm. "Don't. Something's not right about this," he says.

"FAA, CIA—bullshit. But why?" Tori asks.

"Forget them, we have work to do," Vincent says, feeling sick to his stomach as the reality of the past ten minutes sinks in. "Procedures, Flight, let's get video playback up and start figuring this out."

"Uh, Flight, uh, those guys took our SSD arrays."

"What?" Vincent rips off his headset, throws it onto his console, and strides across the room to Sydney Forrester's station, where the empty docks of the solid-state disks, which used to house terabytes of video data, stare back at him. "Are you telling me they took all of our HD video, Syd?"

"I'm sorry, Vince. These guys flashed badges and IDs at us and made it clear that they were armed. What could we do?" Sydney asks, head down, staring at his shoes.

"Not your fault, Syd. Those bastards caught us all by surprise, and they knew exactly what they were doing." With this, Vince climbs up onto Sydney's desk to address the room. "Okay, everyone, start combing through your data. Anything, and I don't care how seemingly insignificant, *anything* out of place, I want to know about it."

"Brian," Vincent calls out to Brian Lane, who had first warned of the invasion, "check with everyone who was outside. See if anyone shot video. We need to see what happened, anything we can get, even if it's shaky cell-phone shit." Vincent steps down from the desk.

Tori walks over to Sydney, who is still sulking. "Those bastards! I'm going to start making some calls," she says.

"What in hell is going on, Vince?" Tori asks.

"I don't know, but it doesn't change the fact that we have to figure out what happened to our ship."

November 18
Willow Springs, California—Incident plus 48 hours

Tori and Vincent are joined by other principal team members. They've watched the available video at least a hundred times, and no one can explain what they're seeing. It doesn't help that the three recovered clips were from handheld phone video. SAS-One's exhaust is a bright, white-hot dot against a pale blue, cloudless sky. In an instant, the white dot explodes outward in a blue-flame doughnut that grows like a pond ripple until it simply vanishes.

The search-and-recovery-team coordinator reports back to Tori that they have covered 80 percent of the area where the expected debris field should have been, but none is found. With a sigh, she hits the End Call button on her phone. "It just doesn't make sense," she says to the small group. "By the time SAS-One had attained three hundred and thirty miles, it'd burned most of its ascent fuel. Even if filled to maximum fuel capacity, it couldn't have generated an explosion powerful enough to completely disintegrate."

All share the same frustration that not a single error or significant anomaly can be found in the data. There is simply no reason for SAS-One's failure.

Tori's phone chimes. She hopes that perhaps the recovery team has found some trace of SAS-One. "Tori here," she answers.

The voice on the other end has a slight country twang. "Ms. Navarro, I am General Oswald, CO here at Edwards, and I'd like to meet y'all to discuss your situation."

"I want my SSDs! You had no right stealing that hardware," Tori says as the low-quality video of SAS-One's demise replays over her shoulder. "Your two men, Walker and Smith, stole my data and video array, and I want my property, damn it!"

"Ms. Navarro, we can discuss all that and more. I'm in a unique position to help you overcome the unfortunate turn of events y'all have experienced," General Oswald says in a calm, measured voice.

"Did you shoot down my rocket? Did you? Because we sure as hell can't figure out what we're seeing in the videos!"

There is no immediate response, and Tori assumes the general is covering the phone because she can only detect his whispering and some muffled responses. Suddenly, she can hear more clearly; his hand must have moved. A familiar voice says, "We got it all, sir; we're certain." It's Walker!

Vincent sees Tori's face redden and shoots her a questioning look.

"Walker," she mouths to Vincent.

"I tried for more than two hours to track those guys down, getting the runaround from the grunts who answer the phones over at Edwards," Vincent whispers back.

The general turns his attention back to Tori. "Now, Ms. Navarro, why don't you do yourself and all those good-hearted, hardworking folks a huge favor? Come see me and let us help you get over this rather daunting hurdle."

"Are you going to return the hardware and data you stole from me?"

"Ms. Navarro, we can discuss the entire matter. In fact, why don't you and Mr. D'Angelo join me for lunch tomorrow. I have a nice private dining room, and we can sit and talk over all of this until we're blue in the face. Please, what do you say?" pleads General Oswald.

She covers her phone and whispers to Vincent, "He wants you and me to come for lunch tomorrow." Vincent shrugs in reply. "Very well, General, we'll come see you tomorrow, but be advised, a whole lot of people will know where we're going and with whom we're meeting," Tori says.

"That's just fine, Ms. Navarro, just fine. I'll send my car for you; it'll be outside your front entrance at eleven-thirty tomorrow morning. I look forward to meeting you and Mr. D'Angelo." He hangs up without waiting for acknowledgment.

⚬⚬⚬

November 19—11:30 a.m.
Mojave, California—Edwards Air Force Base

As promised, an air force staff car sits idling, manned by a senior airman holding the rear door open. Tori gets in as Vincent walks to the opposite side and climbs in next to her, never taking his eyes off the airman's. No words are spoken, and the normally thirty-minute drive whisks by in less than twenty. After a brief pause at security, the car continues across the sprawling facility toward a beige, rectangular building. It sits near a gargantuan hanger painted the same nondescript color, almost blending with the surrounding desert. Pulling up to the front doors, an airman first class, or AC1, opens the door on Tori's side as the car halts. Vincent opens his own door and climbs out before the driver has a chance to assist him. Vincent moves next to Tori, and the AC1 says, "Follow me, please." He leads them to a bank of elevators, where they enter and ascend to the top floor. They follow the AC1 down a dizzying array of indistinguishable corridors, all connected at right angles, with linoleum flooring polished to a high sheen underfoot and fluorescent lights blazing overhead. They round another corner, and the hallway widens. At the end, the AC1 opens wooden double doors, which lead to a waiting area. Upon entering, Walker and Smith are standing in front of them. No pleasantries are

118

exchanged. The men's appearance is unchanged from their previous encounter—stoic, clad in dark suits, wearing glasses and earpieces.

"Where are my SSDs!" Tori demands.

It appears that neither man is going to respond, but before Tori can say another word, a door opens behind the men. A colonel steps out and says, "Ms. Navarro, Mr. D'Angelo. Please come right in; General Oswald is expecting you."

They walk past the men into the general's office—a large space replete with rich, deep colors and dark woods. Oswald rises from a high-back leather chair adorned with brass tacks behind an oversize desk and comes around to greet them. He extends his hand to Tori. "Ms. Navarro, it's nice to meet you, though I wish the circumstances were different."

Tori shakes his hand, saying nothing. The general extends his hand to Vincent, who follows Tori's lead.

"Please, have a seat," he says, gesturing toward more high-back leather chairs arranged before his desk in a semicircle. Tori, Vincent, and the colonel seat themselves. The general sits on the corner of his desk; behind him, a floor-to-ceiling glass wall affords a sweeping view of the base, with runways that seem to go on forever and numerous craft of all sorts baking in the desert sun. "May I offer you some coffee or a soft drink?"

Despite not wanting to accept any sort of amenity, Tori answers, "Coffee would be nice, General." Vincent nods in agreement.

"I've got it, sir," says the colonel. "Cream? Sugar?"

"If you have sweetener, I'll take one; if not, black, please," says Tori.

"Black, please," says Vincent.

The colonel heads for a silver coffeepot resting on an engraved sterling tray atop a dark-wood credenza. The general opens the lid of an obviously expensive humidor, turns it toward his guests, and offers, "Cuban, anyone?"

Tori, annoyed at feeling a bit intimidated, musters up her nerve and says, "General, where are my SSDs and my data? What is this all about?"

The general nods. "Right to business, okay." He stands, walks around his desk, sits in his chair, and reclines. "Ms. Navarro, I'm afraid there's been a mishap. I'll make certain you leave here with your hardware today …"

"But?" Tori interjects.

"But your disks were accidentally exposed to a magnetic field, and your data is lost. I am very sorry."

Fuming, Tori exclaims, "What is going on here? Why did you destroy my video? What in the hell is happening?"

Hearing the intensity in her voice, Vincent places a hand on her arm.

"Ms. Navarro, I can't replace what we accidentally deleted."

"Accidentally?" Tori remarks sarcastically.

"But we are prepared to make things right by you."

Tori's eyes are focused on the far corner of the room. She can't bring herself to even look at this caricature sitting across from her. The colonel returns with coffees and reclaims his seat.

"We're listening," says Vincent.

"Now, you know we spend piles of money on secret projects. Well, we've been very interested in some of the technologies you've developed in your ventures, both hard and soft assets. What I'd like to do is broker a deal with you that will keep you in the space game; advance our technologies beyond those of our adversaries; and make you very wealthy in the process," says the general with what Tori's dad would have called a shit-eatin' grin.

"What is it you want, General?" Tori huffs.

"What I want is a size increase in your ship and engine design by a factor of four. I want it scaled up to a Delta IV Heavy, with all the benefits of your lightweight composites, clean-burning engines, artificial intelligence, and—"

Tori cuts him off. "My interests are not in politics, or weapons, or militarizing my life's work! What you're talking about will take years of development before ever achieving a test phase. We're ready to fly now; our second ship is nearly complete. We're going to the moon, General, just as soon as we figure out what happened."

Oswald sighs. "No, Ms. Navarro, I'm afraid you're not," the general says in a grave tone. "If you want to build rockets, this is your only path to do so. And if you choose not to partner with us, I'm afraid you'll find nobody, anywhere, who will want to work with you or Mr. D'Angelo."

"What are you taking about?" Tori asks, overtaken by a sense of dread.

"What I'm talking about is releasing the findings of *our* investigation, detailing your failure to reach space, your apparent hubris in launching a craft so poorly designed and manufactured that it disintegrated the moment it faced dynamic stress ..."

"That's a lie! Our data reflects nothing wrong with that flight! Everything was functioning perfectly within expected norms!" Tori protests.

"Yet, where is that ship? Your craft was at throttle back, a critical point for dynamic force, when it broke up—broke up so badly that you can't find a trace of it," the general sneers. He grabs a cigar, bites off the end, and noisily spits it out. Lighting it, he stares Tori down until she looks away.

Regaining her composure, Tori slowly and methodically asks, "What was on that video, General? That video you intentionally destroyed." With less restraint, she adds, "I don't know what kind of shit you're trying to pull here, but I can assure you—"

Oswald interrupts and blusters, "You're in no position to assure shit. Now think about it. You can walk out of here with a fat government contract that will keep all your folks in gravy for years to come, or you can walk out and face scandal, charges of criminal negligence, bankruptcy—get the picture?"

Tori wants to cry, her head is spinning, but she won't give this pompous asshole the satisfaction. "Why would you do this to me? Why?"

Vincent stares into space as he considers what he just heard.

A long silence ensues.

"I don't see any alternative," Vincent says to Tori in a hushed tone. "You know losing the ship is more than a setback, Tori. It's almost certainly the end for us."

"God. Damn. It," says Tori.

"Ms. Navarro," Oswald says, again using his friendly general voice, "imagine, returning to your little launch site in Willow Springs; imagine how thrilled your people will be when you tell them that their efforts so impressed the United States Air Force that you obtained a seventy-five billion dollar contract to design and construct the most bad-ass rocket this world has ever known. Sure, it's a delay in getting back to space, but you'll explain to them that everything happens for a reason." He studies her face, seeing no readable emotion. He's reasonably certain he'll get what he wants. "Now that's a much better story to share than to go back and look into all of those disconsolate faces and say, 'We failed so miserably that the government will never let us fly again, and we're out of business.' Don't cha think?"

"Son of a bitch," Tori says under her breath. "My father was a man of integrity; that's what he taught me. It's something I got from him and neither you nor anyone else can change that."

The general's mood is confrontational again. "You go ahead and act on your integrity. That and a few food stamps will get you dinner."

"I don't care what you say about me or do to me—"

Again, Oswald cuts her off. "You may not, but I'm sure as shit that all those people working for you, all those people who have invested their life savings, I'll bet they care! Now stop thinking about yourself and step up for those depending on you! This is a one-time offer."

Tori looks into Vincent's eyes and says, "How can I?"

"How can you not?" he replies quietly.

"I can't. I just can't," Tori says softly, her voice trembling. "What is this, General? Really? Did you shoot down our ship just to coerce us into this?"

Tori and the general lock eyes. This time, she's determined not to look away first. The only sound in the room is the tick-tock of the grandfather clock in the corner. Surprisingly, Oswald breaks off the stare down and gravely says, "Look, Ms. Navarro, I'm going to level with you."

This gets both Tori and Vincent's attention.

"What I'm about to tell you is beyond classified." Oswald nods to the colonel.

"Excuse me, please," the colonel says. "I'll be outside if you need me, sir." He snaps a salute to the general, who returns it reflexively.

They watch the colonel cross the room and exit as Wilson and Smith enter and approach.

"I am going to ask both of you to swear an oath," Oswald says, pulling documents from his desk drawer. "What I tell you can never be repeated or discussed outside this office." He slides papers in front of each of them. The forms are straightforward top secret boilerplate, already prepared with their names, home addresses, and social security numbers. "Simply sign these documents; then you're both to place your right hands on the Bible that Agent Smith is holding."

Tori and Vincent acquiesce, signing the papers and placing their hands on the Bible.

"Repeat after me," Wilson says. "I hereby swear that I will never repeat, in whole or part, any of the conversation that takes place hereafter, so help me God."

The pair comply.

"You are right, Ms. Navarro; your ship did perform flawlessly; it didn't explode, and *we* didn't shoot it down," Oswald says, inhaling deeply. He studies his cigar, slowly rolling it between his forefinger, middle finger, and thumb. "The world as we know it is going to change in just a few years." He lets those words hang in the air. "The Bible calls it Armageddon. We're going to be in the mother of all fights for survival as a species—the whole world. Right now, there are global efforts underway to unify us—bring us together as a single people to face what's coming."

Tori and Vincent look at each other, but it's Vincent who breaks the silence. "What's coming?"

"An armada from another world, another galaxy—maybe Canis Major or maybe even closer. We've known for some time now. They could've been traveling through space for generations.

They're moving near the speed of light. Astronomers initially thought it was a cluster of asteroids, but they've now seen evidence of maneuvering, changing speed. They're ships. Big ones."

"Oh my God," says Tori.

"God's got nothing to do with it. They got small ships too—scouts—that can move faster than light speed—a lot faster. That's what took out your spacecraft. They've been testing their weapons on us."

Vincent asks, "You're sure? They're hostile, for certain? We can't try talking to them ..."

Oswald shuts down Vincent's line of questioning and restates, "Yeah, no question, they're hostile! But some world leaders still want a parley. That's why we're working to get out there and meet them before the fate of the planet itself is in jeopardy. Our best hope lies in what people like y'all can come up with."

"So that's why you knew our facility layout and where to go for ..."

"Yes, Ms. Navarro, I'm afraid we've been keeping pretty close tabs on you and your progress. We need your technology."

"So now that you've disclosed this to us, may we see the video?" Tori asks.

"I'm sorry. It really was destroyed. Believe me; I was as angry as you when I found out," says the general.

Vincent says, "Excuse me, General, may I ask a question?"

"Shoot."

"How is it going to be possible to unite the nations of the Earth? It seems like an impossible task, given the mistrust and outright hatred between so many nations."

"Behind closed doors, at the highest levels, talks have been going on around the clock. To foster this cooperation, nations will be encouraged to recognize the UN as a global government, representing the interests of all nations. The ones that won't submit will be ..." Oswald exhales then inhales and says, "made to comply." He raises an eyebrow as he makes this remark. "The major players—Russia, China, the UK, and what's left of the EU—have already signed agreements. But we're running into trouble with the Islamic states and Israel."

"Why's that?" Vincent asks.

"Because the major nations have agreed to let the Vatican run the show," says Oswald.

"The Pope?" Tori asks.

"The one and only," replies the general. "The smallest sovereign nation in the world will lead us. There are enough lawmakers and rulers who feel that putting the godliest man on Earth in charge will give us the best opportunity of dealing with these beings, if we even get the chance—assuming they don't just obliterate us and take the planet."

On their return to Willow Springs, Tori finally breaks the silence. "Airman," she says to the staff-car driver, "would you please drop us at the Bridgeport Inn?" Glancing at her in the rearview mirror, he nods in the affirmative. Turning to Vincent, she explains, "We need to get on the same page about how we're going to deliver the news about the contract."

"Yeah, and I could use a libation," Vince replies.

There is no further conversation in the car. As the driver pulls away, Tori says to Vincent, "Turn off your phone."

He does so without question, and they proceed inside. The barstools are empty; they take two at the far end. After exchanging pleasantries with the barmaid and placing their orders, Tori says in a low voice, "He's lying."

"Oswald?" Vincent asks.

"Tori nods. "I'm sure of it. You don't believe for a minute that they destroyed our video, do you?"

"Well, there's not much we can do about it now," Vincent replies.

"No, I suppose not, but moving forward, we have to assume we're under constant surveillance—offices bugged, phones tapped. Those assholes knew the entire layout of our place and right where to go for our drives. And what kind of bullshit was that with those oaths that already had our names and personal information on them ..." Tori stops speaking and smiles as the barmaid places their drinks in front of them. "Thank you," she says. Tori sips at her vodka Gibson until the barmaid is out of earshot. Finishing her thought, she adds, "That was all about intimidation, nothing else."

"Quite effective. Color me intimidated. I have to tell you, Tori, I was beginning to fear for our lives. I was afraid you were going to push back too hard. We'll go along, but one slipup and either or both of us could meet with an untimely accident. In fact, let's make this our place to meet for discussions, but going forward, whenever we do meet, our phones get left behind," Vincent suggests.

"We should probably have a secret word ..." Tori begins.

"Moonshot," says Vincent.

Tori chuckles at his quick retort and agrees, "Moonshot it is."

Now that they have a scheme to communicate privately should the need arise, they go about planning how best to sell their fabricated story with the big government contract to their employees—why it's now such a grand and wonderful strategy to give up the moon and build the SAS-X4. Neither is enthused, but there's really no other option. They both believe Oswald would have no qualms about dealing with them in a most lethal manner.

December 24—3:00 a.m.
Willow Springs, California—Tori's home

"Tori Glory," says the comforting, deep voice.

"Daddy?"

"Tori Glory."

"Daddy, is that you?" Tori mumbles. She feels him take her hand, just like when she was a little girl, although even as an adult, her hand always felt tiny in his. He places something in her palm, folds her fingers over it, and cradles her closed fist in both of his.

"Oh, my Tori Glory ... noon, night, and morning glory," says the voice.

Tori smiles in her sleep and stirs. "You haven't called me that in so long; I haven't heard that phrase, since ... since ..." Now coming to the surface from her slumber, she finishes, "Since before you died." She opens her eyes to see her hand enveloped by two others—a man's hands. In the thick fog of awakening, her eyes trace up an arm to a shoulder ... Agent Smith is staring down at her; she can see his eyes—no glasses. His eyes seem to glow. She gasps, propelling herself backward; her back is up against the headboard, her legs pumping feverously against the fitted sheet. She pulls the top sheet and blankets up to her chin, trembling, ready to scream, but suddenly realizing she's alone. Nevertheless, she cannot control her shaking. She scans the room, terrified of what she might see, but no one else is there, only the usual moon-bathed shadows of her bedroom and its furnishings. The terror of the dream was intense, but she refocuses on her father's voice. It *had* been him; she heard it so clearly. She thinks of him and takes a few breaths, remembering him holding her close, how his chest felt as she lay her head on it. Recalling the scent of Old Spice. She begins to relax and then realizes that there's something in her clutched fist. She opens her fingers to reveal a black USB thumb drive.

The ringtone on Vincent's phone cuts through the quiet like a freight train. He grabs it from his nightstand, taps the answer icon, and puts it to his ear, but before speaking, he hears Tori's voice.

"It's almost six; aren't you up?"

"I would have been in another ten minutes, thank you very much," Vincent says.

"Oh, well, sorry for waking you. It's just that I'd like to share some ideas for a future moonshot," she says.

Upon hearing their code word, adrenaline pumps the sleepiness right out of his system. Being careful not to disclose their prearranged plans, he replies, "Okay, I'll make sure you're first on my agenda at nine." He hopes anyone eavesdropping will buy the ruse. Vincent abbreviates his usual morning routine, grabs his keys, and sets his phone on the table by the front door.

A short distance away, Tori is already on her way to the Bridgeport Inn, leaving her phone and computer on the bed. On the passenger seat next to her sits her old laptop; it hasn't seen the light of day in half-a-dozen years. It had started acting up, and after buying a new one, she decided to have it repaired, keeping it as a backup—unnecessary until now.

Vincent arrives to find Tori seated at a corner booth. "What's with that?" he says, nodding toward her computer.

"It's my old one ... haven't used it in years. Pretty sure it's secure; well, you know, safe. If Oswald's goons thought to bug this thing, then we're screwed far worse than we ever imagined."

"Coffee," Vincent says excitedly, righting the cup on the saucer in front of him, grabbing the pot Tori had ordered, and pouring to the brim. He's experiencing an odd mixture of fatigue and excitement. "I have no idea what you could be up to," he says, sipping through a stifled yawn.

"Slide around next to me," Tori instructs. In a quiet tone, she asks, "Do you believe in angels, Vince?"

Vincent cracks a little smile as he looks at her. He's known her long enough to realize that no empirical or theological discussion is either wanted or expected. She's the cat who swallowed the canary. "I'm guessing you want me to say yes?"

She pops the thumb drive into the USB port. Its icon appears, and she opens the drive. On it are two video files: playMeFirst.mp4 and playMeLast.mp4. She double-clicks on playMeFirst.mp4; the video player fills the screen—a high-definition video. At first, Vincent doesn't recognize what he's looking at; the image is blurred and shaky, but then it sharpens to crystal clarity. It's a tight shot of SAS-One. The camera operator had zoomed in to gain focus, a common technique. Now the camera widens its field of view, showing the entire rocket blazing its way upward. Before Vincent can process what he just saw, the blue-flame doughnut is hurtling out in all directions. He snaps his head around to look at Tori, his mouth hanging open. Smiling smugly, Tori gingerly extends an index finger to his chin and pushes upward. Her smile broadens to a grin.

"How? Where ... did you get this?" Vincent asks.

"An angel," says Tori.

Vince scans her face for any sign that she's joking but finds none. "Play that again, please," he says.

"One more time at normal speed, then I have to show you something," Tori says.

Once again, Vincent watches the close-up come into focus on SAS-One; the view pulls back for several seconds and then—an awful but magnificent ring of blue fire. "As if it vanishes," he says quietly to Tori. "It's there one second, and the next, it's just gone."

"No, not *just* gone ... you see the explosion, but watch this again at one-one-hundredth speed," Tori says, selecting the slow-motion option.

Vincent's eyes are glued to the monitor. The blurry close-up, the fine focus, the pullback, and then he sees it. SAS-One's nose crumples inward as the rest of the ship pushes forward, but it never gets beyond that point. It disintegrates under its own force, as if held in place, the last few fragments incinerated in an instant as the remaining fuel explodes. "Tori, what am I looking at? What is happening here? I don't understand. It looks as if it hit a brick wall that isn't there," says Vince, trying to keep his voice calm. Then he lowers his head toward her and whispers, "Is it *them*? Did it hit a cloaked alien ship in our orbit?"

"I've been watching this for the past three hours. You saw what I saw. Our ship *hit* something—first thing we thought seeing the video. It *hit* something! The disintegration, the explosion, the fireball ... fire ring that spread out in all directions, *but only laterally* ... nearing Mach 5 at three hundred thirty miles altitude; it *hit* something," Tori reiterates.

"My God, Tori, what could it have hit?" Vincent asks.

Tori takes a deep breath and says, "You know my father wasn't religious, but he had faith. He used to tell me that science is merely agreed-upon arguments, as much faith as actual evidence.

Like him, I don't go to church, but I pray. When I was little and he encouraged me to pray, I asked him why ... know what he told me?"

Vincent shakes his head.

"He said, 'If humankind is the product of some accident of evolution and the greatest thing in all of this vast universe, we don't deserve God.'"

Vincent sits with his thoughts for a moment and asks, "You know I'm an atheist, don't you?"

Tori closes the video of SAS-One and double-clicks on the file named playMeLast.mp4. It opens with a man standing at a lectern. Before clicking the Play icon, she looks at Vincent and says, "Not for long."

The man at the lectern seems to be quite tall, with an athletic build and dark eyes, appearing almost black. He has a thick head of coal-black hair, olive skin, and a charismatic aura. He's wearing a dark suit and shirt with no tie. Behind him on a large screen is a Bible verse: Psalm 11:3—*If the foundations be destroyed, what can the righteous do?*

"Who is he?" Vincent says, nodding toward the image on the laptop monitor.

"Matteo Pasquale. If you Google his name, you'll find snippets of him being described as a laicized Catholic priest; although he was never defrocked, just left on his own. He's also a former astronomer and professor of physics at the Catholic University of America," Tori replies.

"All he's missing is the collar—still looks like a priest," says Vincent. "Okay, let's hear what the good father has to say."

Tori clicks Play.

Pasquale looks out over the crowd. The camera stays on him and the Bible verse. "So what does it mean?" he asks.

"'If the foundations be destroyed, what can the righteous do?' If you believe the Bible is the Word of God, then you must believe that it is one of the foundations of our relationship with Him. No different than believing that the church is His house; the congregation, His flock; His Son, our Savior. If someone wanted to undermine our relationship with Him, wouldn't any of these fundamental beliefs be a great place to start ... inject some doubt? Were I Lucifer, in my quest for the souls of His faithful, perhaps I'd order my minions to start weakening these foundations, find places to introduce uncertainty. Then, as the root of a tree can eventually displace and crack solid concrete, over time rendering that foundation uneven ... broken ... unable to support having anything built atop it, I could begin to destroy those foundations one by one."

"He sounds as if he's giving a sermon—still sounds like a priest," Vincent comments.

Tori replies in a whisper, "He only left the church, not his faith."

Pasquale continues, "For centuries, our ancestors knew exactly what the essence of our world was. It tells us very clearly in Genesis: God made the heavens and the Earth; He then made us in His image to preside over the creatures of His creation and live in peace—our only obligation, to worship Him. Then, of course, we all know what happened in the garden." He smiles. There's laughter from the audience. "But for centuries, we knew, *we knew* that God put us at the center of His universe. Then Nicolaus Copernicus in the mid-1500s and later Galileo Galilei in the early 1600s came along with their theories, telling us that we've had it all wrong and championing the heliocentric model. Imagine the consternation at the time. What? The sun doesn't revolve around the Earth? Earth spins in space around the sun? These many centuries later, we all accept this, right? It's hammered into us beginning in preschool. Yes, the Earth revolves around the sun. But the Bible is the Word of God, right? Where does it describe Earth revolving around the sun? The short answer is—nowhere. Not a single mention of Earth moving through space, nor described as a sphere."

Vincent darts a look at Tori. "Just listen," she whispers.

"We all remember Genesis 1:1, 'In the beginning God created the Heaven and the Earth.' It then goes on to say that the Earth was without form; darkness was upon the face of the deep. Sunday school stuff; you all remember, right?" Laughs and nods from the audience. "Then God commanded that there be light, and He separated light from darkness, calling one day and the other night. Then in verses six, seven, and eight, it gets interesting. Verse six: 'And God said, Let there be a firmament in the midst of the waters, and let it divide the waters from the waters.' Verse seven: 'And God made the firmament, and divided the waters which were under the firmament from the waters which were above the firmament: and it was so.' Verse eight: 'And God called the firmament Heaven. And the evening and the morning were the second day.'

"It then goes on to describe Him creating land, separating it from the oceans, but then in verses fourteen through sixteen, He creates the sun and the moon and places them *into the firmament* to divide day and night, with the sun and moon to rule those periods respectively—very important jobs for each of those celestial bodies." Nervous laughter. "Then, at the very end of verse sixteen, the Bible says, 'He made the stars also.' Think about that for a moment. He made the stars ... *also*. An afterthought."

The background slide changes to an ancient Hebrew text containing an illustration of Earth as a flat disk enclosed under a dome filled with the sun, moon, and stars.

"Now, can't you just imagine God admiring His creation? 'I like my work here, nice firmament; I'm good with my sun and moon ... hey, I'm going to throw in some stars just to dress things up.'" Laughter from the audience. "An *afterthought*. No big whoop. He made the stars *also*." Pasquale lets everybody sit with that thought for a moment. "Modern astronomers will tell you that our universe is jam-packed with stars. In fact, they'll tell you that it's abounding with galaxies, each of those chock-full of stars, and around those stars orbiting planets. They also tell you that there exists more than one universe, called the multiverse. In essence, they're telling you that we're not special. I've heard them say those very words: Earth is *not* special. In fact, by their measure, there are billions upon billions of other earths out there, and none of them are special either. And I know this for a fact because I once bought into the Copernican Model. So why would anyone want you to believe that Earth is not special; that we are not special, and that you are not special? What would be the benefit of making the entire population of the world believe that there is nothing special about any of us? Hmmm?" he says, scanning the audience. There is high anticipation, but his pause continues. Finally, he proceeds, "Because by getting us to accept the multiverse, it injects that first bit of doubt into whether we can believe God's Word—that *we are* special, that He made us the *center* of His universe."

"Tori," Vincent begins.

She pauses the video.

"Are you trying to tell me that you're buying this?" Vincent asks.

"Vince, I'm asking you to watch and open up your mind," Tori replies. She clicks Play.

"So," Pasquale continues, "according to mainstream astronomy, we're not special, and we're probably not alone. Remember a decade or two ago when no scientist would even consider life beyond our world? Too controversial, not even when a fossilized worm was discovered in a meteorite from Mars. Why, it would wreak chaos! But, boy, things have changed." More laughs. "These days, we've found evidence of microbial life in space, Mars too, and there are so many other earthlike planets out there. We can't be alone, right? Why do you suppose science did such a one-eighty? In my opinion, because, like every other fact they declare, it suits some ulterior purpose."

The background slide changes to display a quote:

> Today's scientists have substituted mathematics for experiments, and they wander off through equation after equation, and eventually build a structure which has no relation to reality.—Nikola Tesla

"Scientists haven't practiced science for many years. The quote behind me from Nikola Tesla states that he experienced the same frustrations in his day. Today, if I'm an astronomer and I have a theory, I am no longer required to conduct experimentation to prove it. No, I merely need to come up with a mathematical formula. Makes it convenient, if you have something to prove but not the scientific means to do so."

A new slide appears:

> For there is nothing hidden that will not be disclosed, and nothing concealed that will not be known or brought out into the open.—Luke 8:17

"My intention is not to preach the Bible, but rather to point us back to it as what we all *thought* we took it for—the Word of God. So, if the Bible is true, it means we live beneath a firmament. If the sun, moon, and stars are all within that firmament, then why would science want us to believe in the multiverse? What purpose would it serve to believe that the universe is teeming with life and we're not special? Well, let's break it down. Okay, we're not special; we're a biological fluke of evolution … same thing has happened on billions of other worlds. We hear top scientists today telling us that God doesn't exist. God has been slowly eradicated from science, public places, and our schools. There are still groups working feverishly to change our currency and remove any mention of God. For decades now, we've heard politicians speak of the new world order, which many believe is the globalization of the planet— one world, one government. But the *one* they fail to mention is *one ruling cla*ss. In his farewell address, President Dwight D. Eisenhower warned us of the military-industrial complex, and what have we seen? Wars, weapon development, and a self-serving cycle. They've got black budgets that run to trillions of dollars annually. They've got us believing their lies, but the only part that hasn't come to pass so far has been the one-world model. Who are 'they?' Did you know that possibly the only United States president not genetically linked to King John Lackland of England was our eighth president, Martin Van Buren? Yes, that includes Kennedy, Obama, and the Bush family. The jury is still out on Trump. He's no more forthcoming with his DNA sample than his tax records, but all the others are verifiable. So we definitely have a ruling class groomed to step in, but we don't have that utopian one-world government. *Yet.* What would it take to get us there?"

A new slide appears behind Pasquale:

> In our obsession with antagonisms of the moment, we often forget how much unites all the members of humanity. Perhaps we need some outside, universal threat to make us recognize this common bond. I occasionally think how quickly our differences worldwide would vanish if we were facing an alien threat from outside this world.
> —President Ronald Reagan, Speech to the United Nations General Assembly, 42nd General Assembly, September 21, 1987

"How about an alien invasion? There's a motivator." Laughs again. "For decades, we've been told by politicians and even shown by Hollywood filmmakers that by banding together, we could defeat an extraterrestrial threat. Now, if we're not on a spinning globe circling the sun but rather at a fixed point under a firmament that contains everything we see in the heavens, how is an alien invasion possible? Well, folks, it's not. Therefore, those in power must convince us that what they say is the truth and what the Word of God says is fiction. Have you ever investigated the symbolism used by our government and its space agencies? Just take the time to check out the Apollo mission's symbolism, the freemasonry of the Apollo astronauts—all rooted in Satanism. But that's another lecture. All your lives, you've been told lies. Ever wonder why rockets don't go straight up? They always arc. NASA would have you believe it's for the space shuttle to slip into and achieve orbit or for deep-space rockets to slingshot around to use the Earth's gravity. No, it's to put on a show. They know that if they shot a rocket straight up, it'd hit the firmament and be destroyed. Think I'm kidding?"

A soundless video showing a fiery blueish ring expanding outward from a central white point of detonation plays behind Pasquale. The ring expands until it dissipates.

"Check out Operation Fishbowl, when our government detonated nukes against the firmament in 1962. And again, hiding the truth in plain sight, naming the exercise Operation *Fishbowl*—really?" Laughter and applause ring out.

Vincent looks at Tori, the color has drained from his face. "Look at that, it looks just like ..." he says.

Tori nods in agreement.

"It's coming, folks," says Pasquale. "The government is going to tell you that it's an alien invasion, that we have to join together to fend off the attack, capitulate to a central authority—the ruling classes' dream for centuries. The result will be enslavement under a demonic regime. Those of us who believe the Word of God will join His legions and resist. It will be a global holocaust. Sound familiar?"

"Armageddon!" shout audience members.

"Armageddon," says Vincent simultaneously, Oswald's voice in his head.

"That's right," Pasquale concurs. "Scripture states that only the Father knows the date and time of Christ's return. And, while that is very true, it's becoming more and more difficult for the government to keeps us in the dark. Technology is empowering individuals like never before. The danger is in becoming enslaved by it and too dependent on it, but used as a tool, we can communicate faster, more efficiently, see further, and document more readily than ever before in history. There are a growing number of credible people posting well-crafted and quite scientific experiments to social media sites. Many are very impressive. More people are questioning the status quo by the hour. Just to give you an example: Does anyone remember a little event that took place August 21, 2017? I believe it was called a total eclipse." A surge of agreement from the room. "Did anyone out there," Pasquale gestures to the audience, "understand NASA's explanation of how a planetary body, our moon, which is *two thousand miles across,* can cast a shadow only seventy miles wide? When's the last time you saw an object cast a shadow smaller than itself?"

On the screen, an official NASA release of the eclipse's path shows the moon's shadow narrowing as it falls across the Earth. Pasquale points to the path of totality. "This narrow strip is seventy miles wide; yet the moon is two-thirds the width of the United States. How is it possible that only these few Americans are in the dark? Someone isn't telling us the truth, folks."

Vincent asks Tori, "Can you stop it there, please?"

Tori complies and asks, "You okay?"

Vince exhales. "Not sure. I want to be, Tori. But all the math, all the study … the years … my world is upside down right now."

"You know it's true though, don't you?"

"I don't want to believe it—not a word," says Vincent. "It goes against everything, *everything* I've ever believed. After our meeting with Oswald, unlike you, I sort of thought things fell into place, but then I started thinking about it and became uneasy. The more I thought, the worse I felt. And right now, I'm looking backward over a career that was plagued with so many unanswered questions, a career where "This is need-to-know only" was as common as a simple yes or no. Oh my God, Tori, it's all making sense."

Tori embraces Vince. She can feel him shaking.

"What do we do now?" Vince asks.

January 10
Business World Network, Studio A—New York, New York

"Happy New Year and welcome to *Net Worth*. I'm your host, Steve Kardon, coming to viewers around the world live from our studios in New York. Today we welcome back Tori Navarro." Brief applause from the stagehands. "Tori, the last time you were in our studio, you were planning a moonshot with an unmanned spacecraft. I'm sorry to let our viewers know that the launch didn't meet with success. However, it's my understanding that despite the failed launch, your team netted a substantial joint-venture contract with the United States Air Force and NASA. So I guess you could say it met with a certain level of success. Initial appearances can be deceiving, wouldn't you say?"

Tori smiles and says, "Steve, you're not going to believe the magnitude of your understatement …"

DREAMER

Best Friend

The night is cold, dark, almost black. The narrow path ahead leads to the school's side entrance and the location's only illumination. A single industrial lamp, protruding from a cinderblock wall above the metal door, creates a stark, inverted V of light, just enough to outline a square concrete step. The outside light also casts long, crisscross shadows from the adjacent chain-link fence onto the nearby playground, where a swing set is partially hidden in the murk.

The door is open. He leans against the jamb. The metal frame is cold to the touch; he can feel the uneven texture of the surface, the result of frequent repaintings over the decades. He peers into the locker-lined hallway. It is dimly lit by a series of florescent tubes, some working, most not, and further down, a few flickering in their death throes. Despite the light from a few surviving fixtures, he cannot see the floor. It's as if the luminance is being consumed before it can reach the linoleum tiles to complete the institutional scene.

To his left, a darkened stairway both ascends to the floor above and descends to the one below, offering no invitation of light from either direction, both sets of steps retreating into blackness. Straight ahead, at what appears to be the midpoint between his position and an identical door and set of stairs at the other end of the hallway, an interior door is open. A soft, off-white, slightly yellowish light is spilling out. There's an odd scent in the air.

Without the actual desire to do so but compelled by an uncontrollable urge, he steps into the hallway. The scent becomes a strong odor ... copper. Or it *smells* like copper. It stings his nostrils and stimulates his salivary glands. Unwilling to bear the thought of swallowing, he spits.

As he takes another step, he feels something underfoot. In the darkness, he cannot see what it is but can sense that it has some give—not rigid or hard. He repositions his foot, and it slides through a viscous substance. He reaches out to steady himself against a locker. The hallway seems to grow longer with every labored step. Each movement forward is exactly like the last. Multiple unseen obstacles block his way; his footing is unsure. Finally, he wriggles his foot free until he feels the sole of his sneaker hit the floor. Then he gently shifts his weight, trying not to slip in the thick liquid covering the tiles.

He tries to maintain a steady pace, keeping his focus on the open door just ahead on the right. There's no point looking down; he cannot watch his step because his feet are invisible in the gloom.

Drawing closer, he's almost at the door, maybe another ten feet. But now the light from inside the room reveals more obstacles—body parts and the source of the copper smell ... blood, appearing black in the dimness. For a moment he stands still, staring at the severed limbs, but not just severed ... chopped. No whole arms, legs, or torsos. Only pieces, most no bigger than a few fingers or half a foot. At the sight, his heart races, and his own blood runs cold.

Through the open door, he can see shadows emanating from the room, and he moves to look inside. It's the nurse's office. There on an examining table sits his best friend. A nurse is tending to the stub of his right arm. Her white uniform is stained deep red in some spots, pink in others, from closing the horrific wound. Why can't he remember best friend's name? For God's sake, he recognizes the familiar face. They've been through everything together—and now this.

No words are exchanged. He and best friend just stare at each other as the nurse finishes her work. It must hurt like hell, but best friend's face is stoic. Nothing more to do here, best friend is being taken care of. "Have to move on," says the same uncontrollable urge that made him come this far in the first place. It's now directing him to the far end of the hallway.

He no longer smells the copper, but it's in the air. He has just become inured to it. As with the first part of the hallway, he treads carefully, trying not to think of what or who he is stepping on or over.

Now he can see something in the distance, a single, distinct shadow by the far staircase, just in front of the exit. He doesn't want to but moves forward. He wants to run in the opposite direction; he wants to scream—a stifled instinct since first seeing the carnage— but he tamps it down and continues.

The flicker from a dying fluorescent tube backlights the shadow enough to make out its shape—a man, a huge man, a *man-monster* with a bald head. Almost upon him, the man-monster pauses under a humming yet working light. Now he can clearly see that the beast is enormous. With its overall bulk, massive bullet-shaped head, and gigantic belly, the formidable freak almost fills the height and width of the hallway. In the light, the brute appears to be naked, at least shirtless. Maybe whatever the man-monster is wearing for bottoms is lost under the folds of flesh that hang off it like curtains. There's no time to further study the gruesome giant. The man-monster raises its right arm and out of the darkness emerges an axe. The berserker joins its hands on the shaft and begins swinging. Sparks fly from the axe head as it strikes the cinder-block wall. The next swipe produces a loud, high-pitched screech from metal-on-metal contact with a locker on the opposite wall. The behemoth lunges forward, but with a quick duck, he avoids the axe blow by less than an inch and darts past the man-monster.

Reaching the end of the hallway, he finds the door leading to the outside locked. He turns to face the mountain of sweat-covered flesh. As the colossus raises the axe once again, it knocks out one of the few remaining fluorescent tubes, resulting in a loud pop and a shower of milky shards. The gargantuan beast doesn't seem to notice as it lunges forward.

The blackness explodes with light and gunshots, again and again—six times in all as best friend steps down from the stairway on the right and unloads the .38 caliber rounds point-blank into the side of the man-monster's bullet-shaped head. With a great sloppy, sloshing sound, it falls forward onto the floor.

Best friend tucks the pistol into his waistband and then extends his remaining hand. With best friend's assistance, he readies himself to step over the man-monster's body and onto the staircase. Halfway over the mountain of flesh, it grabs his ankle.

Baby Doll

The rain has stopped, but the ground remains wet, and the red and blue flashing and swirling lights refract off the slick pavement. Fire trucks and police cars must be surrounding the scene, but he sees only the strobing lights cutting through the blackness of this night. There is no one else; he is alone.

Directly ahead lay the remnants of his parents' mobile home. It had been a beautiful triple-wide, warm, pale yellow in color with white trim on the exterior. Over the years, his mother took great pride in how comfortable she made the place. The interior was decorated in seafoam green, with a wood-burning fireplace in the living room. The kitchen was open with a cooking island and bar-style seating. It had been decorated with a lifetime of memories: school photos of him and his three siblings, images of his father's boat, citations from his parents' service in the army air forces during the Second World War, and countless other miscellany from their forty-plus-year marriage. His mother's favorite room had been the one where she kept her dolls, probably over a hundred. She was simply born to be a mother, and after her kids were grown and gone, she found surrogates made of plastic, fabric, and ceramic. She adopted these beautiful foundlings from garage sales and flea markets, always cleaning them with the greatest of care and restoring them to better than their original condition. She made clothes for them—every stitch a labor of love—on her Singer sewing machine, one that she'd owned for decades.

Gone. All gone.

He walks up the driveway toward the ruins, a smoldering and scorched foundation capped by partial walls, perhaps two or three feet high at most, with jagged, sawtooth, soot-blackened tops. The driveway is painted in a yellow herringbone pattern—a popular trend in the mobile home park. It extends under the carport and terminates at the screened porch. The carport, however, is no more. The roof is gone; there are only the vertical aluminum poles that once supported it. Leading up to the screened-porch door is a single concrete step painted to match the driveway. Though all the screen is gone, melted away by the intensity of the inferno, the metal door and its frame remain.

He steps up, places his hand on the screened-door handle, but before opening it, he peers through the empty frame. The porch floor is bare concrete. That's strange; his father had put down a covering of some sort … wasn't there a blue wall-to-wall outdoor carpet? Regardless, it is bare concrete now, its wet surface refracting the lights from the unseen emergency vehicles.

In the middle of the porch, something catches his eye—one of his mother's dolls. She's a typical-looking baby doll—short, curly blond hair, wearing a pink-and-white plaid dress with ruffles around the shoulder straps and hem. She's looking away from him, her slightly raised chubby right arm bent at the elbow, and her left slightly lowered. She is unscathed. Untouched. Pristine … amid total destruction.

How?

Confused, he stares. Suddenly, the doll's arms reverse position; the left raises, and the right lowers. Then her head pivots toward him. Her bright-blue plastic eyes lock onto his.

She Storm

The day is gorgeous. The sky is a perfect sheet of uninterrupted blue extending beyond the distant treetops. Everyone in the park is enjoying the picnic and other outdoor activities. A ton of people have showed up, but it doesn't feel at all crowded. He's reminded of his youth and those fun times when his extended family—siblings, cousins, girl- and boyfriends—all got along, before the complications of business, family politics, and in-laws. This is like one of those idyllic days—everyone having a wonderful time. He cannot possibly feel happier.

There's a *girl*. She's sweet and beautiful and makes him tingle from head to toe whenever she looks his way. He can't really describe her, other than to say that she is perfect. She seems different each time he looks at her, but no matter, because every time she's still perfect, just in a new, distinctive way. When she speaks to him, he can't quite understand her words, but she's smiling, *smiling at him*, and that makes his heart race. She extends her hand to him. She's beckoning him to follow. Where to? It matters not. He can hardly believe it. How can she possibly want *him*? He takes her hand, and they run through the grass under this perfect sky, the sun shining high above.

There's a structure in the distance. She's heading toward it; he follows along. It's a white house with light-blue trim and lots of windows. She leads him into the living room, and they sit next to each other on a sofa replete with thick, floral-patterned cushions. His bare knee is resting against hers; she moves nearer to him, and now his knee rests against her thigh. They kiss, and his heart races with the excitement of roller-coaster ride. He places his hand on her waist to pull her closer; her mouth opens and, as their tongues meet, a door slams.

Out of nowhere, the picnickers from the park race inside, a buzz of excitement in the air. Hearing only sentence fragments over the din, he directs his attention to the north-facing windows. Outside, the clear-blue sky gives way to a menacing amber haze, and towering black clouds boil into the atmosphere. In the distance, twisters descend from the cloud bottoms. They dance and wreak destruction.

From another room, a frantic radio voice pleads with listeners to take cover. The cloud towers are reminiscent of toy soldiers, marching in time to some unheard orders as they rumble overhead. Down below picnickers scream in terror, praying for the tornadoes to pass by.

He pulls her toward the base of a wall for safety, but there are too many windows. The radio voice in the other room is silenced by the sound of breaking glass, splintering wood, and blood-curdling screams. Debris flies everywhere; all is chaos. He attempts to cover her with his body, but she disappears. Everyone does. He is alone.

From his vantage point lying on the floor, he can see blue sky through the cracked and broken window glass. He lifts himself up to get a better view of the outside, only to see the next approaching storm. It is bigger, blacker, and angrier than its predecessor. A funnel forms rapidly, descending directly toward him; there's no chance to seek cover.

The Elevator

He walks to the elevator bank in the hotel lobby and pushes the Up button. Illuminating, it is pale yellow. The lobby is large, open, and very dark. There seems to be no one else around. He considers taking the stairs. After all, he only needs to walk up to the third floor, and riding elevators isn't exactly on his list of favorite things to do. Before he can turn and walk to the staircase, the Up button darkens; the elevator bell dings, and the arrow next to the copper-colored metal door comes to life in vibrant white. The doors part and slide into the walls.

He steps in and pushes the 3 button. The doors slide shut. There's a weighty feeling in the pit of his stomach as the elevator cab ascends, but while it glides upward, the discomfort eases. On the panel above the doors, the 2 illuminates, then darkens. He refocuses on the doors' vertical seam in anticipation of his exit, but there is no sensation of deceleration. The 3 button lights, then darkens, but the doors don't open. He can feel the car continuing to rise.

Now the elevator cab begins a rapid acceleration upward, the momentum making him feel heavy. The speed increases; the light through the door seam flickers as the floors rush by faster and faster. Without warning, the car stops. He is hurled into the air, landing hard on the floor. None of the numbers on the panel are lit; there's no way to tell how many floors it climbed. As he regains his feet, the elevator compartment begins to plummet with such velocity that he is lifted off the floor, free falling within its confines.

After what feels like minutes but is more likely mere seconds, the elevator stops, and he is once again slammed onto the floor. He reaches up and presses the emergency button, to no effect.

In an instant, the car is climbing, this time even faster … higher, but something is different. This is not a straight, up-and-down motion as before. Now it feels as if the bottom is swinging to and fro. It has come loose from its cables. After several terrifying moments, it stops. He's tossed into the air and predictably lands hard.

The doors open.

He wastes no time scrambling out through the doors and collapses onto a metal floor as the aperture slams shut behind him. He hears the elevator car descend. Catching his breath, it appears that he is now outside, no longer in the hotel, but high atop a metal structure—an observation platform. The metal railing is cold and wet to the touch. As he raises himself up, he peers over the railing, awed by the height. There are steps, but they only go up to a higher platform. The higher one is enclosed by a glass-and-metal box, protecting any sightseers from the dewy, frigid night air. He decides to climb up.

Once inside, the space is well-lit and offers a panoramic view, although there isn't much to see on such an inclement night. Looking for a way back down, he has no option other than the elevator. He trudges back down the stairs and steps in front of the doors. He pauses, ponders, and then presses the button. Immediately, the directional triangle glows red.

A piercing *ding* announces the arrival of the car. The doors slide open, and stepping in, he realizes that the interior is somehow smaller, the ceiling at an odd angle. No matter, he's committed. He presses the L button and the doors close … the descent begins. The drop is at a normal speed, and the elevator cab no longer feels as if it is swinging. It's going down. He watches the floor indicators count down to L. Its light does darken, but the elevator does not stop—the downward course continues.

After several moments, the elevator stops. Behind him, doors he hadn't noticed before open. He can hear machinery sounds, and the air is redolent of electricity and grease. He peeks out the open doors and sees a cavernous concrete shaft, where elevators on both sides continuously ascend and descend but all at a normal speed. There must be a half-dozen on each side of the enormous space. He thinks for a moment about stepping out; it's only a short drop down onto a concrete floor, but he's afraid of being trapped. After all, this inside set of doors appeared out of nowhere. How could he be certain they'd remain? So instead he crosses back to what had been the front of the elevator car and again pushes the L button.

He breathes a sigh of relief when the doors open. He sprints out, not taking a chance on them slamming shut.

This time, he takes the grand staircase. It's carpeted, thick and dark-red, with a wide wooden banister in the center painted a smooth, glossy white. He rounds the second-floor landing and begins his trek to the floor above, only to meet a ceiling. The stairs go nowhere.

He turns to walk back down, only to find that the stairway no longer descends to the lobby, but rather to a dead-end hallway with yet another set of elevator doors.

They open.

He steps in.

Chocolate Milk

He's dead on his feet, unsure if he's awake or what time it is—no sign of daylight outside. Nevertheless, he plods to the kitchen in the fog of sleep, opens the fridge, and retrieves a newly purchased gallon of milk. The jug's textured-plastic handle is cold in his grasp, almost enough to shock the drowsiness away, but not quite. He's thirsty and doesn't really want to wake up yet. Still, even in his wonky limbo, he wonders if the fridge temperature is set too low.

Before closing the door, he spots and liberates the chocolate syrup—a recently rediscovered childhood favorite, purchased on a whim during his last shopping trip. He places both on the counter.

With the refrigerator door closed, the kitchen is almost completely dark. The only illumination spills in through the blinds from the yellow security light outside. He doesn't require much light; he knows where things are. Turning in the opposite direction, he pulls out a tall glass from the cabinet above the double stainless-steel sink.

He pops up the top of the chocolate syrup container. He licks a drop off the thumb and forefinger of his right hand as he squirts the thick liquid into the bottom of the glass with his left. It looks black in the dimly lit kitchen. After peeling the plastic tab from the milk-jug cap, he lifts and pours from the heavy container, his hand shaking due to its weight. He opens the drawer in front of him, retrieves a long-handled spoon, and begins to stir, trying not to spill.

He raises the glass to his mouth, and though wanting to savor the rich flavor, his thirst overwhelms him, and he chugs down one mouthful, then another, and another. It's cold—very cold—sweet, and decadent.

Taking the last gulp, he feels something in his mouth—a lump. His first thought: a chunk of frozen milk. The fridge *really is* too cold. Expecting to dissolve the lump, he pushes it against the roof of his mouth with his tongue. Something doesn't feel right. He spits it back into the glass. Taking the long-handled spoon, he fishes out the clump and places it on the countertop.

He opens the fridge to fully illuminate the counter. As the chocolate milk runs off the lump, he sees a small, dead mouse with large black eyes and small rounded ears. Its fur is a lighter brown than the chocolate.

Despite the wee carcass before him, he's still extraordinarily thirsty. Compelled by a force beyond his control, he squeezes more chocolate syrup into the glass, picks up the milk container, pours generously, and observes several more lumps splash into the glass.

Using his spoon, he removes four more dead mice.

He drinks.

Bike Ride

Since his divorce, cycling—more specifically, mountain biking—has become an increasingly important part of his life. The freedom, adrenaline rush, and increased fitness are all strong allures, but by nature, he makes important decisions gradually. Increasingly though, he always takes the bike with him, and more and more often, when the opportunity arises, he will tackle a new trail.

Though he has never ridden in this park before, it feels comfortable, even familiar. Atop a hill, he mounts his bike—a soon-to-be-replaced, inexpensive department-store purchase from his early, noncommittal days. The trail up ahead is narrow and steep.

As he starts down the bumpy dirt slope, he notices another rider just behind him and off to his right. Though close, the other cyclist is not cramming or pressuring him. Gaining speed, he studies the route ahead. About a quarter mile down the trail, at the bottom of the hill, the path makes a sharp, 180-degree right turn and then runs parallel to a ledge that abruptly drops down the mountainside. He already knows he's traveling too fast. The bike is bouncing along the rough, compacted dirt and not making enough contact for adequate braking.

Entering the curve, he leans into it, brakes fully applied, but inertia is carrying him off the trail, through the patchy grass, and toward the edge of the cliff just a few feet away. Despite his best efforts, in another moment, he is airborne. He closes his eyes and begins to free fall.

He's stunned when his bike impacts a hard surface. It's not pretty, but somehow he managed to crash onto a boulder protruding from the mountainside. He's dropped perhaps ten feet. It could have been much worse.

As he stands, he brushes himself off. Above, he can see the rider who had been behind him. From his vantage point atop the boulder, the other rider appears to be quite tall. He has dark skin and very sharp-angled bone structure in his facial features—American Indian, perhaps? The man says nothing but merely straddles his bike and observes.

After checking himself for injuries, he looks at his bicycle. He can clearly see that the back wheel is bent. Nevertheless, he believes the bike is still ridable. Looking up to the Indian, he shouts, "It seems I bent my wheel."

The man shouts back, "You've *always been* riding with a bent wheel."

Looking up, he sees the man is riding a Gary Fisher mountain bike. He yells, "Maybe I'll get myself a good bike like yours." He throws his bike up next to the trail and begins to climb up off the boulder. By the time he reaches the top, the Indian is gone.

He mounts his bike and begins riding once again. He starts up a hill just as the Indian crests the top, turns around, and comes barreling back down directly at him. He dismounts, pushes his bike to the trailside, and narrowly avoids a collision. The Indian circles back around and, though maintaining a distance, starts to follow.

Remounting his bike, he attacks the steep hill. Once over the top, the trail leads onto a boardwalk-type structure and then into a densely wooded area. The thick tree canopy obscures the railings, walkway, and adjacent benches so completely that they all fade into the blackness a short distance down.

He begins to ride over the planks, followed by the Indian. He can feel the sticky wisp of spider webs clinging to and tickling his face and neck. He turns his head to avoid taking another in the face and sees a hand-size, black-and-white spider bouncing in a web ahead of him; he tears his way through.

After he passes unscathed, he stops because right in front of him is another enormous web with another gigantic spider—this one black and orange.

As he cleans his face of the cotton-candy-like substance, he peers further down the boardwalk into the gloom. Every few feet, he can make out more webs, each as substantial as the one he's now facing, and each occupied by creatures that would dwarf a tarantula.

He turns around and begins to head back to the dirt trail. As he approaches the Indian, he says, "Too many spiderwebs to go that way."

The Indian replies, "Too many spiderwebs."

They ride on.

CURRENTS

December 7, 2015
Associated Press—Port Canaveral, FL

Coast guard helicopters and other aircraft have launched a search for containers lost from the cargo vessel *Columbia Elizabeth*. The three-hundred-forty-foot ship was en route to Puerto Rico from Port Canaveral, Florida, when the captain noticed a number of containers askew and hanging over the side. The barge diverted to the Port of Palm Beach and remains moored there, since no recovery efforts have yet commenced. According to a coast guard spokesman, perhaps as many as twenty-five containers were lost and may represent significant navigational dangers. The spokesman went on to say that hundreds of these containers are lost each year, most eventually sinking to the ocean floor.

Present Day
Friday, 2:00 p.m.

"You're late. You said you'd be home by one," Marilyn says, not turning to face Ken as he enters the bedroom.

"Don't start," Ken says. "I left as soon as I could. Just as I was headed out at twelve-thirty—"

She cuts him off, "I *know*, they presented you with the case of another wrongfully charged, upstanding pillar of the community."

"Marilyn, I mean it, don't start," Ken pleads.

Marilyn continues packing his overnight bag. "For tomorrow evening, I put your blue blazer and gray trousers in the garment bag, along with my dress. I also packed a couple Tommy Bahama shirts for knocking around on the boat. Do you have a preference on which two pairs of swim trunks?"

"Black and gray," Ken replies. He watches as she retrieves items from the dresser drawers and places them into his duffel. Amazing. Seven years later, and she's still as beautiful as ever. Now she is packing her own weekend clothes. Her sheer-lace top and harem pants almost obscure the bikini. "You're wearing a thong?"

She stops, looks over her left shoulder at him, her long chestnut curls spilling over her right, and says, "So?"

"A bit much, don't you think ... or *little*, depending on your viewpoint ..."

"Are you saying I don't have the body for it?" she asks, already knowing his answer.

"No, I'm just saying, we're going to a funeral, and there will be other people—"

Marilyn interrupts, "First of all, spreading your father's ashes on the ocean isn't a funeral. Secondly, what *people*? We're going to be with your obnoxious brother and catty sister-in-law. Go change." She resumes packing.

He fumes but complies, removing his jacket and tie. Nothing has really changed for him since first meeting her. She's gorgeous, and she knows it; she loves the attention of men—always has. Many an evening, when they were dating, he had to deal with the occasional brazen drunk—or *six*. She loved clubbing, and though loathing it himself, he'd take her anywhere she wanted to go. Far too often, he'd show up the following morning for a law-school class at Nova Southeastern University sporting a green-and-purple shiner. But on those mornings, he'd also be spent—very spent. Her *apologies* made it all worthwhile, back when he aspired to become a big shot attorney, marry the beautiful coffee-shop waitress, and live happily ever after.

"So who's the latest scumbag they've saddled you with?" Marilyn asks matter-of-factly.

Ken sighs, knowing she speaks the truth. "Suspicion of burglary, resisting arrest, assault on a police officer—long rap sheet—and the kid's only twenty." He shakes his head.

Marilyn zips up his duffel with exaggerated movements, conveying her irritation with his long-hour, low-pay job. Nothing he hasn't seen before. "I don't understand how you can take it, dealing with vermin for next to no money," she huffs.

"Can we *please* not do this right now? Can we just get through the weekend?" Ken again pleads.

The drive from their two-bedroom, two-bath condo on Davie Boulevard to his brother and sister-in-law's house isn't far, just off Las Olas Boulevard, but the two couples are worlds apart. Their Ford Fusion makes the turn from Southeast Sixth Avenue onto Ponce de Leon Drive and follows it back into the Venice of America, the canals of Fort Lauderdale. The streets narrow as they snake their way to Dale's house—really a six-bedroom, six-and-a-half bath, seventy-seven-hundred-square-foot monstrosity with three hundred feet of waterfront dockage, more than enough for his new fifty-two-foot yacht. They reach Southeast Eighth Street and turn into Dale's travertine driveway. Coming to a halt, they notice that one of the three garage doors is open, and just inside they see the ass end of a new Bugatti Divo. "Jesus, the extravagance," Ken says, shaking his head.

Marilyn casts *the look* in his direction, that same one she deploys every time they visit Dale and Audrey—something that doesn't happen all that often. Ken can count on one hand the number of times he's seen his brother and sister-in-law since graduating law school. His older brother, Dale, is also a Nova Southeastern University alum but chose a path in corporate-finance law, graduating three years ahead of Ken. But there's *the look* from

Marilyn, the one that says, "You don't have to be a public defender. You could have money too."

Ken sighs and drops his head.

As they get out of the car, a voice booms from the portico, "Kenny Boy, my baby brother!" Dale walks into the bright sunlight, arms wide. He wraps Ken in a firm bear hug. "Good to see you," Dale says. Ken pats his brother on the back.

They disengage, and as Ken goes to retrieve their luggage, Dale turns his attention to Marilyn. "Hey, gorgeous!" he says, embracing her, one hand dropping to her waist. She turns her head, allowing him to kiss only her cheek. He first lifts her off the ground, then sets her back down. With no positive response from Marilyn, Dale looks back to his brother. "Let me help with the bags, Ken. What can I take?"

Ken hands him Marilyn's overnight bag and makeup case. "Here, grab her highness's war paint, willya? he says.

Marilyn wastes little time getting away from her husband's brother. She is already steps ahead of them on her way to the house. The whole time, Dale's eyes remain transfixed on Marilyn's derrière. "Whew, love that butt floss," he says.

Ken sighs and shakes his head. Attention from men in general is one thing, but from his own brother … he already regrets complying with Dale's plan. He should have known it'd be another weekend of having his face rubbed in his older brother's wealth and success.

Inside, Audrey is striking a pose—hands clasped at her waist—in front of the round mahogany table in the grand foyer decorated with a large vase of fresh-cut lilies. "So lovely to see you, Marilyn," she says, staying in place and forcing Marilyn to approach her—an obvious attempt to establish herself as the alpha female. Audrey leans in and plants an air kiss on each of Marilyn's cheeks, accompanied by a *mwuh*.

"Lovely to see you too, *Aud*," Marilyn says, beaming her best fake smile.

Audrey raises an eyebrow at Marilyn's forced familiarity. "You're looking … well," she says, noting Marilyn's scantily clad curves beneath her swimsuit cover.

Marilyn returns the compliment, though observing the evidence that Audrey has been having some work done. Still an attractive woman, with lustrous blonde hair, she is thin as a waif. She's nearly a decade older than Marilyn, a resentment that Audrey works hard to conceal, not always successfully.

As the men come into the house, Dale pauses to close the door. Ken walks over to Audrey. "Hi, Audrey," he says, leaning in and kissing her cheek. "You look great, as always."

Turning to his brother, Dale commands, "Don't set anything down. C'mon, we'll take everything straight to your cabin."

He follows Dale across the cool, white marble floor, the expanse interrupted occasionally by a handwoven area rug. They pass the kitchen—all white, glass, and stainless except for the mahogany crown molding and cabinets. They walk through a set of double sliding glass doors that lead to an enormous travertine patio, which, of course, matches the front drive. Beyond the gazebo, hot tub, and infinity pool is the dock where Dale's latest acquisition, a new Azimut 50 motor yacht, the *Seaductress* is moored. The hull is dark navy blue; the cabin and flybridge gelcoat glistens white in the sun. They descend a few steps, and the dock is level with the dive platform on the stern, making boarding easy.

"Wow, she's a beauty, Dale!" gushes Ken.

"Thanks, I've been dying to show her off to you. I was afraid they wouldn't deliver her in time for Dad's send-off and that I would've been forced to charter a plane. Less than twenty hours on the engines, she's as brand-new as they come." Dale beams.

Dale opens the sliding glass doors, and they enter the main saloon. On his right is a seating area featuring white Italian leather; opposite is an entertainment center that conceals a sixty-inch flat screen, which rises out of its hidden compartment. Just forward is a dining area in the same finish, a down stairway in the middle, and on the right, auxiliary controls for the interior cockpit. Ken follows Dale down past the galley and toward the bow. Opening the teak door reveals the vessel's guest stateroom—a V-shaped space with a queen-size platform bed and private access to one of the two heads.

"Gotta admit, Dale, this is pretty spectacular," Ken says, quickly calculating that the boat probably has more square footage than his condo.

"Here, throw your shit on the bed; let me show you the rest," Dale replies.

My shit, Ken thinks to himself.

Reversing direction back down the hallway, on the left Dale points out another stateroom, smaller with bunk-style beds and the other head, both with walk-in showers. A few steps down, they're standing in the master stateroom, a space that utilizes the full width, or beam, of the boat. A king-size bed is brightly illuminated by a series of large windows on both sides. There are also built-in dressers, nightstands, a wardrobe, and yet another sixty-inch flat screen.

"Good Lord," says Ken in amazement. Then, noting a combination lock on one of the panels, he asks, "Hey, what's that, a safe? Shouldn't that be hidden behind a painting or something?"

"Oh, gun locker," Dale explains.

"You have an armory onboard?"

"Damn right. There are real-life pirates, little brother, and law enforcement is scarce on the open seas. Got two .45s and an AR-15, along with plenty of ammo."

"Jesus!" exclaims Ken.

Dale leaves the stateroom and starts down the corridor toward the back of the boat. "Here's the engine room, and back here is the crew quarters," he says, gesturing toward the stern end of the deck.

"You have a crew?" Ken queries.

"No, but if we ever wanted to hire a professional captain for a long or complex voyage, we could. C'mon, let me show you the sundeck!" Dale is practically giddy as he leads Ken back up through the saloon and up the stairs to the flybridge. The main cockpit has an impressive array of electronics. There is a wet bar, and the rest of the space is comfortably padded for sitting or lounging, with a table that can be lowered to provide even more space, all surrounded by bright chrome work. Looking forward over the top of the windshield, the bow is padded as well, all of the cushions sporting built-in cup holders.

"Dale, this thing was built to party!" Ken exclaims.

"She hauls ass too. Her Volvo diesels can churn out over eighteen-hundred ponies, capable of zipping along at over fifty miles an hour," Dale says. "An upgrade I insisted on. She's the fastest 50 afloat, and, not only that, next month, a custom *Breedendam* will be delivered."

Ken gives Dale a quizzical look. "Lifeboat," Dale responds.

"Permission to come aboard, Captain?" Marilyn shouts from the dock. Audrey is standing next to her, shielding her eyes from the bright afternoon light, despite wearing six- hundred-dollar Gucci sunglasses.

"Permission granted," Dale shouts back. "I was just giving baby brother the fifty-cent tour. Ready to get underway?"

"Just let me double-check that the house is locked, and the alarm is armed, but yeah, now that we're all here, let's go," Audrey shouts back up to the bridge.

Dale starts the blowers and switches on the electronics. He programs the GPS for Bimini and taps Go. He pushes the start button, and the starboard engine roars to life, then the port. He sees Audrey walking back down to the dock and flashes her a thumbs up, which she returns. "Kenny Boy, would you undo the lines?"

"Sure," Ken replies, first moving over to the swim platform and then hopping down onto the dock. He unties the spring line, then the bow and stern. After jumping back onboard, he gives a hard shove to propel the yacht away from the dock. He hears Dale engage the bow thrusters as he pulls up the bumpers. Climbing back up to the flybridge, he stands behind his brother. Dale eases the throttles forward and takes her out.

"We'll head straight down here, take the Stranahan River to Port Everglades, and then it's a straight shot to Bimini. We'll be there in time for dinner." Dale smiles.

Cruising down the Intracoastal, the yacht is just passing beneath the Seventeenth Street Causeway when the girls emerge onto the bow, beach towels and piña coladas in hand. Audrey is wearing an otherwise conservative white one-piece, except for the plunging neckline that shows off her augmented cleavage. Her shoulder-length blond hair is fashioned into a bun. Marilyn has shed her outer layer and pulled her reddish-brown tresses back into a braided ponytail, looking not the least bit self-conscious about her bikini top and thong, which leave little to the imagination.

"Oh, Christ," Ken blurts out.

"What? She's gorgeous, and she knows it. Let her enjoy herself," Dale admonishes.

"Stop drooling over my wife," Ken says humorlessly. "Drool over your own."

"Who, Twiggy?" Dale asks. "She is so damned skinny that her hips leave bruises when we fuck. She's been lipoed, had ass fat injected into her lips, and insisted on these fucking hard-as-rocks implants. Trust me, you're lucky."

"I'm not saying otherwise. I just don't enjoy her need to flaunt it, ya know?"

The girls take seats on the cushions in front of the saloon windshield and lean back.

"Now that's a nice view," Dale comments, nodding in approval as he scopes out the girls' tops. "Those fuckers may feel like baseballs, but they sure as hell look good. Whaddya say we see if we can make them bounce," Dale says with a sly grin, turning the yacht toward the inlet and pushing the throttles forward. *Seaductress* responds as the diesels pound below decks. In a moment, she's on a plane, throwing a rooster tail of white foam over the emerald water. The girls wrestle with their towels as the wind rushes over the bow. They soon get things under control and smile up at the guys. The seas are calm, with only gentle rolling swells that *Seaductress* slices through with grace.

"Check this out," Dale says, flipping a switch. "Autopilot."

"Seriously?" Ken asks.

Dale smiles and nods affirmatively. "She uses GPS and radar to avoid other boats … Shit, she can practically dock herself. Hey, wanna beer?"

"Sure."

Dale walks over to the wet bar, returns with a pair of ice-cold Heinekens, and hands one to his brother. "Cheers!" he says to Ken, clinking bottles.

Ken cannot help but notice Dale's Rolex Sea-Dweller—twelve grand, at least. "So you said the engines have less than twenty hours on them; how many hours do you have operating her?" Ken asks.

"About two with the pro captain who delivered her. They shipped her over from Italy via cargo ship and then he piloted her to my place. We sailed up and down the Intracoastal for a while and then I put him in an Uber to the airport," Dale replies with a dismissive wave.

"Two! Two *whole* hours? And you feel qualified to take us to Bimini … fifty miles offshore?"

"Hey, it's not my first boat, Ken."

"It's not like you've made this trip before … I hope you know what you're doing!" Ken says anxiously.

"Look, just relax and enjoy the ride. There you go, just look at *that*." Dale nods toward the bow, where the girls are lying on their stomachs. "Damn," says Dale unintentionally. He looks at Ken, who stares back with displeasure. "Oh, lighten the fuck up, Little Bro. Audrey's ass isn't as nice as Marilyn's, but c'mon, you can't tell me that you haven't thought about prone-boning her, and you know it. Bitch loves it when I have her on her belly and take her from behind."

"One of these days, your arrogance is going to come back and bite you in the ass." Changing subjects, Ken asks, "Where's Dad?"

"Storage compartment in the saloon. Didn't wanna take a chance leaving him behind," Dale replies.

"So what's the plan when we get to the island?"

"Once we're docked, we'll clean up, have dinner at the resort, and maybe play around at the casino. What do you think?" Dale asks.

"Sounds good."

"Tomorrow, we'll sleep in, have a nice leisurely breakfast, and at midday, take Dad's ashes out to his favorite fishing grounds and spread them," Dale adds. "I've already put a deposit on a center console with a shallow draft—perfect for getting into the bonefishing spots."

Dale taps the touch-screen controls, and Credence's "Fortunate Son" blares forth from hidden speakers. The girls turn back toward the flybridge and respond with four thumbs up. The gesture brings attention to Marilyn's top, wildly askew and barely containing her ample breasts.

Over the sound of the bow spray and rushing wind, Audrey yells, "So how have the two of you been?"

"Oh, fine. Ken's always overloaded with cases and working at the call center keeps me busy. How about you and Dale?"

"Well, he's spent the past four months obsessing over this boat, sweating every detail from the contract signing to delivery. It has to have *this*, it has to have *that*, only the best of the best—you know how he can be," Audrey replies.

"And what have you been doing to keep yourself busy?" Marilyn asks.

"Between my civic organizations and taking care of the house, I hardly have any downtime, and of course once this thing got here, I was in charge of décor and stocking ... I wasn't going to leave that to Dale. He's fine at picking out the boat, but God help us if he decorated," says Audrey, shaking her head.

Marilyn smiles and nods, all the while thinking, *Bullshit. You have staff for the house and personal shoppers to do your legwork. You've been spending your time getting a nip here and a tuck there. Bitch.* But instead she says, "It certainly is a gorgeous boat, most beautiful I've ever been on."

"Oh, have you been on many *yachts*?" Audrey asks, damned well knowing the answer. It's just one more of her thinly veiled digs to flaunt her wealth and status under Marilyn's nose, her only counterpoint to Marilyn's youth and natural beauty.

"Boats, sure. Yachts, not so much," Marilyn answers with her sweetest smile. She sits up and adjusts her top, *accidentally* allowing her left breast to slip out. "Oops!" she says, slipping it back in, adjusting both with an exaggerated flourish, pushing them together, and creating double D cleavage that makes Audrey's implants look like pimples. From the corner of her eye, she can see Dale staring over the top of his shades and smiling. She cannot see Ken; he must be reclining in his seat. So she decides to push the envelope. Turning to lie back down on her stomach, she pauses momentarily on all fours, drops to her elbows, sticks her heart-shaped ass high in the air—directly in Dale's line of sight—and then resumes her prone position.

Audrey turns her head away and rolls her eyes.

Dale drops back down into his captain's chair.

Ken stares into the distance off the starboard side, oblivious to what had just transpired.

Friday, 5:50 p.m.
Bimini, Bahamas

Dale keys the radio mic and announces their arrival. "Resorts World Bimini Marina, Resorts World Bimini Marina, this is *Seaductress*, whiskey-delta-alpha-niner-o-four-eight, on channel sixteen, over."

"*Seaductress*, Resorts World Bimini Marina, switch to channel sixty-eight, over," comes the reply.

"*Seaductress*, switching to sixty-eight, over," Dale says.

Ken listens to the exchange as Dale obtains a slip at the posh resort and requests dock hands to secure the boat. *Seaductress* is far from the largest vessel in the marina, but she's substantial. Ken strolls to the aft deck, while Dale maneuvers the boat into the slip, backing her in gingerly. Ken throws the bumpers over the side, and the hands tie off the lines. With the yacht in place, Dale kills the diesels, steps down from the flybridge, thanks the dock hands, and slips each a twenty.

Dale walks over to Ken, slaps him on the back, and says, "Let's have some fun; c'mon, let's get the girls and grab some grub."

The men enter the saloon, Dale's hand still on Ken's back. Dale stands about six-four, six inches taller than his younger brother, and likes to drop subtle reminders to Ken of this and other differences, most notably wealth. Marilyn and Audrey climb up from below decks. Marilyn is wearing a form-hugging red dress with lace inserts at the waist, low-cut enough to accentuate her breasts without being tasteless. To complete her look, she wears nude stockings and red stiletto pumps. Her hair is down, cascading over her shoulders. Behind her, Audrey is decked out in a white dress, no less tight, open over her cleavage with straps that crisscross over her shoulders and plunge down her back. She's wearing silver heels; her hair is again in a bun, accentuating her slender neck. The men stare admiringly, but before they can comment, the women in unison demand that they shower and change into evening clothes. The brothers obey without protest.

The view from their restaurant dinner table is spectacular as the sun drops below the horizon, far enough from Florida that the expanse is nothing but blue. Dale observes, "You don't get this view just anywhere in the States; typically, one would have to be in Cali to watch the sun setting over the ocean to the west." He motions to their server for another round.

"I've got to say, Dale, Dad would have loved this—coming here on that amazing boat of yours, I mean," says Ken.

"Eh, he was such an old salt; he'd probably have complained that she's not rigged for fishing," Dale replies. Then, doing his best impersonation of his departed parent, says, "Too deep of a draft for chasin' bones."

"Good point," says Ken. They share a brief laugh. Ken raises his martini, "To Dad, may he never have another one *that got away.*" They toast.

"Ah, I miss him," says Dale. For just a moment, Ken sees a crack in his brother's arrogant façade. "Sixty-one is just too young, but he's with Mama now."

"I don't think he wanted to be here without her," Ken insists. "He wasn't the same after she passed—that embolism, so sudden, totally unexpected …"

"He died of a broken heart?" Audrey chirps, taking a sip of her Manhattan.

"No," says Dale, "he died of complications due to pneumonia, but that doesn't take away from the fact that he barely lasted a year after Mama died. There was so much more he could have had out of life."

"Like *grandchidrun* … " Audrey says, beginning to slur. She downs the remainder of her drink and flags the server for another.

"Let's not pull at that thread," Dale protests.

"*Arways* what *you* want," slurs Audrey. "*Dudn't* matter; my window *ish* closing anyway." She turns to Marilyn, "*Whaevuh* you do …" She stops herself midsentence.

Ken, noticing Dale's discomfort, interjects, "Hey! Let's check out the casino; whaddya say?"

Dale motions for the check.

The server with Audrey's drink makes a quick U-turn, grabs the bill portfolio off the server station, and delivers both to the table. Pleased with herself, Audrey sips eagerly at her Manhattan and hums an upbeat tune. Dale scans the check, opens his wallet, and stuffs a wad of bills into the portfolio. Not waiting for Audrey to finish her drink, Dale stands and proclaims, "Let's go break the bank." They all rise from their seats and head to the gaming tables.

Ken glances at his watch—nearly two in the morning. He hadn't realized how long he'd been distracted by the slots. He looks around for Marilyn but doesn't see her. Strolling toward the front of the casino, he spots Dale among a group of guys crowding the craps table and makes his way over. As he approaches, Marilyn's head pops up after throwing the dice. He stops and watches as the stickman pushes them back to her. Bending to pick up the cubes, her breasts press hard against the top of her dress, and the back rides up to her upper thighs. Not a single pair of eyes is on the dice as she shakes, blows, and then flings them toward the far end of the table. The stickman says something Ken cannot make out. A cheer goes up from the crush of men surrounding her. He watches the game continue and, on the third toss, notices one of the men holding his phone to capture images of Marilyn. She sees the device and blows a kiss. Ken can no longer hear the raucous casino sounds, only the beating of his heart. He pushes his way through the gamers, grabs Marilyn by the arm, and begins dragging her away. In heels, she stumbles a bit trying to keep up with him. As he swings a door open to step outside, he can hear a chorus of boos from behind them, and one fellow with a distinct Aussie accent yells, "Fuck you, mate, ya bleedin' killjoy!"

"You're going to give me a stroke; ya know that?"

"I was only having fun," Marilyn insists.

Back in the stateroom, Ken lies on the bed with only the top sheet covering him, his hands behind his head. He stares intently at the ceiling, when suddenly an almost imperceptible creak draws his eyes toward the door leading to the head. Marilyn steps out, wearing only her red fuck-me stilettos.

"Sorry, I took so long, kitty needed a touch up." Sauntering toward the end of the bed, she runs her hand down her stomach and over her shaved pussy. She bends down, intentionally letting her long, reddish-brown hair block Ken's view of her breasts. She begins bunching up the sheet with her fingers, slowly pulling it off Ken. Climbing onto the bed, she lets her hair and breasts brush against his ankles, shins, and knees as she moves over him on all fours. She pauses over his crotch, lowers her head, swings her hair from side to side, and watches his cock harden. She rubs it first with one cheek, then the other. Next, she gently bites and kisses the shaft and head.

Ken moans.

She crawls forward a bit more until it's in her cleavage then makes short forward and backward motions. "I love how your hard cock feels between my tits. Is it good for you, baby?"

Ken groans, "God, yes."

Ken reaches for her. She pushes his hand away. "Uh-uh, you relax and let me do all the work," she whispers, kissing his chest and continuing to massage his manhood between her breasts. She moves forward until his face is nestled in her cleavage; she reaches back and strokes him. "Ooo, baby, you're so hard," she purrs. Straddling him, she slides back and works his cock inside her. She moves her hips back and forth, pressing against him, getting his cock deep within her. She leans forward, bracing herself with her hands on his biceps, as she rides him relentlessly.

Ken moans and thrusts upward matching her rhythm, her hair tickling his face. He can take no more; his climax is intense, and he feels Marilyn orgasm several times.

She collapses onto him, her breath warm in his ear. She bites the lobe, giggles, and whispers, "Am I forgiven?"

Ken sighs.

Saturday, 11:00 a.m.

The quartet arrives at the Big Game Club and Marina with the ashes of Dale and Ken's father. Audrey carries a bouquet of calla lilies. As promised, a twenty-foot center console with a ninety-horsepower Yamaha engine and fore and aft fishing platforms awaits them. It's a perfect shallow-draft bonefishing platform, but no gear is necessary for this trip. They don't even bother with refreshments. The ride to the bonefishing area is quiet, except for the engine hum and sea spray. Entering the shallows, Dale slows to near idle speed. Schools of fish dart hither and thither beneath them.

"Wow, would you look at all the bones running through here?" Ken marvels.

"We definitely brought Dad to the right spot," Dale says, opening the cardboard box with the crematorium logo.

"How do you want to do this?" Ken asks.

"How about we take turns dumping his ashes and saying a few words?" offers Dale.

"No, just you boys," says Marilyn.

"I agree, just you two," adds Audrey.

"Okay," Dale responds, pulling a thick, clear plastic bag from the box and opening one end. "Okay if I go first?" He looks at his brother.

"You're the firstborn, go ahead," Ken says with an accepting shrug.

"I'm also better looking, taller, and richer. I was just being polite." Dale chuckles, despite a total lack of either humor or humility.

"Yeah, well, you were his favorite too," Ken acknowledges.

"Jealous little prick." Dale smirks as he begins to pour the contents over the side. "Dad, thanks for all you did for me as a kid and even as a young man as I began to make my way in the world. You were a good man and always there for me. I'll miss you." He hands the bag to Ken.

Marilyn fumes at Dale's remarks. She hates the way he can be so abrasive, using humor as a weapon. *Given a chance, I'll fix his ass,* she thinks to herself.

Ken sprinkles the remaining portion. "Goodbye, Dad. I hope you and Mama are together again and that you're both at peace. Tell Mama I love her."

A teary Audrey hands Marilyn a bunch of the lilies, and they bend to lay the flowers on the water.

They all stand quietly for a few moments.

Ken breaks the silence, "Are we ready to head back? I'm hungry."

"In a hurry?" Dales asks.

"We did what we came to do," Ken replies.

Dale shakes his head and cranks the key. The Yamaha outboard turns over. He idles into the deeper water and opens up the throttle. Just like the ride out, the return trip is without conversation.

After lunch at the marina, Dale and Audrey head into Alice Town and take in some of the local color. Ken and Marilyn decide to find a quiet beach spot. All agree to meet back at *Seaductress* before dinner.

Saturday, 6:30 p.m.

Ken and Marilyn board *Seaductress*. "Hello? Anyone here?" they call out. No reply.

"Hmm, I wonder where they are?" says Ken.

"Do you want to try his cell?" Marilyn asks.

"Nah, let's just get cleaned up and head to the restaurant. Our reservations are for seven-thirty, so I imagine they'll be there," Ken replies.

Ken, sporting gray trousers and a blue blazer, is waiting on the aft deck when Marilyn emerges from the companionway. "Holy Christ," he gasps as she steps out wearing her little black dress, and little it is, covering her only from bust to crotch. Her hair is down, flowing over her bare shoulders. Her cleavage is prominently on display, thanks to a deep, plunging neckline, ending just above her navel and held in place by a crisscrossed lace. Her only accessories are gold hoop earrings and the thin gold chain Ken gave as a birthday gift the year after they met.

"I'll take that as a compliment," she says, smiling.

"Good lord, Marilyn, if you as much as sneeze, you're going to give everyone a show!" Ken protests.

"Good, they can eat their hearts out," Marilyn says with defiance.

He knows there's no point in arguing. If they wind up in a fight, she'll just go alone. "Ugh," Ken sighs, anticipating another night of gawkers eye fucking his woman.

They walk into the restaurant, finding Dale and Audrey already seated. Dale is sipping an obscenely overpriced single malt, and Audrey has a Manhattan.

"Have a seat; I'm buying," says Dale.

"You're already lit, big brother," says Ken with a laugh. But Dale doesn't even acknowledge him, instead jumping up to pull out Marilyn's chair.

"My, my, don't you look fantastic!" Dale says.

"Why, thank you, kind sir," Marilyn replies, taking her seat.

"That's a lovely eyepatch you're almost wearing, dear," comments Audrey.

"Well, I want to look good for my hubby; you know, while I still can, before the years start to take their toll," Marilyn snarks back, smiling.

"Looks to me more like you're trying to *land* a hubby," Audrey mutters, still audible enough to be heard.

"If I weren't married ..." Dale starts.

"If you—well, remember, asshole, *you are* and *she* still *is!*" Audrey shrieks, slapping Dale's shoulder with the back of her hand.

Ken shakes his head slowly and says, "Here we go." It's obvious to him that Marilyn enjoys getting under Audrey's skin, but Dale's ogling is making his blood boil.

Ken finally distracts Dale's attention from Marilyn, sharing a story about their father. Afterward, family anecdotes told myriad times ensue. They honor their old man's memory with multiple toasts.

"I feel like we should do something other than sit here and drink," Ken says.

"Gotta go with our strengths," Dale replies, laughing. "Wanna hit the casino again?" he suggests. "You stole my lucky charm from me last night. Cost me about eleven grand, you asshole. You owe me."

"Eleven thousand?" gasps Marilyn. "God, you know how long it would take us to save up that much money?"

Audrey sees an opening, and with a dismissive wave of her diamond-encrusted hand, says, "Darling, this man has to invent ways to burn through what he makes. It's practically a full-time job."

"I pretty much lost all I can afford to last night," Ken admits.

"Well, I can give you some cash to play with ..." Dale begins.

"Absolutely not. I'll stand or fall on what I earn, thank you," snaps Ken.

"Hey, little brother, just sayin', I got plenty ... and it's not like you *earn* all that much. I mean, my money works for me; I don't work for my money ..."

As the server sets another round on the table, Marilyn says, "Excuse me, I need to powder my nose."

Both men stand, but Ken blocks Dale from assisting with Marilyn's chair. "Let me help you with that, darling," Ken offers.

Dale makes no attempt at subtlety as he watches the gyrations of Marilyn's ass on her way to the restroom. He turns back to the table. Audrey's eyes glare at him. "What?" he asks in an annoyed tone.

"You're a fucking pig," Audrey replies in a sharp, whispered voice. "And she's a cheap tramp."

"Hey, Audrey ..." Ken starts.

"Ken, how can you put up with those outfits and her attitude?" Audrey asks.

"Do you really have to ask?" Dale chimes in with a laugh.

"When Marilyn gets back, I think we're going to call it a night," says Ken.

"Nonsense, it's not even ten," Dale protests. "Let's take our drinks into the lounge. They probably need the table for other diners."

As Marilyn returns, Ken waves to her from their new location. "I've got your drink here, honey," he says. "Think you're ready to call it a night?"

"Oh, not yet. Maybe after the next round," she answers.

"That a girl!" says Dale. "C'mon, Marilyn, come shoot craps with me."

"Well, last night was fun, so okay," she replies, rising to her feet. She walks over to Ken, gives him a peck on the top of his head, and coyly pleads, "I just want to play for a little bit, okay?" Dale offers his arm, but she pretends not to notice, and they head to the casino.

Ken shakes his head as Audrey looks on.

"And why, pray tell, do you put up with this?" Audrey asks.

"I love her. I want her to be happy," Ken says, sighing. "We don't go out very often; she seldom gets to show off like this. When she does, it's always a concern that some asshole will take things too far, but I put up with it because, honestly, there's not a lot else our lifestyle can afford her."

After several more rounds, accompanied by stilted small talk, Audrey looks at her watch. "Been more than an hour, should we go find them?" she asks.

"Sure," says Ken, feeling a little woozy from all the booze.

They walk into the casino, and Ken immediately sees a replay of the night before, except Marilyn's dress is black, and Audrey hasn't returned to the boat and gone to bed. Marilyn stands to Dale's right, shaking the dice over her head. Her rack bounces up and down to the great delight of the guys around the table. She kisses the cubes, leans over the rail, and lets them fly, giving the men in front an unobscured view of every bit of her magnificent cleavage, and for the ones behind, every possible inch of her shapely legs. Ken sees Dale with a fistful of bills clenched in his left hand and swatting Marilyn's curvaceous ass with his right. Ken has had it.

He walks over, leaving Audrey to watch, arms folded, struggling to remain upright, and says, "Enough."

Marilyn pouts and says, "I'm just having fun."

"Enough," Ken repeats.

"New shooter," the stickman orders, and Marilyn relinquishes the dice.

Marilyn smiles at Ken and bounces over to him, throwing her arms around his neck and planting a kiss on his lips. "Can we have a nightcap before we go?" she asks.

The foursome returns to the lounge and reclaim their seats.

"Damn, Ken, this girl is my lucky charm. I've nearly made back what I lost last night!" Dale boasts. "This is for you, little lady." He palms a wad of hundred-dollar bills, places it in her hand, and folds her fingers around it.

Marilyn looks at the bills and throws them back at him. "I don't want your fucking money!" she snaps.

"You're dressed for it," Audrey quips louder than intended and followed by a stifled hiccup.

"You're just jealous," Marilyn snarls underneath her breath, "because your husband desires me. You know it and so does he." Marilyn is sitting directly opposite Dale. She crosses her legs, giving him an unobstructed—pantyless—view. Audrey rolls her eyes, gets up, and walks toward the exit.

"Ooo, commando! I thought as much when I slapped you on the ass," Dale says with a drunken grin.

"Fuck this. Come on, Marilyn, we're going back to the boat right now," Ken insists. "I can't take any more of your flirting and their pretentious, bullshit snobbery!"

Ken is passed out on the bed. Tonight, there'll be no apology from Marilyn. She looks at his prostrate form, hoping she didn't push things too far. If she did, well, she can fix it. She always does. She decides to go up on deck for some fresh air and stargazing. Exiting the saloon, she walks aft barefooted. As she passes the crew cabin, someone grabs her arm and pulls her inside.

"Hey!" Marilyn yells, surprised to be facing her brother-in-law.

"Did I scare ya?" Dale asks.

"No, but you startled me," Marilyn complains. "What are you doing in here; why aren't you with that mousy bitch of yours?"

"She's passed out. Fuck, for all I know she's dead from alcohol poisoning," Dale says, then laughs. "I just stopped in here to use the head. I'm having cocktails on deck … Join me?" He suddenly realizes he's still holding her left arm. "You were making me pretty crazy tonight; you'd better hope Audrey doesn't remember some of the shit that went down."

Marilyn pulls her arm free and then places both of them over his shoulders. She's on tiptoe to get her lips close to his ear. "I enjoyed making you crazy and watching your wrinkled, old cunt squirm while I made you drool," she whispers. "But, you know, I could only ever love you like a brother." She laughs.

Dale bends to kiss her and is surprised when she kisses him back, her tongue darting into his mouth.

"I just wanted to give you something to think about next time you bang the Crypt-Keeper," Marilyn says. "Now I'm going to bed. Nighty-night, you pompous asshole."

Dale glares into her smiling eyes. He pulls her past him, quickly spins her around, and pushes her facedown onto the bed. Marilyn protests and attempts to get up, but he pushes her down again as he unbuckles his belt and unbuttons his trousers. Pulling up her dress, he thrusts his hand between her legs, forcing them apart. He enters her from behind, slamming himself into her again and again. He grabs her hair with his right hand and pulls her toward him—hard, bending her back. He reaches around with his left, pulls down her dress and grabs her breast, squeezing as hard as he can. He moves his hand up to her throat. "Tease me, cunt? You've forgotten, haven't you?" he growls.

Marilyn can only make guttural sounds, his hand closing her throat, making it hard to breathe. Dale releases his grip and places both hands on her hips, pulling her into him, his thighs slapping against hers. As he reaches climax, he pulls out and unloads all over her hair, back, and ass. She can feel his seed. She reaches around with her left hand and pulls a white, sticky glob from her disheveled tresses. "You fucking asshole! What the fuck is wrong with you?"

With his right hand, Dale turns her around to face him. He lifts her left leg and reenters her; his left hand is on the back of her neck, pulling her into him as hard as possible. Marilyn pushes against his chest with both hands, but her resistance only incites him to pound harder. "That's it, bitch. Fight me. C'mon, try and stop me," he exhorts through clenched teeth. This time, he cums inside her with a groan.

Dale pushes Marilyn back down onto the bed, her dress now covering only her waist. "You may want to clean yourself up before crawling into the sack with my little brother," he advises, pulling his pants back on, walking out of the cabin, and leaving the door wide open. Marilyn draws her knees to her chest and sobs.

Sunday, 9:30 a.m.

Ken awakes to a pounding headache. He looks over to see Marilyn sleeping at the far edge of the bed. He assumes that if he rouses her, she'll be hungover too, and decides to let her sleep. He slips out of bed and dons a Tommy Bahama floral-pattern shirt and cargo shorts. He debates whether he should go to the head, the potential for puking still a very real possibility. He decides to take his chances; odds are that fresh air will make him feel better. He exits the companionway into the saloon. Audrey is sitting on the aft deck, sporting her Gucci sunglasses, with a scarf covering her hair. He steps out to join her.

"Good morning," Ken says softly.

Audrey smiles and nods.

Dale appears from behind, carrying a pair of highball glasses filled to the brim. "Well, about time you got your ass outta the sack. Bloody Mary? A little hair of the dog? Fuck me, Ken, that shirt's a little loud, isn't it?"

"Are you fucking kidding me?" Ken asks. "You're drinking *again?*"

"More like drinking *still*." Dale laughs. "Seriously, it's no old wives' tale, a little pick-me-up will get you through," he insists.

Now Ken thinks he may puke, just the thought … He puts it out of his head. "Any coffee?" he asks.

"Sure," Dale says, nods, and disappears back down to the galley.

"You okay?" Ken asks.

"Been better," Audrey whispers back.

Moments later, Dale returns with a pot of coffee and service for four. No one speaks as they go about the business of caffeine preparation, but as soon as he has a sip, Ken asks, "What time are we heading home?

"Soon as I finish that Bloody and this coffee," Dale replies.

True to his word, he sets his cup down and strolls through the saloon to the auxiliary cockpit, where he flips the switches that start the blowers. He walks back to the table and refills his coffee cup. Returning to the captain's chair, he starts the engines. "Ken, man the lines?"

"Sure."

"Need any help? I can call the marina …"

"Nah, I know the drill," Ken answers.

The engines rumble below decks. Ken liberates *Seaductress* from the dock, pulls up the bumpers, and rejoins Dale at the controls. As soon as the yacht reaches navigable waters, Dale wastes no time pushing the throttles to full. *Seaductress* slices through the waves as smooth as silk, with maybe a bit more chop than the ride over.

Ken takes a seat on the aft deck, but despite *Seaductress's* clean-burning diesels, the fumes and motion get to him. His first thought is to bolt and puke over the side, but he's within eyeshot of Dale and Audrey. The last thing he wants is to arm them with more fodder for their nouveau riche scorn. He decides to move quickly to the crew stateroom. He remembers it being equipped with a private head. Entering, he closes the door behind him, hits his knees, and retches. Having eaten a light dinner, it isn't long before he tastes bile. After a series of dry heaves, he wads up some toilet tissue, blows his nose, and wipes his eyes. He depresses the vacuum pedal, and last night's meal and this morning's coffee disappear with a *whoosh*. He takes a few moments to collect himself, to make certain that the next wave of nausea will pass without incident. On his way back out to the aft deck, he notices the disheveled sheets on the crew bed and something laying on top. Marilyn's gold necklace ... broken.

When Ken walks into the stateroom, Marilyn is sitting at the vanity in a white terrycloth robe emblazoned with the navy-blue *Seaductress* logo on the breast pocket. In the mirror, she sees him hold out his hand. In his palm is her necklace. She pulls the robe collar up around her neck as she watches his eyes trace a line from her to her little black dress, laying crumpled on the cabin floor. She can see the color drain from his face. He takes a few steps toward her. She averts her eyes and pulls the robe tighter. He throws her necklace to the floor and storms out.

Dale may be a financial wizard, but he's not very creative. Ken walks into the master stateroom, making a beeline to the gun vault. He punches in the code—o-four-one-six-eight-oh, Dale's birthday—and the door unlatches. Ken grabs a .45, pops the clip to make certain it's loaded, shoves it back in, tucks the gun in the back of his waistband, and heads to the saloon. Emerging from the companionway, he sees Dale working on another Bloody as the *Seaductress* autopilots them toward Port Everglades, still hours away. "We need to talk right fucking now," Ken says coolly.

Dale raises his drink to take a sip. "Da fuck is your problem?" he sneers, suspecting the worst. Over his glass, he stares into Ken's eyes.

"What happened between you and Marilyn last night?"

"Leave it, little brother ..."

Ken smacks the glass out of Dale's hand, shattering it and spilling its contents all over the controls. "What happened?"

Hearing the glass smash, Audrey moves into the saloon, removing her sunglasses.

As Dale gets up from the captain's chair, Ken produces the .45 from his waistband. "Not so fast, asshole. You think I don't know you can take me in a fair fight?" Ken deliberately exaggerates taking the safety off.

Dale sits.

"What's going on? Ken? What's the matter?" Audrey asks, voice quivering.

Ken turns his head toward his sister-in-law and instructs his brother, "Go ahead, Dale. Tell your wife what's going on."

Staring into Ken's eyes, Dale says, "I think Kenneth here has come to find out the truth about Marilyn."

"Oh, God, this is awful, just awful," says Audrey. "No one ever wanted to hurt you."

"What?" Ken says, turning to Audrey.

With the momentary distraction, Dale starts to lunge at his brother, but Ken gets a bead back on him. Dale sits once again. "Look, Goddammit, put that thing down before someone gets hurt, and we'll talk about this! Let's just sit and talk!"

"Let me get this straight; you, me, and *your* wife are going to sit and talk about you fucking *my* wife? How ridiculous does that sound?" Ken's voice is strained and cracking.

"Ken," says Audrey, "we're sorry; we only wanted to protect you. We were always so afraid this would come out. It was so long ago; it doesn't matter anymore."

Ken feels woozy again, but it's not alcohol-related this time; it's personal and emotional. Unable to process what Dale and Audrey are saying about Marilyn, his head swims. He flips the safety back on, lowers the gun, and tosses it onto a cushion in the dining area.

Dale gets up, reaches over to retrieve the pistol, and backhands the right side of Ken's face. "Don't you ever point a fucking weapon at me again unless you intend to use it, fuckhole."

Audrey is sitting on the sofa just behind the cockpit. Dale grabs Ken's shoulder and shoves him in her direction. "Sit," he commands. Ken obliges. "I'm trying to be cool here, Ken, but understand, you just pointed a gun at my head."

Ken doesn't speak. Unable to make eye contact, he stares at the carpet.

"Now one of the things I love about you, little brother, is your naiveté," says Dale. "You could be making good money but instead feel some moral obligation to defend society's scum, for peanuts!

Maybe that makes you a better man than me. Hell, sometimes I think it goes beyond naiveté and borders on plain fucking stupidity, or maybe denial, or perhaps all of the above."

Ken looks at his brother.

"You must have realized at some point in your *relationship*," Dale makes air quotes, "with Marilyn that she had been waitressing in that shithole coffee shop long before your ugly mug ever graced the halls of Nova University. You weren't the first to want to tap that hot, little hash-slingin' ass … right?"

Kens eyes are back staring at the floor.

"Fact is, little brother, when you brought her home that Christmas break—stars in your eyes—how could I tell you that the woman you were so deeply, madly in love with was just a local cum dumpster?"

Mouth agape, Ken's eyes widen and lock onto Dale's. Furiously, he barks, "How fucking *dare* you?"

"Ken," says Audrey, "Dale's as blunt as ever, but you need to know the truth." She looks over to Dale.

Dale takes the handoff and continues, "She was trying to hitch her wagon to a lawyer, that's all. She saw all those guys, mostly well-to-do, running in and out to get amped up on caffeine for late studies and finals and knew, given her hotness, she could have her pick. Well, little brother, that's where you and I are most definitely alike. My eyes were filled with those same stars …"

Ken puts his hand to his forehead. "Are you telling me that you and Mar—"

"There's more; now keep hold of yourself 'cause this is going to be hard to take, but you may as well know it all. Shortly after finding out we were brothers, she tried to blackmail me."

"What!" Ken shouts.

"It gets worse," says Dale. "Anyway, that's when I confessed the whole thing to Audrey, even though I didn't know her when I was … was … *seeing* … Marilyn. I didn't want to hide anything from her, Ken." Dale inhales deeply and confesses, "There was a baby—well, a pregnancy."

Looking at his brother in consternation, Ken stammers, "That's not possible. Marilyn can't ... We had tests done; she can't conceive."

"Ken," Dale says, exhaling noisily, "She had an abor ... a procedure, but there were complications. Expensive ones. I had to ask Dad for help."

"Jesus! Dad knew?"

"Only that I got a girl in trouble. He never knew it was Marilyn, I swear," Dale assures. "By the time you brought her home, that was a distant memory. I was with Audrey, and Dad was never the wiser." Dale pauses and then continues, "But the old man gave me a dressing down that I'll take with me to the grave. All he ever wanted was grandchildren, and what I did destroyed him inside. I could never even think of having a kid after that."

Audrey spots Marilyn peering in from the companionway, still in her robe. "Ears burning, dear?" Audrey asks with an evil grin.

Ken looks over his shoulder, sees tears streaming down Marilyn's cheeks, and then looks back down at the floor.

"Ken," whispers Marilyn, "I don't know what they're telling you about me, but you need to hear my side ... please."

"Well, so far I've learned that I don't really know you at all. You're a Goddamned gold-digging tramp who lied to me, tried to blackmail my brother, and God knows ... Ah, fuck, and we haven't even gotten around to the events of last night!"

"Last night?" inquires Audrey. "What happened last night?"

Dale begins to say something, but Ken interrupts, "Apparently, sister-in-law, dear, your husband, my esteemed brother, and my whore of a fuck-happy wife had a sloppy, little reunion in the crew quarters."

"He raped me!" shouts Marilyn, rushing forward and pulling open her robe to expose purple-blue handprints on her neck. "That's how I got pregnant in the first place, because he raped me!"

"This is bullshit! Who are you going to believe, me, your own flesh and blood, or some gash?" hollers Dale at Ken and Audrey.

Audrey is now standing, openmouthed and wide-eyed at Marilyn's accusation.

"I have never once had consensual sex with anyone but you, Ken. I swear to God! Before I ever met you, he took me out to dinner and on the ride home, pulled into a wooded area near Sunrise Boulevard. I told him I'd never had sex before. He didn't believe me. I begged him to stop. He kept insisting that I was lying because of the way I flirted with the law-school guys. I tried to explain to him that regular waitress wages were shit, and the only way to make any real money was good tips. Being friendly meant better tips. He didn't care. He held me down ... He did it three times before he agreed to take me home!" Marilyn sobs.

Ken and Audrey glare at Dale, who looks as if he's going to take a swing at Marilyn.

"Ken, I swear, before you, there was only Dale, and no one but you ever since! Dale's right; I wanted to marry money to get out of there, but I love you, and although I gripe about it, the money really doesn't matter!"

"I don't understand, what's the blackmail he's talking about?" Ken queries, pointing at Dale.

"When I told him I was pregnant, he said it couldn't be his. He insisted I had been with other guys, but it wasn't true. I only threatened to go to his ... your father when he abandoned me! And it's true—I had the abortion; things went wrong, and it left me scarred and infertile," Marilyn explains, tears rolling down her cheeks.

"Jesus, God!" Ken exclaims, putting his hand to his head. "How could you keep this from me?"

"How could I tell you? How many times did I turn you down when you asked me out back then? I knew you were *his* brother, but the more I got to know you, the more I learned how different you are."

"How could you even be around him, if that's true?" Ken's asks, eyes tearing up.

"Because, if I wanted to spend my life with you, I *had* to make peace with it," Marilyn replies, sniffling.

With no one manning the controls or keeping watch, *Seaductress's* radar fails to detect the barnacle-covered cargo container just below the surface on her current heading. Running wide open, she strikes it going over fifty miles per hour. Her bow is thrust into the air, and her twin propulsion pods strike the tractor-trailer-size hunk of submerged metal and are torn from her hull. She splashes back down on her starboard side, nearly capsizing but righting herself and gliding to a near stop ... only moving with the currents.

Ken is first to come to. The saloon is filled with smoke. There are lights flashing on the console and buzzers wildly blaring through the acrid air. He makes his way to Marilyn. She blinks her eyes open, looking around startled. "Are you okay?" he asks.

"I think so," she replies, smoothing her robe and getting to her feet.

"We're on fire!" Dale yells from the other end of the saloon.

"Audrey, you okay?" Ken yells.

"I'm not injured," she replies.

"Ken! Quick, the engine room!" Dale instructs.

The two dash below deck, toward the aft section, where the Volvo-Penta diesels smolder. They grab the extinguishers and spray the area. There is a loud *pop* as the electrical harness explodes, sending sparks and more smoke into the room. The lights go out. The alarms and buzzers go silent.

"Fire's out; let's get out of here," Dale says, coughing.

The two couples move out onto the aft deck.

"What the fuck was that?" Ken asks.

They scan the horizon, no other vessels in sight. "We hit something," Dale says, stepping back into the saloon. Smoke is still pouring from the open sliding glass door. Moments later, he reemerges with fins and snorkel in hand. "I need to check her bottom," he says. He slides into the crystal water off the swim platform at the stern. Within a couple minutes, he's climbing back up. He sits on the edge, his shoulders slumped.

"What did you find? Are we sinking?" asks Ken.

"No, no ... at least I don't think so. Our propulsion pods have been completely ripped off—right out of the hull. In short, we have no propellers," Dale says, shaking his head in disbelief.

Ken climbs to the flybridge, keys the mic, and calls, "Mayday, Mayday, Mayday!" But the radio—all of the electronics—are dead. He flips switches to no avail. He opens the minifridge in the wet bar—no light. No power at all.

"Okay, so we're dead in the water. No power, no radio, no hotspot, so our cells are useless. How long before we're listed as overdue?" Ken asks Dale.

"Whaddya mean, overdue?"

"Dale, come on, you're the sailor, but even I know enough to file a float plan before taking a boat out. Are you telling me you didn't file our itinerary with the fucking coast guard?" Ken fumes.

"For a short hop to Bimini and back? I didn't see the point," Dale says as he scans three-hundred-sixty degrees around him—no land in sight. "Feels like the Gulf Stream has already picked us up in its current."

"Oh, shit. We have no idea if we're even close to a shipping lane. Okay, okay, everybody think for a moment; did any of you tell *anyone* else about our plans for this weekend?" Ken asks. "Is anybody going to have a clue as to where to start looking for us when we don't show up at work tomorrow?"

The others shake their heads.

"Well then, dear family, I guess we're going to have some time to work out our little problems," says Ken.

CAM4

Saturday

The wireless security cameras and base station arrived a few days ago in the all-too-familiar box with the iconic smile. Michael could hardly wait for the weekend to set everything up.

Finishing his morning coffee, Michael reviews the instructions and immediately commences installation—four cameras in all. Steps one, two, and three: download the app to his phone, set up the wireless base station, and get them synchronized with one another. Done. Now, open the weatherproof camera case and install two lithium AA batteries. Done. Now, assign each camera an identity. *Easy enough,* he thinks, *Cam1.* He repeats the process with the remaining three, numbering them respectively.

Michael installs Cam1 and Cam2 to cover the comings and goings in the front of the house—one over the front door and the other over the garage. He then prepares to set up the remaining pair in the backyard—one over the screen door, but the fourth? Now he is facing a dilemma. With Cam3 placed over the screen door, it will catch the face of anyone entering through the porch, but where should he install the last one to best cover the ground-floor windows? It needs to be far enough back to capture those in both the living room and master bedroom.

"Aha!" Michael exclaims as an idea pops into his head. He retrieves his six-foot ladder from the garage, leans it against the oak tree just off the back deck, and ascends. Once mounted firmly into trunk, he taps the Live button to activate Cam4. Success! A bright, full-color, live video of the back of the house and yard.

Sunday

Stepping out of the shower, Michael hears the phone alert. One of the cameras detected motion and shot video. He dries off as quickly as possible, anxious to see what or who was caught—a porch pirate, maybe? He unlocks his phone, opens the app, and quickly comes to a realization: installation was the easy part; management might prove a bit more challenging. All four cams have been triggered, and the app is displaying warnings for high battery usage and imminent depletion. Eager to see the cause of such a commotion, Michael does a quick review, which shows megabyte after megabyte of him mowing the lawn. "You stupid ass," he scolds. "Note to self, disarm the system on yardwork days."

Wednesday

Over the intervening days, the only images captured are of him backing his car out of the driveway every morning and pulling it back in each evening. *I should consider myself lucky, really,* Michael thinks. *It'd be far worse to be emailing video to the cops because someone broke in.* He decides to see the glass half full and not lament the lack of capturing anything even remotely interesting.

Thursday Evening

Michael barely hears the app alert; his phone is charging in the kitchen. Setting down his seltzer, he walks into the room and unlocks his phone. Cam4 has caught something! He selects Cam4 and taps the play icon to find a shaky night-vision video of two squirrels chasing each other, their claws noisily scratching the bark as they skitter and chatter. The last second of video, accompanied by a loud thud, is an image of the base of the oak.

Flipping on the floodlights out back, Michael sees Cam4 pointing straight down. "Damned squirrels," he huffs. He considers the best way to reorient Cam4. *The deck is probably high enough to reach it with a broom handle,* he thinks. *If not, I'll have to drag the ladder out again.* Leaning out over the railing, he *is* able to push Cam4 back into its proper position. A quick live check confirms that, once again, it is covering the four ground-floor windows.

One Week Later

Michael fidgets with his cell phone; he launches the security app, trying not to be disappointed in the lack of activity. He scrolls the list of cameras, and to his surprise, finds the message "offline" where Cam4's default image should be. "Damn it!" he exclaims, walking to the back door and switching on the floodlights. "Squirrels," he hisses. However, peering out the back door, he quickly notices that Cam4 isn't out of adjustment. It's *gone!* "What the hell?" he shouts, unlocking the door to get a better look.

Passing through the screened porch and onto the deck, Michael can see the still-attached mount, but Cam4 is nowhere to be found. He descends the three steps from the deck into the yard and circles the tree several times, trying to estimate the falling unit's trajectory and maximum distance it could have traveled. "Where are you, Cam4?" he says quietly. "Where did you get to? You couldn't have gone far."

Michael considers getting a flashlight, but the evening is brisk, and he didn't bother to grab a jacket and shoes. Besides, it'll be more convenient hunting in daylight—easier to spot Cam4's black exterior, especially if it has bounced beneath the deck.

As Michael closes the back door, locks it, and turns off the floodlights, he hears a ping from his phone; one of the cameras captured something.

Launching the app, Michael sees that Cam3 caught him going out and coming back. "Shit," he utters. Then he notices something else; Cam4 is no longer offline. He taps the icon to transmit a live shot, but when it loads, all he sees is a blurry gray night-vision image, nothing discernible. "Hmm, are you laying lens down, or did some creature use you as nesting material?" he asks the image. "I think you'd be too heavy for a squirrel to carry into the treetops, but maybe a racoon or possum dragged you under the deck."

Friday

Arriving home after work, there's still enough daylight for a more thorough search of the oak-tree roots. Michael grabs a flashlight for exploring under the deck. He again plods around the tree several times. The flashlight beam reveals nothing below the planks. "Where in hell did you go?" he groans in exasperation.

Checking his phone, Michael sees that Cam4 is still online. "Okay, so if you're still online and transmitting, you have to be close enough to the base station, which means you weren't stolen and are still around here somewhere," he deduces aloud. Daylight is waning, and the air is getting chilly. Perhaps tomorrow. He taps the Live icon, only to get the same blurred grayscale image with no sound.

Saturday

In the morning, Michael searches the backyard unenthusiastically. "Ugh, screw it," he says. "I'll pony up another hundred-twenty bucks for a replacement." He walks back inside and orders the replacement online in less than a minute. The quest to recover Cam4 is over and done with. It's out of his mind. Well, honestly, not completely. But today, it will not eat into his precious time with his daughter, Penny. His handful of hours with her—two weekends a month—is worth far more than the price of a new camera. He proceeds to the shower, still trying to repress his obsession with Cam4.

An afternoon of shopping, dining out, and seeing a movie with his baby girl easily distracts him from the mystery of Cam4.

Now it's time to take her back to his ex. Dropping Penny off at Tanya's house, Michael escorts her to the front door, walks back to the street, and climbs into his Honda Civic. It occurs to him that he hasn't turned his phone back on since entering the movie theater—a flick based on a short story about a young geologist who explores Mars and, in the process, meets God.

The screen on his phone illuminates, and Michael sees an alert from Cam4: Motion Detected. He taps the alert, and a five-second video loads. The image is still night-vision gray, but the picture is crystal clear. Cam4 is on the ground, on its back, and aimed up into the oak where it had been attached.

Michael's first thought: it must have fallen from a nest. "Gotcha! Now, I know exactly where you are," he exclaims in celebration. "Figures you'd show up after I ordered the new one. Oh, well, I'll find a place for it," he says to the image but then notices some audio has been captured as well. He turns up the volume to full and clicks Replay. The image doesn't change, only a few oak leaves move in the breeze, but he can clearly hear breathing—guttural exhalations. "What the ...?" he asks.

9:48 p.m.

Arriving home, Michael pulls into the garage bay and hurries through the house to the back door. He flips on the light and heads to the spot where Cam4 should be laying, but there is nothing. He finds himself walking in circles around the tree's base once again. In frustration, he pulls out his phone and taps Live. He notes that Cam2 observed his return, and Cam3 was also tripped. Cam4 shows the earlier blurred grayscale image. He looks up into the tree and shakes his fist. "You little bastard. You took it back up, didn't you?" he curses at the squirrel, raccoon, or whatever.

11:33 p.m.

Michael is awakened by an alert. He had fallen asleep on the sofa, his phone on the table next to him. With the volume still turned to full, his heart jumps. He picks up his cell; on the screen is displayed a message from Cam4: Motion Detected. He taps the icon. The Cam4 image is sharp, taken from the ground and pointing up into the oak, but this time, the vantage point is the opposite side of the tree, nearer the deck steps. "Whatever critter stole the cam must have dropped it from a nest up in the branches again," he conjectures. "If I move quickly, maybe I can grab it before the little beastie recovers it!"

As swiftly as possible, Michael scrambles to the back door, switches on the floodlights, and heads out onto the deck.

Nothing.

"Can't be!" Michael knows he's got the right spot because he recognizes the same branches from the video. He's been meaning to trim them; they're growing too low, creating a fire risk when lighting the barbecue grill. "You have to be here, right here!" he yells at the vanished Cam4.

Determined not to spend another moment perusing the tree roots, Michael returns to the living room and plunks down on the sofa in front of the TV. *Weather Wrap Up* is calling for the possibility of snow. Figuring he'll watch the morning edition, he grabs his phone and taps Play. This time, the breathing is louder and more pronounced. The sound is creepy enough, but he swears that during the last few seconds, the breathy growl turns to laughter.

Despite being unsettled by the maniacal sound, Michael taps Live. Blurry. Gray. Indiscernible. "What the hell is going on?" he whispers.

12:59 p.m.

"Jesus!" Michael hollers, his phone alert chirping. "You stupid ass, you forgot to turn down the volume again." He really doesn't want to but *does* read the Cam4 screen alert: Motion Detected. He's unsure whether to be annoyed or fearful. Maybe both. He taps the alert. Crystal-clear, night-vision appears of the gate that opens to the deck, accompanied by that ever-present breathing. If Cam4 fell from the tree once again, this time it landed on the top step. *Is that even possible?* he wonders. Fighting the instinct to stay in bed, he dons his robe and slippers and heads to the back door. He flips on the floods and rushes to the gate, but Cam4 is nowhere to be seen.

Michael retrieves his phone from the pocket of his robe. When he taps Live, as expected, the image is the same blurry gray. "Oh, this is messed up," he gripes, his voice trembling. He turns down the phone's volume before sliding it back into the pocket. He turns and heads back to bed.

Sunday 1:57 a.m.

Despite lowering the volume, the alert instantly wakes Michael. His sleep has been shallow, restless at best. He stares at the ceiling, not wanting to look at his phone. But he knows he eventually will. There it is: Cam4: Motion Detected. Michael taps Play. The breathing, as in the other clips, is easily detectable, and the image is laser-sharp and unmistakable. It's a close-up of his screened-porch door handle. "Whaaaaa ... oh, fuck me," he whines. It makes no sense. The door handle is three feet above the decking. How could the camera be that far off of the floor? "Think, man, think!" he yells at himself. His heart pumps rapidly; his hands are shaking. "This has to be a gag; someone is messing with me, but who?" Michael feverishly processes the possibilities. "A neighbor? Nah. I'm not that close to anybody around here, nor am I feuding with anyone. A joke by one of my twisted buddies? Who did I tell about my security cameras? No one!" He wracks his brain to the point of exhaustion without arriving at any possible resolution or explanation.

Rather than making another exploratory trek to recover Cam4, Michael locks his bedroom door and adds 911 to his one-button presets. *I locked the back-porch door when I came in last night, right?* he wonders, trying to recall. He's sure he did, but doubt nags nevertheless.

He taps Live. As expected—dreaded—the blurred image appears.

3:33 a.m.

His phone chirps. Michael can see the message that popped up from Cam4. He sighs. *Look at it,* he thinks. *No, this is too messed up. No more. I'm done playing. I have to know!* He picks up his phone, unlocks it, and taps the security-system icon. The video loads. As with the others, the video plays, but the image is still. The camera moves neither up nor down, right nor left, but it is a recording, not a snapshot. Clearly, Cam4 is focused on the door that leads from the back porch into the kitchen. The growling, short breaths are more pronounced.

"No!" Michael presses the Disable button to shut off all four cameras. He drops the phone on the nighttable, lies down, and pulls a pillow over his head.

5:02 a.m.

The alert tone chimes. Without looking at the screen, Michael turns off his phone.

10:00 a.m.

Michael pulls into his ex's driveway just as she steps out the front door. "Hey," he says, climbing out of the car.

"Didn't you get my messages?" Tanya asks.

"What? Ah, no," Michael replies, realizing the phone's been off since the incident earlier this morning.

"Penny isn't feeling well. I was hoping to save you the trip over. She wants a raincheck. I can let you have her next weekend; I don't mind."

"Oh, okay. That'd be great. I appreciate it. Will you give her my love and let her know I hope she feels better?"

"Of course. I'll text you about next week just as soon as I look at my calendar, okay?"

"Okay, thanks. Uh, bye," Michael says, climbing back into his Honda.

Sitting at the stop sign at the cul-de-sac exit, Michael presses the phone power button. The screen flashes, and a progress bar begins its creep across the smooth glass surface. He sets it in the cup holder. A few moments later, he hears the familiar security-alert tone. He drives on.

11:11 a.m.

Michael sits in the parking lot at Fountain Pointe Beach—a favorite contemplation spot—staring out at the waves. The wind-whipped sand is moving in ghostly sheets down the beach, and the roiling whitecaps make him shudder despite the warmth of his car. The security app chimes. "Shit," he grumbles, ignoring it for the moment.

Exiting the Honda, Michael pulls up his jacket collar against the wind and walks the half block to a package store. He purchases a fifth of gin and returns. It's been a few years since he's had communion with the Creature, but between the cold and Cam4, he wants a little help to lose the chill and loosen his tangled nerves. The first swig makes him gag, cough, and shake uncontrollably. "Shit," he squeaks in a stifled voice. Regardless, the feeling is warm, calming. He takes a few deep breaths. After one more swig, he recaps the bottle and picks up his phone.

Michael taps the icon. The clips progress from the deck and through the porch. The clip from 7:17 a.m. is just inside the back door of his kitchen, at eye level, but now the video is in color— no more night-vision filter. Listening intently to the audio, there are words he can barely make out, but they sound like, "Oh, Miiiiiichael?"

Whoever this is has to be in my house! Michael thinks. *I must not have locked the back door.*

Clip from 8:53—far side of the kitchen, near the arch that leads into the living room. Michael hears a breathy growl and toward the end, "Miiiiiiiikey."

"I was home then! This guy was in my home while I was there!"

From 11:11—living room, just inside the arch. A more demanding tone, but still encapsulated within a growl, "Miiiiiiiiiichael!"

"He's still there!" Michael says and taps Live. The same infuriating, nondescript gray image comes up.

"What is this?" Michael shouts at his phone. "Oh, God, what is all this?" He dials 911.

"Nine-One-One Dispatch, what is the nature of your emergency?" a woman's voice answers after the first ring.

"My name is Michael Williams; there's an intruder in my home."

"What is the address of the residence?" the woman asks calmly and professionally.

"1595 Lake View Drive," Michael replies. "I'm not there, though. I was alerted by my security system."

"Where are you calling from, sir?" the dispatcher inquires.

"My car. I'm just leaving Fountain Pointe for home," Michael explains.

"Do you know the identity of the intruder?"

"No," Michael replies, not divulging that the intruder apparently knows him.

"Stand by, sir; stay on the phone with me, please. Don't hang up yet." In the background, Michael can hear her repeating the information. "Sir, I have dispatched a unit to 1595 Lake View Drive. If you get there before them, do not enter the premises. Do you understand?"

"I understand. Thank you," Michael says.

Within fifteen minutes, Michael arrives home. Two marked police cars are parked in the street. He pulls into the driveway and observes a uniformed officer emerging from the back of the house.

Exiting his Honda, Michael approaches the officer, who asks, "Are you the person who called in regarding an intruder?"

"Yes, sir, I'm Michael Williams." Extending his hand, Michael looks at the policeman's name tag. "Officer Ryan ... Did you find anything?"

The policeman's radio crackles, and a voice reminiscent of a kazoo buzz interrupts. Ryan holds up an index finger to Michael and says, "Pardon me." He keys the microphone and speaks, "Ryan ten-one-o-one, uh, negative, speaking with Mister Williams now, ten-ninety-seven, will report on departure."

"Ten-four," buzzes kazoo voice.

The second officer has now joined them. Looking at Ryan, he motions with his head. "Mister Williams," says Officer Ryan, "this is Officer Baker."

"Good morning," Michael responds as they shake hands. Baker grins and nods his head in acknowledgement.

"Uh, we haven't found any evidence of an intrusion, no signs of forced entry—"

"I think you'll find I accidentally left my back door unlocked," Michael interrupts.

"No, sir, we checked your doors and windows," corrects Ryan.

"Well, if I left it unlocked, he could still be in there and have locked it from inside. Would you guys mind joining me for a walk-through?"

"Sure, but what makes you so certain someone entered you house?" Ryan asks.

Michael pulls out his phone and shows him the security app. "See these alerts? These are you and the other officer waking around the house." He points to the ones from earlier. "These are from early this morning." He taps the one from 7:17. "See? This is inside my kitchen!" He taps 11:11. "Now he's in my living room!"

"He? I mean, there's no one in either picture. It just shows an empty room," Ryan counters confusedly.

Michael imagines how this must look to the cops. "Oh, I guess that doesn't make much sense," he says, embarrassed. "If you'll follow me …" He leads them to the oak and points at the vacant Cam4 bracket. "You see, that camera disappeared the other day and I can't find it. I, uh, I, uh think maybe whoever was in my house found it and was carrying it. If you listen carefully, you can hear him breathing."

The officers listen, but from their reactions, they don't seem to hear anything aside from ambient background noise. The cops exchange glances that Michael doesn't see.

"Unit nineteen, advise ten-twenty," crackles kazoo voice.

"Nineteen—still with Mister Williams; we're going to check and clear, copy?"

"Copy, Nineteen. Check and clear. Advise when rolling, over."

"Nineteen, ten-four," Ryan replies. "Okay, Mister Williams, would you let us in, please?"

Michael checks the door and finds it locked. He pulls out his keys and opens it. Ryan places his hand on Michael's shoulder. "Let *us* go in. Wait here, please."

Ten minutes pass until Ryan and Baker reemerge. "All clear, we checked closets, under the bed … nothing out of place," Ryan reports. "Mr. Williams, have you been drinking this morning, sir? I thought I might have detected a little …"

Michael flashes back to those days when the Creature invaded his happy home and drove Tanya away. It controlled him, stole his soul, and possessed him like a demon; he became a stranger to his wife and baby girl. His face reddens at the officer's suggestion; he hasn't had a drop since the day she left … until this morning. "Yes, Officer, I did have two small sips just to keep warm, but I promise you I am as sober as a judge."

"Okay, sir," replies the cop.

"All right, well, thank you for coming out and checking. I appreciate it," Michael says with a deflated exhalation.

"No problem, sir. If anything changes, don't hesitate to call," says Ryan. He walks away, letting kazoo voice know that he and Baker are through.

Michael slumps on the living-room couch, a seltzer sitting next to him on the end table. He thinks briefly about the unfinished fifth in a paper bag laying on the passenger seat. *Nah. Not going back down that road. Too high of a price,* he thinks. He picks up the remote and begins surfing. He misses Penny.

1:21 p.m.

Tick. *What was that?* Michael thinks, turning his head swiftly from side to side. It was subtle but audible. A mechanical click. The alert chimes. His pulse quickens as he lifts his phone from the end table to see: Cam4: Motion Detected. "Shit, shit, shit," he grouses. "It's broad daylight; I'm in my own home; I'm a grown man of thirty-eight years, and I want to cry." He taps the alert. The video plays. On the screen, as if taken from the far corner of the room near the ceiling, Michael sees himself sitting on the couch, remote in hand, flipping through channels. "What is this!" he hollers. "Who are you? What do you want?" He looks into the corner of the room where Cam4 would have to be placed to capture this angle but sees only a cobweb flowing in a delicate dance in the heating-register current.

Michael's heart races. *What to do? What to do now?* he thinks. Without an obvious direction, he decides to do the one thing that always calms him down.

"Michael?" Tanya says on the other end of the line.

"I didn't know what else to do … who else to call …" Michael trails off.

"Michael, what's wrong? You don't sound right," Tanya observes.

"Ty-Ty, the damnedest thing is happening …"

She knows there's a problem; he hasn't called her Ty-Ty—a derivative of the initials of her maiden name, Tanya Yates—since well before their divorce. "Michael, what?" she queries.

"I ... I ... I don't even know where to begin, I ... it's so ... it's so nonsensical."

"Mikey, what's going on? You seemed fine when you were here this morning; what's happened?" Tanya asks.

"I don't even know where to start," says Michael. "It's all so unbelievable."

"Start at the beginning," Tanya suggests, trying to remain even and measured despite his frightening tone.

"I installed a wireless video surveillance system, four cameras. The camera I mounted to the tree out back disappeared shortly after I put it up. It's been ... it's been ... uh, I can't. It's just too crazy," he says. He pauses and thinks, *It's been what? Stalking me? If I say that, she'll think I've lost it, or worse.*

"Michael? It's been what?"

"No, never mind ..."

"Tell me, please," Tanya insists.

"It's been malfunctioning and driving me crazy. I just needed to vent. Hey, Ty-Ty, I'm sorry I bothered you with this, especially while you're dealing with our sick little girl. Is she okay?"

"She's running a slight fever but sleeping at the moment."

"Okay. Poor kid. Tell her I love her when she wakes up, and we'll do something extra special next weekend," Michael says, feeling calmer. "Listen, I'll let you go, so you can take care of her."

"She's asleep, so if you want to talk, it's no problem," Tanya replies.

"No, thanks. It's okay," Michael lies.

"Michael?"

"Yeah?"

"If you change your mind, don't hesitate to call me back. Promise?"

"Yeah. Bye,"

"Okay, bye," Tanya says.

He waits for her to hang up and then sets down his phone.

3:33 p.m.

Tick! Michael jumps. He'd fallen asleep on the sofa. The empty Beefeater bottle lay on the floor, shed of its paper cocoon. He hears the alert. He can see the phone screen in the reflection of the table-lamp base. Its mirror image is distorted yet easily recognizable: Cam4: Motion Detected. He reaches over his head and grabs the device.

He taps the alert. His sleeping face fills the screen, accompanied by breathy growling sounds.

5:00 p.m.

After a short trip to the package store, he sits on the sofa waiting. He knows not what for; only that whatever it is, it's going to happen soon. He takes a swig from the already-half-emptied bottle. He taps Redial.

"Michael?" Tanya asks.

"Yeah, isss me again. I'm sorry ..." Michael's voice is weepy; he can't steady or conceal it. "I don't zackly know what's going on, but I juss want you to know that I'm sorry. I'm soo sorry for everything."

"Michael, you're worrying me. What in God's name is going on with you?"

"Thas juss it. I dunno whuss going on; only that iss either gonna end or begin, I juss dunno."

"You're drinking again," Tonya observes, her voice flat.

"Iss not what you think, Ty-Ty, but if thiss iss the end ..."

"Michael," Tanya's voice softens, "what are you talking about?"

"Nothing. I'm soo sorry. There's st-still a part of me that loves you—always will. Pleasss know that. Tell Penny I love her soo much it hurts." Michael disconnects.

Immediately, Tanya's name and number come up on his phone. Michael ignores it. He disarms the security system and switches off his phone.

5:18 p.m.

Tick!

Tanya arrives at the same time as Officer Ryan. He screeches to a stop in front of Michael's house, patrol-car lights ablaze. She whips her Fusion into the driveway. They both run to the front door and hammer, all the while calling out his name.

No response. They fear the worst.

"Do you have a key, ma'am?" asks Ryan.

"I do," Tanya says, fumbling in her purse. "Here!" She wiggles it into the keyhole and opens the door. "Michael!" she shouts.

"Mister Williams?" Ryan heads to the back portion of the house while Tanya checks the rooms in the front.

After determining that Michael isn't in the house, Tanya spots his phone on the end table. It displays 18 Missed Calls Tanya, 10 Missed Calls Stafford Police Department, and just below: Cam4: Motion Detected.

With the phone in her hand, Tanya walks toward the rear area, where Officer Ryan is entering. "I found his phone," she says grimly.

"Huh, okay. Well, no sign of him outside. But let's hope there's a simple explanation, and he'll just turn up. In the meantime, you're welcome to file a missing persons report; no waiting period is required when there's concern that he might harm himself," Ryan says. He then notices something out of the corner of his eye. Pointing toward the oak, he comments, "Oh, I see he finally found his missing camera."

COOKIES WITH SATAN

To my loving brother, Ben.

I'm so sorry. I hope you can forgive me. Please try.

It's been so hard, so lonely since Peggy's passing. I am at the end. I don't want to go on anymore—I can't. We were so unprepared. Everything I could sell, I did, except of course Peggy's beloved Trans-Am. I can't bring myself to do it; she loved that car so. It's the only thing I can look at that reminds me of her, and it makes me smile because whenever she drove it, she beamed. I never—not a single time—saw her unhappy behind the T/A's wheel.

I know my few friends will be disappointed and unhappy with me about my decision to join my love, but at my age, there's no chance I'll ever again have what I had with Peg. Even if I could, I don't want it. I want her; I want to be with her; and in a short while, I either will or won't, but either way, my suffering—mental and physical—will be at an end.

I'm sorry too, Ben, to burden you with the disposal of my home and few remaining possessions, but I hope there'll be something leftover for your troubles. I'm also going to apologize now for whatever condition my body is found in. It might be a while. I'm not very sociable anymore. In fact, I probably talk with you more than anyone, and we only chat every few months. But know, since that wreck took my leg and hand,

I've wanted out of this weak, fragile, flesh-and-blood vessel, and now I'll finally be free of it.

You've been a good brother, and I love you with all my heart. The time you spent with me during Peggy's final days and the days afterward are priceless to me. As much as I wish we lived closer, to this day, I can't conceive of myself leaving our house, even though I can no longer afford it. It was—is—Peggy's and my home. We built it, and I can never part with it.

I understand that selling the house will be harder because of my final act, and again, I apologize. The Trans-Am is worth at least $20,000, and it's yours—do with it what you will. I'll soon be in a place where it won't matter.

My world has become so small and isolated over these past few years. There are likely a half-dozen or fewer who will care I'm gone. My light will simply flicker out, but I know this will be hard on you. My last wish is that you not let it. If you want to mourn, do so for the days back home when we raced our bikes down Lawrence's Hill in summer and exchanged them for our Flexible Flyers in winter. Remember the day we found Dad's old trunk of Playboy magazines and the week we didn't talk after discovering each of us had a crush on Jenny Turney.

Those are the things to mourn, not my broken, aged body and unending emptiness. My release from this hell on earth is to be celebrated.

Aside from my Peggy, what I desire most of all is your forgiveness.

All my love,
David

David trifolds the note, slides it into an envelope with Ben's name written on the front, and then licks and seals the back flap. With the help of a cane, he rises from the table, shifting his weight to his good leg. He wrangles the prosthetic one underneath him. He switches the cane to his other arm and slides the stump into its receptacle. David grabs the large bottle of Knob Creek bourbon, thrusts it under the armpit holding the cane, retrieves the letter, and grabs the keys to his car, as well as Peg's. Over the past few years, he's found all sorts of ways to carry a load. It's a slow hobble to the door that leads to the garage.

Despite holding the letter and keys, David easily turns the doorknob, takes the two steps down, clomps to his Chevy Malibu. It's a newer car, and he wonders if its exhaust system, with all its modern, antipollution devices, will even do the trick. Thank God for the certainty that Peg's classic T/A is up to the job; otherwise, he might have to find another way of offing himself.

Through the open window, David drops the letter onto the Malibu's front seat, relieves his armpit of the booze, and places it next to the letter. He walks to Peggy's car, reaches through its open window, slides the key into the ignition, and turns it. The big V-8 starts on the first crank with a belch of blue-gray smoke from the dual exhaust. A smile comes to his face as he listens to the throaty rumble of the beast and watches the exhaust swirl against the closed garage door.

One more important detail. Just before David wrote the note to Ben, he had placed wet beach towels at the base of the garage-bay doors. Now he must place the last one along the bottom of the door leading into the house.

David limps back, pulls a towel from the shelf, and stuffs it tightly into the space beneath the door. He then sits in the Chevy's driver's seat. He pushes the Start/Stop button, and the engine purrs. David listens intently for a second; it's hard to hear his engine over Peggy's, but it *is* running. His Malibu has been modified to accommodate his disabilities, so he decided dying in it wouldn't hurt the resale value too much. It's already bad enough to be leaving Ben a suicide house—leaving him a classic suicide car would be downright criminal. If necessary, he *can* still drive an unmodified car—having done so yesterday, filling both gas tanks as insurance against running out of gas and ruining his plan. Nevertheless, with his permanent disabilities, the Malibu has definitely proven to be the more practical choice for getting around.

David places the note conspicuously on the dash, tunes the radio to his favorite oldies station, and takes a swig of Knob Creek. The bottle is large and difficult to handle with only one hand and a stump, but it will become easier as the contents empty. He reclines the seat a bit, takes another healthy swig, and leans his head back, enjoying the warmth of the bourbon on its way down. Another swig and another, he can feel it working.

David awakens, sitting in an overstuffed, oxblood leather chair. Its covering is warm-butter soft, with cushions so plush that he experiences a floating sensation. Looking around, the room is austere white. No corners are discernible; the walls seem to go on forever in every direction, and there's no telling how high the ceiling might be with no obvious light source. The space appears aglow. For a moment, he fears his suicide attempt has failed and that he's hospitalized, but room features begin to come into focus. There is a simple, white desk in front of him and behind it a chair like his, except in white. The furniture blends in completely. David has never experienced an environment so sterile, yet so stimulating. He's tempted to stand, but the starkness of it all is disorienting. He feels the floor beneath his feet, but it blends into the walls as if he's in a sphere.

Well behind and to the right of the desk, a door slides open. Its blackness is as monolithically monotone as the whiteness of the room and its contents.

Though entering by way of the door, a woman appears to walk directly through a black wall. There seems to be no transition from dark to light, as if she emerges from nothingness.

David is struck by her beauty. She reminds him of a young Peggy, but as attractive as he always found his wife, this woman's physical attributes are almost beyond description. While he always felt Peggy had a great body, this woman is … perfect. That's the right word, but even so, she *should not* be David's type. She's much taller than Peg, and he's never gone for tall women, being only five-nine. David simply cannot reconcile his immediate attraction, his developing fascination, and now his unadulterated animal *lust* for this stranger with the deep-felt passion he still feels for Peggy. Nor can he stop himself from watching her stroll toward the desk. Everything about this woman—those long, shapely legs, the locomotion of her hips—are reminiscent of the brazen sexuality that earned women the label "broads" in the early part of the previous century. She has a tight, trim waist and ample bosom, all form-fitted into a short, scarlet cocktail dress with matching pumps. Her azure eyes, one partially obscured by a stray lock of spun copper, twinkle invitingly. The open back of her dress is largely concealed by her long, auburn hair. Despite his best efforts to look away, he cannot stop ogling her. But what makes the situation even more heart pounding? Well, astonishingly, she *is* leering back at him and smiling! She's on display; she knows it, and she's enjoying the attention. For the first time in more than three years, David is fully aroused.

The door slides shut without a sound. Once again, the wall is seamless and white. The woman glides to the chair behind the desk, sits on the arm, crosses her legs, and clasps her hands in her lap. A quick whip of her head tosses the wayward curl back into place. She's still smiling at David, her eyes locked onto his. He is watching her every movement intently. Her incredibly long, auburn bottom lashes seductively touch her high cheekbones, and the top ones caress her eyebrows only to retreat when she blinks and then reemerge framing those glacial-ice blue eyes.

"Can you tell me what's going on?" David asks. "Who are you? Where am I? What is this place?"

"You've got some things to think about, David, some important decisions to make," the woman replies, her voice silky and soothing.

"What decisions?" David insists. There is nothing he can detect about this woman that doesn't ooze sexuality. It's as if her breath is composed of rose-scented pheromones.

The woman uncrosses her legs and stands, every movement grace personified. She executes a pirouette to circumnavigate the chair, extends the slender index finger of her left hand, and traces the edge of the desk with a perfectly manicured, bright-red nail. She slowly walks around, coming toward him. Her dress is a second skin, so much so that David cannot help but watch her muscles inflect and relax beneath.

My Lord, it's as if she's wearing nothing, David thinks. *She's the most beautiful, most sexy creature I have ever seen!* He can feel his face flush as, in the back of his mind, he imagines Peg admonishing such objectification. But he *cannot* rein it in. To make matters worse, the more turned on he becomes, the more she piles on the smiles, and those eyes! "She's loving this!" he whispers.

The woman moves from the desk to where David is sitting; her index finger remains extended. She gently swings her arm forward in his direction.

My heavens, she means to touch me! David gasps. His right hand grips the armrest, the leather submissive to the pressure. A thought thunders in his brain, *Oh, God, no! She's going to touch my left arm, my fucking stump!* He's panicked at the thought of her disgust. He wants to warn her off, withdraw his arm, but he's frozen in place, stunned by her exquisiteness.

The woman's index finger lightly touches the blunt end of his stump, directly on the bulging scar tissue where his wrist used to be. Her smile never wavers. She then uses her middle and index fingers to walk up his arm to his shoulder. She is now standing behind him. She places her right hand on his opposite shoulder and begins to massage. Her movements are gentle yet firm as she works her fingers into his muscles.

"Oh my Lord, that feels incredible," David sighs. "Who are you?"

The woman leans down, her breasts pressing against his back, her ginger hair spilling over his neck and giving him goose flesh. Her lips touch his ear and she whispers, "Call me Veronica."

David, awash in her scent and aura, murmurs, "But *who* are you? What are you here for?"

Veronica lets her head rub the back of his as she moves her lips to his other ear and, in the same tone, tells David, "Anything you want."

"Am I dead? Is this heaven?"

"The answer to your first question is no; so the answer to the second is no as well," Veronica explains, her warm, moist breath both tickling and exciting him.

"I don't understand," David says, allowing his head to bob and weave with the rhythm of her kneading. "And, frankly, I'm not really caring that I don't."

"That's good," Veronica comments softly. "We're going to make our time together all about David."

"What time together? What does that mean?"

Veronica stops working his shoulders and moves in front of him, never letting her left hand lose contact, sliding it from his shoulder down his right arm to his hand. She kneels next to him and places her right hand on his thigh and makes short, gentle strokes. "It means that you'll need to make a very important decision after you've talked with the others, and if you make the right one, we're going to have a lot of fun times together."

David stares into her eyes and asks, "Others?"

Veronica pays no attention to his question, tilts her head just a bit, and explains, "I'm very good at doing what I'm told," she replies with a mischievous pout.

"What others? Who are they?"

Veronica rises, bent at the waist, and leans into him. She kisses his neck; her breasts press against his chest. She kisses his jaw, working her way to his ear, where she whispers, "They just want you to be happy, like I do." She leans back a bit to look into his eyes, then forward. She kisses him on the lips and opens her mouth. David reciprocates, and their tongues entwine. With her right hand, through his trousers, she grips and strokes his hard-on. "My time is up for now; I have to go," she whispers, her lips still pressed against his.

"What? No! No, *don't* stop," David pleads, leaning forward to continue the kiss as she pulls away. His heart is racing.

The doorway has reappeared without a sound. Veronica stands and tells David, "Make the right decision. I promise, we'll have lots of fun."

Veronica turns and walks away. David cannot take his eyes off her ass. Never has he seen fabric undulate so erotically. She never looks back but raises her right hand just over her shoulder, palm facing him, and flexes her fingers to wave goodbye. She passes through the portal. It closes without making a sound.

David's breathing is rapid, his pulse wild. He hasn't experienced such feelings since … he can't think of a time! He's reminded of a verse his mother recited, "I did but see her passing by, and yet I love her till I die." He thinks, *Wait. Am I saying that I'm in love? Can that be? No, not love. But God, I do want her. I want her like no one ever before!* For a moment, he's filled with guilt, thinking of Peggy, but those thoughts quickly fade, and his mind returns to Veronica. "Will she come back? I hope she does …"

Before David can process what happened—really, what *is* happening—off to his left another door opens. Again, there is no sound, and through the door, there is only solid black, until a young girl emerges. From beneath a green beret flows a mane of straight, blond hair, which, aside from her bangs, streams to her waist. Her blouse has a floral pattern, and she's wearing a blue bowtie, a green skirt that matches the beret, and a sash of the same color, draped from her right shoulder down to her left hip, where a box rests beneath her arm. Almost every square inch of the sash is covered in badges.

David greets her. "Hello, little girl."

"Hello!" the girl replies with a chipper lilt.

"I'm David, who are you?"

"My name is Bettina McCormick, but you can call me Tina," she offers enthusiastically.

"Are you one of the *others* that Veronica mentioned?"

"I'm the top-selling scout in my entire troop. In fact, for the past three years, I've been number one in the *nation*, and I plan on being first again this year," Tina reveals, beaming.

"I see, and what do you want from me?" David queries.

"Why, I want you to be happy, of course."

"Do you think I'm unhappy, Tina?"

David sees Tina's eyes drop to his stump resting on the chair arm. Instinctively, he drops it down, out of sight.

"It's okay," Tina insists, her smile transitioning to a sympathetic grin. "Everybody gets unhappy sometimes, you know?"

"I do," admits David.

"When I feel bad, do you know what makes me happy, David?"

"Ponies? Little girls are usually crazy about them," David says, returning his stump to the armrest.

Tina giggles. "No, silly, cookies!" she trumpets, producing a box of Thin Mints, his favorite.

"Oh! I should have guessed that, shouldn't I?" David replies, chuckling.

Pointing to a series of similar badges on her sash, Tina explains, "This one is for top seller in my troop; this one is for my state; this one is for my region, and this one is for the whole country! And I have two more sets just like these!"

"Wow, that's really impressive. You must work very hard."

"Oh, I do. Even my teachers realize that. They let me do makeup exams and projects for extra credit after cookie-selling season ends. I'm the best because I've done everything I can to set myself up for success," Tina explains.

Intrigued by her candor and maturity, David tells her, "I have no doubt that you'll be successful at whatever you want to do as you grow up."

"I already know what I'm going to do," Tina assures him.

"Oh? So what do you want to do?"

Tina stops opening the box of Thin Mints. Her cheerful disposition loses any trace of whimsy as she answers, "I'm going to be president. I'm going to be the most important and powerful person in the entire world."

"I have no doubt," David replies honestly.

Tina takes a cookie and turns the box toward David. The sweetest of smiles returns. "Have some, please ... So are you *really* good at something, David? You know, like something you do better than anybody else?"

"There was a time. In fact, we have that in common. I was the top national salesperson in my company," David reveals, taking a cookie and popping the whole thing into his mouth.

Tina's eyes grow wide. "Tell me about it, please?"

"Gosh, Tina, I haven't thought about it for a long, long time," David confesses.

"Oh, but if I can learn something ..."

David grabs a few more confections, pops one into his mouth, and leans back into the baby's-bottom-soft leather, a proud grin lighting up his face. "I started out as a sales assistant, producing presentations and writing copy for the lead salespeople at a chemical company that markets gazillions of different products. The two guys I worked under were killing it, making a fortune. How did they do it? It was all *me*, all me! I was their secret weapon. They'd come back from the road and take all the credit for my hard work. Finally, I had had enough. I went over their heads to the big boss and told her that I deserved a shot on the front line. Well, she didn't believe me, so I quit on the spot. I spent the better part of another year at a rival company doing the same work. However, this time, the guy I reported to was a decent, honest fellow. He arranged a review of my work with the executive VP of sales, who gave me my first opportunity. I never looked back. But wanna know the best part?"

"Yes, please!" Tina replies.

"My old boss, the woman who didn't listen to me ... She called and offered me a job as a full salesperson because after I left, those two bozos couldn't sell water to a man on fire!" David brags.

Tina claps.

"I took Peggy, oh, uh, my wife, to Europe three times and Asia twice, all on my company's dime for being their top sales rep. That's how much I meant to them. They did everything they could to keep me happy, even made me a VP with stock options.

"Wow, are you rich?"

"Hmm. For a time, I guess. Had about everything we wanted: nice clothes, luxury cars—Peggy got herself a classic. Have you ever seen *Smokey and the Bandit*?"

Tina shakes her head.

"Well, if you ever do, Peg got herself a car like the one in the movie. But we traveled, took cruises, and built a big, beautiful house on a secluded lake with a guest- and boathouse. Yeah, Tina, I guess you could say we were rich."

"I'm going to be rich!" Tina shouts.

"I'm sure you will. You're off to an amazing start. You should be very proud of yourself," says David.

"Oh, I am. You should be proud of yourself too!"

"There was a time, but now—"

"No matter what, David, you did all those things! You did them, and that should make you *proud!*" Tina interjects. "You showed them; you showed them *all*."

David smiles and replies, "Know what? You're right, Tina. You're absolutely right! *I did* do those things ... and *more*. So yes, I am proud, damned proud!"

Tina smiles widely and says, "I'm afraid I have to go now, but it was very nice talking with you."

"It's been a genuine pleasure. You're a very bright girl, and I know you're going to realize everything you could possibly want."

"Thank you, David."

"What do I owe you for the cookies? Oh, I don't believe I have any money on me, so I may have to owe you."

"Oh, don't worry about the cookies. They're … free!" She hesitates and walks back through the portal.

David watches her depart. Bettina's last sentence felt unfinished; something was left off the end—an unspoken thought. *They're free …* for now, *maybe?*

David's peripheral vision catches a door opening on his right. He turns his head but finds himself staring into black space. He leans forward to try and get a better view, but as with the other two apertures, no light penetrates the darkness. After several moments, a sandaled foot emerges. Stepping through is a tall, lean fellow, though he has a bit of a slouch. His hair is a light, sandy brown, shoulder length. His full beard is unkempt, and his attire is reminiscent of a beach bum—gray tee, sans sleeves, and tan board shorts with blue vertical stripes. His pace is beyond leisurely as he shuffles behind the desk toward the chair. Over the course of the entire amble, he never appears to notice David. It's hard to tell for sure though, as his eyes are obscured behind a pair of sunglasses. He walks to the chair, turns around, and falls into it, his back against one arm, legs draped over the other. The man's head lolls to the right as if unable to overcome gravity; his hair falls across face. He's now looking over the top of the desk in David's direction. He pulls his shades down to the end of his nose, exposing his dark-brown eyes and says, "Hey."

"Hey," David replies, uncertain how else to respond to the man's greeting.

Spying the box left behind by Tina, the man nods his head in the direction of the treats. "Those for anyone, man?"

"Help yourself," David offers.

"Fuckin' A, man. Dude, can you slide them a little closer?"

David's a bit surprised at the request, since the box is about equidistant from either of them. Nonetheless, David leans forward and shoves the box in the beach bum's direction. It comes to rest within his reach.

Without acknowledgment, the man pulls out several cookies, pops them into his mouth, and begins to chew. Crumbs fly in every direction as he exclaims, "Oh! These are the best, man!" He takes a couple more and pushes the box back toward David. "Got anything to drink, man; you know, something to wash them down with?"

"Sorry, no," David replies. He watches the man finish the cookies, wipe his mouth with the back of his arm, and cluck his tongue in an effort to swallow the unmoistened confectionary blob. The man exhibits no intention to engage in conversation, so David decides to initiate. Picking up a cookie, David declares, "If I could have my way, I'd prefer to have a little Scotch with these."

The man replies, "Oh yeah, bro. Or some water!"

David eats the cookie as the two study each other. Finally, David asks, "So are you here to talk with me about something? Anything? Do you at least want to tell me your name? I'm David, by the way."

The man lets out a loud sigh. "They call me Ice Cream, man, 'cause I'm chill. Get it?"

"Okay, then, Ice Cream Man," David responds, suppressing a small chuckle.

"No, dude. Not Ice Cream *Man*, man, just Ice Cream. See, man?"

"Oh, Ice Cream. Sorry, got it," David apologizes, doing his best to repress a laugh. "What do you want from me?"

"I'm sure you know that by now, man. I just don't have the energy for all this formal jazz; know what I'm saying, Davey Baby? So why don't you just tell me what went down that made you give up," insists Ice Cream.

"What do you mean?" wonders David.

"Oh, dude, come on. You checked out, you know?"

"What? I thought Veronica said I'm *not* dead, that ..."

"No, man, not that. I'm talkin' about before ... your mental checkout, when you said, 'Fuck it all.'"

"I don't know that I want to talk about it," says David.

"Dude, we're just gonna sit here 'til ya do," Ice Cream warns, sighing. "Tell ya what," he continues, sliding his shades back up to cover his eyes. "Wake me when you figure it out and realize you *have* to talk about it."

David sits; his mind pores over the events that forever changed his life. How long does this process go on? He's unsure; there's no telling in this place. Maybe it has been mere minutes, maybe hours. "Okay," he says.

"Lay it on me, man."

"I had everything: a great relationship and a perfect and lucrative job. Things were great. Peg and I decided to start a family; she was going to be a stay-at-home mom. She'd just left her job, closing the door on her corporate career. She had already started working on the nursery. After making all these life-changing choices, we figured it was time to celebrate. It was a Friday; I had just closed a big contract, so I took her out that evening. We were on our way home. I'd had a few drinks, so I was being careful to stay under the speed limit. Out of the blue, a car headed in the opposite direction crossed the median and hit us head-on. The guy was a repeat DUI offender, without a license or insurance. Because of my elevated blood-alcohol level, my own insurance company refused to pay." David holds up his stump. "I lost my hand and leg. We hadn't arranged any sort of insurance for Peggy; hadn't seemed all that important at the time."

"Dude, that sucks. I'm *really* sorry for you," says Ice Cream.

"That's not the worst of it. My treatment ran to hundreds of thousands and required months of rehab. But if you knew me, you'd get that I'm the guy with the can-do attitude. I mean, I was a superstar in my industry. I felt certain that my company board would do everything in its power to help me out. I was ready for anything, or so I thought. For the first few days after the wreck, I was heavily sedated. My first memories start about day four, as I was being prepped for my third surgery. Peggy was holding my hand, sitting next to my hospital bed. Her head was bandaged. When I questioned whether she was okay, she started to cry. I asked why, and she told me that each time I'd regained consciousness, that was always my first question. Apparently, I drifted in and out a lot during those first days, but she was just so touched that my first thoughts were of her. I really don't know how many times that happened.

"Peg had a serious concussion, but thankfully, aside from some minor cuts and bruises, that was the extent of her accident injuries. However, unbeknownst to us, there was another medical issue. An MRI revealed a brain tumor. I told her not to worry; we'd do everything necessary to beat it and get her well. Again, she started to cry, because I was *again* repeating what I had previously told her. But then she said, 'It's inoperable.'"

"Nothin' they could do, man?"

"Because of its size, growth, and location around blood vessels, *no*. Treatment options were limited, and the doctors offered us no real hope. Over the course of the next month and a half, while I was recovering in the hospital, they monitored its growth. It was growing at an unexpectedly rapid rate. They did everything they could. No expense was spared, but she was gone in less than three months. During that time, she never told me about her pregnancy. I found out when I received two death certificates. I guess she thought I'd never know and tried to spare me the pain.

"Bummin', seriously hard, dude."

"Thanks. I guess that was the day I checked out. Holding Peggy's death certificate in my remaining hand, along with Olivia's … my unborn daughter's … our favorite girl's name. It all came crashing down. Until then, it had just seemed like a bad dream. I pushed everyone out of my life; I wanted no contact with anyone. I did nothing. I seldom bathed or changed clothes. The only remotely constructive thing I did was order groceries online and have them delivered.

"Depression, man; it can happen to anybody."

"It may have started out like that, but it became a lifestyle. My days began and ended watching the same TV shows—every single day; to the point that I could recite some program dialogue verbatim. When the phone rang, which happened less and less, if it wasn't on the sofa next to me … voicemail. My mobility is probably one-tenth of what it could be if I consistently used my prosthetics. But I'd rather order pizza and watch a rerun of *M*A*S*H* instead; it's easier. More than once, I actually bought clothes online to avoid doing laundry.

"Man, you're being hard on yourself," Ice Cream insists. "Take a page from my playbook, man. I conserve my energy; I mostly lay low and don't cause trouble. Half the time, man, people don't even know I'm in the room … avoids conflict. It's a peaceful way to be."

"Honestly, Ice Cream, I don't know if I can handle human interaction anymore. I started hiding out from the world; now I can't stop, but the bottom line is—I don't *want* to stop. I've lost my drive—to do anything."

"It's okay, man. After everything you've been through, you deserve to do what you want, even if that want is to do nothing, man."

"Well, I've certainly done a lot of that," admits David.

"Let me ask you this, man; when you were doing all those business deals and making bread and havin' it all, what did all that get you?"

"It got me here … wherever *here* is," David replies.

"Exactly, man. You played by the rules; you did all that was expected of you and more! And for what, man? Just to have it all taken away. So what did you do? You've changed it up, man. You've put yourself in the position where no one can ever take anything away 'cause there's nothin' for them to take, man! You beat the system. Don'tcha see that?" Ice Cream smirks at David. "Fuck 'em, man! Fuck 'em all!"

David can't hold back his glee. "Ice Cream, *man*, I've got to say, you have an interesting perspective."

Once again, Ice Cream lowers his shades to make direct eye contact. "But do I speak the truth, man?" he mutters.

David nods in agreement. "You *definitely* speak the truth, man."

"All I need to hear, Davey Baby. I gotta boogie, but it's been real, man; it's been real."

Ice Cream moves with an absence of alacrity, slowly getting himself out of the chair, grabbing a few more cookies, and cracking a smile that exposes a mouthful of chocolate-covered teeth. Departing, he says, "Later, dude."

David watches him leave, shakes his head, and comments, "What a character."

As Ice Cream exits, the door closes without a sound, without a seam.

"Hello."

The voice is pleasant, but nevertheless startles David, having come from behind him. He turns to see a woman in a high-neck—what his mother called—granny dress, all buttoned up with a lace collar. Her face is roundish with slightly plump cheeks, and her eyes are bright. She's appears to be in her late twenties or early thirties, looking as if she just stepped out of a nineteenth-century photograph.

"Hello, I'm David." He watches as the woman passes on his right and walks toward the desk.

The woman takes a seat behind the desk and finally responds, "A pleasure, I'm sure. I'm Lizbeth."

They study each other for several moments before Lizbeth breaks the silence. "May I ask you a personal question, David?"

David takes a moment to consider. It's all been so strange, such an evocative, emotional experience; he isn't sure he wants to comply. His conclusion though, as with Ice Cream, is that he *must*. "All right," he sighs.

"Would I be correct that you've been deeply hurt, wronged by another?" Lizbeth inquires with a slight tilt of her head.

"Yes. Yes, I have," David answers.

"May I ask how?"

David takes a deep breath to steel himself and begins, "I lost my family and the limbs on my left side in an accident."

"An accident, you say?" Lizbeth queries skeptically.

David lowers his head and softly replies, "Yes."

"So that I may understand fully, nobody was at fault? Accident implies happenstance," Lizbeth clarifies.

"I've put it behind me," David asserts, head still lowered.

"David?" Lizbeth prompts.

"Yes?"

"Please, look at me," Lizbeth requests with heartfelt empathy.

David raises his head and allows their eyes to meet. There's something about Lizbeth. David can't quite put his finger on it, but she's in his head, triggering a mantra: "She knows; she understands."

"David, what if I told you that I am intimately familiar with the sort of pain you've experienced? Though I am physically intact, I too lost my family in a tragic way."

David replies, "I believe you."

"Tell me who took your family?"

"A man. A drunken man," comes David's sheepish reply. "I've forgiven him," he adds in a whisper.

"I don't think you have, David. I think that's part of the reason you're here. And, might I say, that is all right."

"That's not what I was led to believe. I was told forgiveness was necessary to move on."

"And how exactly did you *move on*, David?"

David has nothing to say.

"Hate is as much a part of being human as love. When love is torn from us, the natural replacement is hatred for whoever was responsible for destroying the love in our lives," Lizbeth assures him.

"He got away with it," David whispers, his voice strained, fighting back emotion.

"Tell me about your experience, David. I want to know everything," Lizbeth says.

David is barely able to form the words. "I can't. I can't go over it again."

"May I share something with you, David? Perhaps, it will demonstrate how facing your pain and embracing hatred can rid you of this emptiness."

David nods.

"For as long as I can remember, David, my father bedded me as well as my sisters Emma and Alice. His carnal lust knew no boundaries. His almost nightly visits started before I was old enough to remember. Even after my mother died and Father took another wife, it continued," Lizbeth explains stoically.

"So the loss of your family, that was a metaphor? I mean, it is tragic—no child should have to deal with that ... " David interjects.

But Elizabeth corrects him, "No, David, I meant quite literally that my family was lost to me in a tragic way. My sisters and I seldom spoke of these violations of us because we were ashamed. For me, it fueled a deep-seated hatred of men—all men. I tried to avoid my father; I spent my free time in our barn. I built a coop for a family of pigeons that nested there. In almost no time, I had thirty. Lovely birds with angel-soft, gray down, and they made the most pleasant sounds. Their coos calmed me. I also found comfort with a friend, Bridget McBain. But I lost her when Abby, that horrid woman Father married, stumbled upon us in the barn when we were in a compromising situation. She screamed bloody murder at us and then ran to tell Father. Bridget fled home in tears. I gave chase after Abby, but in the time it took me to dress, she'd gotten to Father. He was livid. He called me the most terrible things. He told me he'd fix me and stormed out of the house. I hid in my room for hours, waiting for goodness knows what, but Father never returned. As afternoon began to dim into evening, I went to the barn and discovered what he had done. He had taken an axe, killed my pigeons, and destroyed their coop. That was the moment, David, when I embraced my hatred. It came to me as if by divine intervention. My uncle John had just arrived for the night, so I had the evening to ponder the consequences of my plan. The anticipation was almost as delicious as taking the revenge itself. But you didn't allow yourself the pleasure of plotting revenge on that drunken man, David, did you?"

"Oh, yes, I have. I've often thought of killing him if I ever got the opportunity, but nobody knows what became of him," David confesses through his tears.

"How would you kill him, David?" Lizbeth asks.

"I don't know, shoot him?" David proposes, head down, eyes closed.

"Who is this man? What do you know about him?"

"He goes by several names, but the one he used on the night … on *that* night he was Miguel Fernandez Bustos. The investigators told us that he was in the country illegally. He'd been deported several times, each following a DUI arrest. He was already wanted on a charge of involuntary manslaughter for a past offense, but after being released from custody, he had fled the jurisdiction. The district attorney assured me that Bustos would die in prison this time. This was around the time that my psychologist insisted on my forgiving him. Believing he would lose his freedom forever, I did. Less than two weeks later, the prosecutor called to say that Bustos had been released on his own recognizance due to overcrowding and blah, blah, blah. I didn't even hear the rest. My brain shut down when I heard *released*."

"Now he is free to repeat what he did to you, or *worse*, to another family," Lizbeth notes. "And this man, this monster, you'd show him the mercy of a quick and painless death? His victims, your wife, Peggy, your unborn daughter, Olivia, don't they deserve for this man to suffer, David?"

"Vengeance is mine, sayeth the Lord," David quotes. "The shrink used that line a lot."

"God judges a man's soul, David. You have a *good* soul—an exceptional soul. He does not judge the actions of the flesh, the *man*. There are passages in the Bible that speak of an eye for an eye … I'm sure you know of what I speak," Lizbeth asserts.

"I do. It's all confusing."

"Revenge, David, is good for the soul. It brings peace for an injustice done. Do you want to know how I achieved that serenity?"

David nods.

"What is good for the goose—or in this case, pigeon. The same axe Father used to kill my lovely birds served as the implement of justice, not only for them, but for my two sisters and me. While Father was out, I found his horrid wife in the second-floor guest bedroom. She was making up Uncle John's bed. When she turned, I brought the axe down on her head with all of my might. She fell forward onto the floor. I gave her another blow, then another, again, and again! She knew what Father had been doing to us, and each stroke of the blade was a magnificent release. When Father came home a few hours later, he napped on the sofa in our living room. I brought him to justice too."

David looks at her and asks, "Lizbeth? Li ... What's your last name?"

Smiling, she replies, "Yes, it's Borden. Lizbeth is a name I took in later years. At the time, I went by Lizzie. And the rhyme that was written about me to sell newspapers ... well, that was a gross exaggeration. I gave neither Father nor Abby forty whacks. She got seventeen and Father only eleven. And, David, though I stood trial, I was acquitted. I had confided to an investigator about Father's indiscretions. He was aghast at what I told him about Father and Abby. He helped steer the investigation and made sure that certain bits of evidence never saw the light of day. This man, sworn to uphold the law, saw me as a victim. Just as you are. David, no one knowing your circumstances would judge you for wanting to exact revenge. Don't you see? Now, tell me, if I could put this man in front of you, would you really give him the gift of a swift demise?"

"No!" shouts David. "Not even death by a thousand cuts would be slow and agonizing enough! I want his limbs torn from his body! I want to make him watch his family die slow and painful deaths, one by one! I want to make him suffer to the point that he would beg me to end his life, just so I could laugh in his fucking face and scream, 'Noooo!'"

David cries hysterically.

Lizbeth reassures him, "Good, David, embrace it. Direct your hate and desire for vengeance."

Sobbing, David, head in hand, pulls at his hair and beats his left temple with his stump. Lizbeth is standing next to him, her hand on his shoulder. She wears a broad smile that David does not see. Soothingly, she says, "Good, very good. I must leave you now, but you've done well. Remember what you feel; don't deny it and take revenge whenever there is opportunity. Fare thee well, David."

David sobs into his right palm. Lizbeth departs, as she arrived, unseen by David.

Head in hand, David is becoming aware of an intoxicating scent in the room, making his mouth water. Lifting his head, he's no longer alone. Before him on the desk is a banquet—no, that's not the correct characterization. The closest equivalent to the spread before him was one he'd seen on a cruise ship, intended for serving hundreds of guests. A voice from behind the mountain of cuisine booms out, "Ah, finally. I was wondering when you were going to come up for air."

David wipes his eyes, sniffles, and inquires, "And you are?"

"Cook!" comes the cheery reply. "My friend, you could use a little comfort food!"

"Oh, I don't ... I couldn't ..."

"Nonsense!" Cook cuts him off. Walking around the table, David comes face-to-face with a rotund little man sporting a thick, white mustache and wearing proper chef attire. However, clad in stark-white toque, apron, and clothing within the equally colorless room, his body is difficult to discern, and at times his head appears to float around the room. "Food makes us feel better!"

"I'm sorry, um, Cook, but I'm dealing with something just now ..."

"It's dealt with! I know because I've been sitting here watching you!" The little man has a slight accent, but it's not obvious enough to determine his homeland. "When the aromas finally worked their way into your nose, they got your attention. That means you are done focusing on your bothers and now you are hungry!" Cook rubs his belly. "When did you last eat?"

David pauses and then replies, "I'm not sure. I don't even know how long I've been here. I nuked some leftover Chinese for dinner ... I don't think I've eaten today."

"And you are going through a lot, am I right?" Cook inquires.

"Oh my God ..." David begins to answer.

"All right then! So now you eat. You eat and you feel better! These are things one cannot deal with on an empty stomach. Tell me, what is your favorite?"

"Uh, gosh. I don't know. I don't really think about food these days," David replies.

"Oh! How can you say such a thing?" Cook feigns shock, but his puckish eyes make David grin. "Ah, good! I see you have a set of teeth! Good! Good! They will come in handy."

Now David chuckles.

Cook takes a step closer and loudly whispers, "Tell me, my friend, do you have a name?"

"I'm David."

"Ah, a good, solid name," notes Cook. "A name for the ages. Now, David, what is your pleasure? Anything you desire."

"Maybe just a burger and fries? And a Coke?"

Cook rolls his eyes. "Years of creating culinary masterpieces, preparing meals for royalty—from more countries than you ever visited—honing my skills to conquer the most sophisticated sensibility ... and he wants a burger with fries! Mithaecus is spinning in his grave!"

"I'm sorry, Cook. I'm afraid my palate ..."

"Relax! I kid with you! Sometimes the simplest foods are best," Cook explains. "You give me just a moment, eh?"

Cook disappears around the desk, obscured by the artistically styled, mountainous display of food. In mere moments, he returns with a platter holding David's meal. He passes the serving dish to David, who awkwardly sets it on his lap. David one-hands the burger, lifts it to his mouth, and takes a bite. "Mmmmm!" David exclaims, chewing voraciously.

"Is good, no?" Cook queries rhetorically.

"When I was a kid, we had a burger joint—Gino's—a few blocks from our house. They made my all-time favorite burger. Everybody loved Gino's; they were the absolute best. The kids I grew up with could all attest to how amazing their burgers were. There was some kind of family tragedy, and they went out of business. I swear to you, Cook; this tastes *exactly* like their signature burger, the Giant! I never thought I'd have a burger that good again!"

"I don't know this Gino's, but I am glad this meal makes you happy," says Cook.

"It's fantastic!" David raves, taking bite after bite, not wanting to waste any more time touting its virtues but instead just devouring it. He swigs the Coke, swallows, and jams fries into his mouth. "Mmmmm!"

"Almost done already, would you care for another?" Cook asks.

With a full mouth, David playfully pleads, "Yef, pleave!"

Without missing a beat, Cook replaces the empty tray with a fresh serving as David finishes the first round. "Thank you, Cook!" he says, stifling a belch.

"It is good to see a healthy appetite," Cook replies, gleefully accepting the compliment.

"This is even better than the first!" David says, covering his mouth and trying not to lose a single morsel.

"It does me well to see you enjoy your meal! A third helping is no trouble," Cook offers, tempting David.

"Oh, I couldn't …" David protests, then acquiesces. "I can't tell you how long it's been since I've eaten this much food!"

"In this place, you can eat all you want! Never get full, never get fat!" Cook explains. David is well into his third burger when Cook suggests, "Now you try something a little different. One of my primo dishes!" Cook strolls around the desk, out of sight. As David finishes the last of his third burger, Cook reappears with another plate of food. "This is a classic and never fails to please a true carnivore."

"Lordy, that smells incredible!" David exclaims.

Cook immediately grabs a fork and steak knife and begins to slice. "My world-famous, ten-ounce, bacon-wrapped filet mignon," Cook proclaims, beaming as he finishes cutting. "Garlic potatoes and french-cut string beans. All done to perfection! The filet is served blue rare, not a spot of color beyond the palest pink, and wrapped with a thick-cut slice of applewood-smoked bacon. The potatoes are hand-smashed with garlic, butter, and a dollop of cream. The string beans are young and crisp, picked just hours ago. Lastly, a freshly baked dinner roll—hard crust, butter-soft interior—to sop up the au jus."

David is indulging ravenously while Cook regales him with recipe secrets. He half-listens, nods, and chews.

"It is wonderful to prepare a meal for someone who enjoys his food!" Cook declares "Now I have you try something extra special." Again he walks around to the back of the desk. This time, when he reemerges, he takes David's empty tray and hands him another gastronomical delight. "You didn't mention whether you like Southern cooking, but I think you do. This is my crispy fried chicken with piping-hot cornbread and collards. I have brought you an ice-cold pitcher of sweet tea too."

"I really shouldn't. I mean, how am I not sick after all I've eaten? But the aroma is making my stomach rumble," David admits, staring incredulously at a golden-brown drumstick, breast, and thigh.

"Come, my friend, David, eat, eat," commands Cook in the friendliest of tones.

David slowly raises the drumstick and bites into it, his eyes rolling back in his head, followed by a satisfied moan.

"Ecstasy! Is it not?" whoops Cook.

"I never cared for the dark parts before, but this is amazing! The skin is so crispy, and the meat so tender … the flavor! I don't have words to describe how incredible these collards are, and the buttermilk cornbread … *perfect*," David gushes.

"Ah, yes, the cornbread … You'll notice it doesn't fall apart when you soak up the collard juice," brags Cook. "You finish enjoying that. I'll be back."

When Cook swaps out the empty plate for a full one, it takes no coaxing at all for David to grab and stuff as much of the world's largest and most luscious Reuben into his mouth.

Cook chuckles as he hands David a mug of beer and, for immediate use, a linen napkin to wipe the Russian dressing from the corners of his mouth. David studies the napkin for a moment, appreciating the fine craftsmanship. He dabs and then trains his attention back onto the sandwich.

"Those are homemade potato chips. They're quite delicious and complement the Reuben nicely," Cook boasts.

David chomps down on one, and his eyes grow wide. In a mouthful-muffled voice he asks, "How did you make these? The insides are light and fluffy … They actually taste like a baked potato!"

"The tricks are: first of all, a thick cut, then flash-fry just long enough to sear the outside, and finally, don't cook them all the way through. The potatoes must be of a proper size and age so that the starches have begun to break down into sugar. However, if aged too long, you will lose flavor," Cook explains.

"Incredible. I can't wait to see … well, *taste* what's next!" David says.

"Excellent! I am so happy to hear you say that because next comes dessert! I'm afraid our time together is nearing an end," Cook remarks.

As David finishes his Reuben, he's hard-pressed to understand how he managed. *When I first picked that thing up, I couldn't help but notice its weight. It had to be several pounds!* he thinks, gazing at the empty plate, munching the last perfectly salted chips, and washing it all down with a swig of small-batch lager from a frosted mug.

Cook rounds the desk pushing a dessert trolley loaded with confections of all sorts. "My friend, I leave you now, but it does my heart good to know you have been fed well. This gets your mind off of other things."

"I can't believe how much I've eaten," David confesses, taking inventory of the cakes, cookies, parfaits, fudge squares, ice cream, and brownies oozing with melted chocolate icing. "This has been wonderful, Cook. Thank you for going to so much trouble."

"David, it was my pleasure," Cook replies with his enigmatic smile. He is pleased that David's eyes never leave the desserts and doesn't seek permission to begin sampling the delicacies.

David, transfixed by the sweets, does not see Cook's departure. Every succulent morsel he puts into his mouth tastes better than the last. It isn't until there's nothing left that David realizes he's been eating nonstop—with no inkling about the passage of time.

To David's right, a door slides open. Stepping through is a large fellow resplendent in an off-white linen suit, an ivory vest, and bolo tie with an onyx set in its clasp. His toupee is as black as the gemstone. Despite the illusion of Southern gentility, on closer inspection, the fellow is slightly disheveled; his face is flushed with beads of sweat pocking his brow. He dabs at his forehead with a linen pocket square, turns to David, and declares, "I'll tell you, son, I really get goin' when the Spirit's upon me, which is why my flock continues to grow." He approaches David, extends a meaty right hand, and introduces himself, "Son, I am Reverend Hargrove W. DuBois."

David stands as they shake hands and replies, "I'm David. David Baker. Nice to meet you, sir."

"Sit down, son, please," the reverend gently orders. He walks over to the desk and leans against it, all the while dabbing at his forehead.

David complies.

"Yes, my boy, my congregation just loves it when I'm animated; though, I must admit, that kind of preaching takes a lot out of me," says DuBois. "I'm not a young man anymore."

"You've been a reverend a long time?" David inquires.

"Yes, over forty years, but fifteen years ago, my ministry really took off," the reverend replies. "That's when I began employing the miracle of TV, reaching the shut-ins. Why, once people no longer had to go to services, and the church could come to them, why … well, son, it just exploded. Today, my flock is over six million strong and growing every week. Why, since this social media thing has come down the pike over the past eight or nine years, I've more than doubled my staff!"

"So you're online as well as on television?"

"Ha! You bet. We do a full-hour broadcast every Sunday morning from eight to nine, and then we air a podcast Monday, Wednesday and Friday. Our premium membership offers access to live chat twenty-four seven, three-sixty-five, and we're constantly loading YouTube with inspirational video messages and special blessings!" DuBois boasts.

"What are special blessings, if you don't mind my asking?" David queries.

"Of course not! For a small donation, one of my staff will post a video prayer session for a premium member who might be in need of a little additional support. We'll pray 'specially for them—or a loved one—and entreat the Holy Spirit to come into their hearts and bring them peace," the Reverend explains.

"What about people who aren't premium members?" David asks.

"Oh, we have tons and tons of free content, and of course our weekly service is broadcast across the airwaves for free," Dubois emphasizes.

"Reverend?" interjects David.

"Yes, my son?" replies Dubois.

"Why are you here … speaking with me now?" David asks. "I'm not really religious and haven't attended church since becoming a teenager. I certainly don't see myself signing up to become a premium member in your flock. This just seems a bit strange."

"Son, I have to assume that *everything* you've experienced here has been a bit strange," the reverend observes. "Am I right?"

"You could say that, yes."

"David, while I'm a man of the cloth, I am also a man—a very *successful* one. It's my understanding that you were once a very accomplished man as well. I guess it's my quest to see if you can reclaim what my pappy called that fire in the belly."

"You mean, you want to know if I still have the capacity to make money?"

"Not exactly, son. I want to know if you still have currency flowing through your veins. This is more than ability; it's an innate passion for attaining and building wealth, knocking down walls, and grabbing opportunity with both hands," DuBois rants, grinning wildly.

"Well, Reverend, I used to be in sales. It takes a certain temperament, as you know, a thick skin. I was quite good at what I did because I knew my products. I also studied my prospects closely. I could always connect the dots for them—show them the benefits of buying from me. Is that what you mean?" asks David.

"My boy, being good at what you do is commendable, but being shrewd, polished, isn't what I'm getting at. Let me phrase it another way. I know sales; you might say I'm a salesman too, and the products I sell are comfort and peace of mind. These days, I have a staff of dozens helping me, but there was a time when I was a solo act, without the benefit of either mass or social media. Those were tough times; I worked hard and struggled to reach a few souls. Do you understand what I'm saying?"

David nods.

"When you were selling, son, did you travel a lot? Eat fast food, sleep in strange beds?"

"Yes, sir. At times, slept in airport terminals," David replies.

"And what was it that kept you goin'? What force drove you not to chuck it all and try an easier lifestyle?" DuBois queries.

"Oh, that's easy," David replies firmly. "My wife. Well, her and our plan to start a family."

"I see. Plan, you say? What sort of aspirations did y'all have?" DuBois asks.

"Well, Reverend, we were waiting for the right moment, when we had enough savings and a nice place to live. Then Peggy would quit her job, get pregnant, and become a stay-at-home-mom. Well, we finally made it. I reached the point where my salary alone could provide for all our needs, and our new, exciting life was about to begin."

"I see. So you had all of that in place?" The reverend raises an eyebrow.

David leans back. "This is starting to feel a bit interrogative, sir."

With a hearty belly laugh, DuBois reassures him, "No, son! Not at all. We're just spitballin' ... I just want to learn more about who you are. You know, what makes David Baker tick? I don't mean to get too personal. I may be a man of the Bible, but I'm also a businessman who thinks in terms of dollars and cents. Why, heck, bringing the good Word to folks would be impossible if I didn't keep a watchful eye on cash flow, son. And after meeting another person who has figured it all out, why, I just want to know how you did it." DuBois is leaning forward with his hands on his knees and a broad grin full of the whitest teeth David has ever seen.

"Sorry, this has been the strangest ..." David pauses. Strangest what? Hour? Day? Week? " ... strangest experience of my ... life." Again, unsure of the right word.

DuBois leans back and folds his arms across his chest. "I don't want to make you uncomfortable, but I'd still like to know how you accomplished what you did."

"Sure," David says, exhaling. "We'd set a goal of having a quarter-mil in liquid assets. From there, fifty grand went into securities—the emergency fund—locked away in safe, low-yield bonds. A hundred-fifty went into a land purchase and the construction of our dream home on the lake."

DuBois interrupts, "'Scuse me, son, that doesn't sound like a lot of money for a lake house."

"You're right. We took out a mortgage. We talked about what it would take to do it all free and clear, but we were anxious. At times, we talked about forging ahead prematurely, but in the end, we stayed disciplined, hit our goals, and pulled the trigger. The remaining fifty would be for contingencies, what Peggy called 'must haves,' though we pledged to maintain a cushion of at least twenty-five thou." David's mind drifts to a debate with Peggy about whether a pontoon boat or ski boat was better qualified as a must-have.

"Okay, now, that must have been quite a mortgage. I believe you mentioned a guest house?" DuBois asks.

David remembers mentioning that to Tina, not DuBois. No matter, nothing surprises him anymore. "Yes, sir. We also built a covered boathouse. The mortgage was for eight-hundred-fifty thousand."

DuBois whistles. "So you had a million-dollar home. Impressive, son! Now, you said you had a plan and you did, but it seems to me that a lot of families—like those in my flock— live on a lot less in much smaller homes. What is it that made you so certain you could handle a four-thousand-and-change monthly mortgage payment—assuming a traditional thirty-year fixed rate— and all the expenses of a family?"

"I was pulling down well over two hundred grand annually, plus bennies. I was also made an officer in the company, which gave me shareholder status," David replies, feeling a little full of himself.

"My boy, you make it sound as if you had 'em throwin' money atcha," DuBois observes enthusiastically.

"Ha!" David barks. "Can't say it was quite that easy, but I was starting to get where I wanted to be."

"And where was that?"

"The top, of course."

"To be the company boss?" DuBois inquires.

David takes a deep breath and replies, "Well beyond."

"Is that right?"

"Yes, sir, that *is* right." David is unaware of mirroring the reverend's smile. "I was one of five people in our firm—the four others were C-level—working to bring about the forced sale of our company to a top competitor. The only thing bringing them to the table, frankly, was *me*. I was outselling them in every major market. They were feeling it in their bottom line and wanted that ground back. Had it gone through, my income would have quintupled."

"So that fire in the belly was certainly there!" DuBois exclaims. "You were more than just a budding family man, weren't you, David? You were an up-and-comer! Not content to just go to work, do a job, and go home. You, son, were willing to do whatever it took. I see that now; you had passion, mo-ti-va-tion!"

"I don't deny it," David replies. "As much as I had, I wanted more. Hell, I wanted it all." David is suddenly pensive. "I never thought it could … suddenly vanish."

"What's important, son, is as I suspected, there's a lot more to you than meets the eye. You had the fire; I think you can get it back. For now, I must take my leave, but I surely have enjoyed our time together, David. Surely have. A man of the gospel never really gets a day *of rest*, and I'm afraid I must be goin', but again, it has been a gen-u-ine pleasure!" Moving from his leaning position, DuBois grunts, stands, and extends his oversize right hand.

"A pleasure for me too, Reverend," David remarks and shakes. DuBois exits to David's right without looking back. As the big man walks away, David pauses for an instant as a thought pops into his head: *Of all the various ways he referred to himself, he never said 'man of God.'*

Just when I think this place can't get any weirder … David thinks. He closes his eyes and lets his head fall back against the chairback. He thinks of Dorothy's line from *The Wizard of Oz*: "My, people come and go so quickly here!" He next thinks, *But do they? Is it quick? There's no perception of time. Are they even people? Did I really meet Lizzy Borden? Where did they all come from or go for that matter?*

"Hello, David." He immediately recognizes the voice and opens his eyes, blinking several times in disbelief. In front of David stands … well, *himself*, arms folded, slowly shaking his head. David is speechless.

"Surprised to see me?" Other David inquires.

"Uh, you could say that!" David replies. David studies the man—*himself.* As the shock passes, David becomes aware of their differences. Other David is clean-shaven, trim, athletic, and wearing a hand-tailored Italian suit. But there's something else. He is wearing a wedding ring, something David couldn't ... Because Other David has two hands! And two legs! "Who are you!"

"Man, you've lost your edge. Who do you think I am?"

"Well, at first, I thought you were me, but you can't be."

"Why not?"

"You have your limbs. I *do not,*" David observes.

Other David removes his blazer, folds it carefully, and places it on the desk. He undoes his right cuff link. David recognizes it, a congratulatory gift from Peggy after making salesperson of the year. Other David rolls up his sleeve, turns his elbow toward David, and asks, "Look familiar?"

It does. David has the exact same scar, a memento of an epic bike crash, when he and Ben plowed into each other—at top speed—on Lawrence's Hill. David was certain that getting eleven stitches was the only thing that spared him from his parents' wrath after seeing the two Schwinns, gifted four months earlier at Christmastime. "How is it possible? How can you ... I be standing here talking to me ... you ... uh, what the fuck is this?"

"I am here to answer your questions. How often have you wondered what could have happened if the wreck didn't occur, if Peggy didn't die, and if you'd gotten the seven-figure salary? Well, I'm your answer, buddy. I'm happily married, two kids—girl and boy, just like you both wanted—with another girl on the way. We rent out the *old* lake house these days. You should see the new one we built on the west end of the lake, pretty spectacular," Other David brags.

"I don't understand. How can that be? How could you have all the things I was denied? It doesn't make any sense! It's not fair—"

"Fair!" Other David chimes in simultaneously. "Life's not fair, David; you know that. In fact, didn't you utter those exact words to Peggy when you told her about the plan to force the sale of the company? I believe you did because it was *me* who said it!"

David sits, staring at this alternative version of himself—whole, wealthy, happy ... perfect! "So what do you want from me?"

"Ha!" Other David laughs. "What the fuck could I possibly *want* from you? You have nothing! Your career is a smoldering dumpster fire; your wife is in an urn on the mantel of a soon-to-be-foreclosed-on house, and it takes you half an hour to button a shirt or tie a shoelace. Are you kidding?"

"Then what! Why are you here? Why do you torment me? Goddammit!"

"Hey, hey, relax, okay? Sorry, I should have realized that it's been a while since you were the hotshot with all the answers. To me, it's very clear, but I need to consider the past several years of your existence. You're not the same man you were; I get that now."

"Then you admit you're *not* me!"

"Ugh, this again? Yes, David, I *am* you. Do I need to drop my drawers and show you my ... *our* appendectomy scar? Or maybe the freckle on the shaft of my dick? Maybe a game of twenty questions? I'll get the answer on the first try every time!"

"Fine. I'll rephrase; why are you here?"

"Like the others, I am here for your benefit," Other David responds.

"I'm so lost. What benefit? I haven't figured it out yet, but I either committed suicide or am in the process ... It's been a lot of years since Bible study, but as I recall, taking one's own life is an E-ZPass to hell—a mortal sin," maintains David.

"David, c'mon, I think you know a little better than to take all that hellfire and brimstone shit seriously. I mean you've— I've—seen enough to know that life is a crapshoot. There are no predetermined outcomes. It's eat or be eaten."

"There's something more to it. Otherwise, why am I here? What is all of this for or about?" David probes.

"For all you know, none of this is real. Maybe it's the last few synapses firing as your brain gives in to carbon-monoxide poisoning and bourbon—Knob Creek, nice choice, by the way. But you'll be happy to know that nowadays I only drink Woodford."

"I can't explain it, but it feels real," David insists.

"Look, if you're calm now, let me show you a few things, okay?"

"Sure," David answers.

Other David pulls out a smartphone, taps the screen a few times, walks over to David, and squats down so both can view the screen. "Here's Peg four months after you last saw her," Other David says. David sees his wife posing with an enormous baby bump, her unforgettable smile more beautiful than ever. Other David swipes the screen. "I shot this as we were leaving for the hospital." He taps Play and a shaky video shows Peggy navigating down the lake house stairs to Other David's new Benz, all the while laughing and threatening revenge for capturing her in her present condition.

David, unaware of tears flowing down his cheeks, lights up at the sound of her voice.

Other David shows him images of Peggy and their baby girl, Olivia, at the hospital, coming home, and lounging on the lake house deck. With another swipe come images of Other David's new office after the sale of the company and Peggy in nothing-left-to-the-imagination lingerie, a nightie David had never seen. She had purchased it specifically for the intimate, candle-lit lovemaking that should have followed a delightful, celebratory meal. But, of course, it was never worn because of the life-altering events that actually ensued. More images: breaking ground for the new lakeside mansion, Other David posing next to his new Maybach, Peggy with another baby bump, Olivia posing next to the new cabin cruiser, and then Olivia holding Lucas, her new baby brother. More events, more extravagance, and another baby bump, whose name would be Aidan.

"Stop! Stop! I can't take any more!" cries David at the top of his lungs. "I can't believe everything I've lost! It was bad enough just imagining it, but to see the images, hear the sounds … If I'm not dead, I hope I soon will be!"

"*Dave?*" scolds Other David.

"Oh, fuck you! Fuck you!" hollers David. "You smug, arrogant, cocksucking son of a bitch! How dare you throw this in my face, telling me you're here for my benefit! You fucking piece of shit! All you're here to do is hurt me! I would give anything, *any fucking thing* to have what you have!"

Other David, with an exaggerated motion, raises the Rolex Cosmograph Daytona—at least $23,000—on his left wrist up to his face. He says, "Well, I've heard what I needed to; I have to be going. Try not to let your envy consume you … me, David."

"Go fuck yourself! All of that should have been mine! Mine!" David seethes. The images of the family he never had flash in his mind as he collapses, head in hand, and sobs.

A rustling sound draws David's attention. Lifting his head from his palm, he sees Bettina's smiling face, framed in blond hair, on the opposite side of the desk. "Hello again, David!"

"Tina?"

"Yes, I'm back!" Tina announces as she slides a box of Thin Mints across the desk. "I see you need cheering up again. If you have a cookie, I promise you'll feel better."

Projecting a weary countenance, David forces the semblance of a grin and takes a cookie. "Okay, sweetheart. Oh, probably shouldn't call you that … I can never keep straight what's politically correct anymore," he mutters.

"Oh, I don't mind! You can call me sweetheart. I think it's nice!"

"Why are you back?" David asks.

"Well, do you remember when you met Veronica?"

David focuses on the cookie and absentmindedly responds, "How could I not! I mean, yes, I remember."

Tina titters, catching him in an uncensored moment, and asks, "Do you remember she said you'd have some important decisions to make?"

"I do."

"Well, it's time to decide," Tina explains.

"What am I deciding?"

"Whether you want to stay with us," says Tina.

David takes a few more cookies and, with a mouthful, inquires, "Who is *us?*"

Tina smiles. "*Us*, silly. You, me, Veronica, Ice Cream, Lizzie, Cook, and the reverend. But you *won't* have to see yourself again. That's the best part! You'll get to be you, but the *new* you—your hand and leg will be made whole!" Tina reveals.

"Is that truly possible? I can have my limbs back?" David queries, feeling his heart beating faster.

"Yes! Your hand and your leg—like it never, ever happened!" Tina announces.

"What about Peg, my kids?" David wonders.

"They'll still be alive, not like you," says Tina, regretfully. "But you'll have Veronica to keep you company! I know you like her!"

"There's a lot there to like, Tina, but I love my wife, and Peggy is not alive. She passed away several years ago, so I'm a little confused," David admits. "Can't I be with her?"

Tina adjusts herself in the chair, dons a serious look, and says, "David, you're being given the offer of a lifetime. Well, afterlife time. Don't you understand what this place is? You have the chance to be whole again and enjoy an eternity in Veronica's company— your every wish her command. I can be the daughter you never had; after all, we're so much alike! You'll have friends like Ice Cream and Reverend DuBois, who understand and support you, and best of all, Cook will make you the most wonderful dishes— anything you want—and you'll never get full or fat!"

"Don't get me wrong, Tina; that all sounds so wonderful, but without Peggy, I don't have any interest," David explains. "Tina, I cannot go back to being the man I once was. In my time here, I've reflected on some of the terrible things I've done."

Tina's voice is low and grave. "David, don't you understand that if you don't take this opportunity, you *will* die. None of us will be able to help you. You have proven to each of us that you are worthy and deserve to be here. This is not the time to have a change of heart—change who you are!"

"I don't care. I'd rather fade into oblivion than not have my Peggy. I'm sorry, Tina," David says. "May God forgive me!"

"Fine!" Tina's voice is that of a growling beast. "We offer you what the world could not! This is your last chance! What do you choose?"

"I choose to die," David declares.

"So be it!" Tina hisses.

David's head spins; he is about to pass out.

David's eyes open. The room is brightly lit. Before him stands a bearded man with a pleasant smile and olive skin who appears to be the source of illumination. He reaches and takes David's left hand into his own and says, "David, welcome, we've been expecting you."

David's eyes begin to focus. Standing next to the bearded man are his mother and father. David cries out, "Mom, Dad! Is it really you?" He rushes toward them.

"It's really us, dear," his mother assures him as the three of them share hugs. "And look!" David's mother places a hand to his chin and turns his head to the right where he sees Peggy and Olivia break into a run toward him as he runs to them just as fast as his two legs can carry him.

ACKNOWLEDGMENTS

I don't know if anything will ever come from this book-writing endeavor, but should any of the stories within receive recognition, it should be known that it didn't happen in a vacuum. To that end, I'd like to express my love and appreciation to the following folks:

My wife, Nicole. My toughest critic and greatest inspiration far beyond my storytelling. She doesn't always care for my stories, but she cares about me and encourages me to keep improving, both in my fictional realms and the real world. I love you more than I could ever promise.

Dani Aved, Nicole's best friend from their college days. Dani's been my sounding board, typically reading my stories in their rawest form and giving me feedback before anyone else sees them. She questions me when I'm unclear and lets me know specifically where material needs to be punched up. She's also great at picking up on what I thought were clever subtleties hidden between the lines.

I enjoy writing; it's fun not knowing what my characters will do or say until their deeds and words miraculously appear on the screen. But writing is a pastime for me, and without large chunks of time to devote to it, I found myself going round and round trying to write a novel. I must thank my buddy, Frank Troscher, who, after reading "Long Fall," suggested that I write a series of short stories instead. I really enjoy the various short forms from flash fiction ("The Day Earth Died") to novella ("The Abandoned").

My proofreader and editor, John Young, whom I have yet to meet in person. I found John via nextdoor.com, and to date, our exchanges have all been strictly via email. John is no-nonsense when he digs into a manuscript—old school. Exactly what I wanted, and more importantly, needed. John, thank you for the great suggestions and hard work!

Johnny "Dr. Buff" Bufano—pharmacist to the skiers, surfers, and stars, for his thoughtful, detailed feedback and constant encouragement to add sex scenes.

Cynthia Greene, a dear friend we miss greatly since her relocation to Florida with her hubby, Harvey (a fellow curmudgeon) and their giant pup, Barney. Cynthia often reviewed my writing and offered suggestions.

Just for the record, I do not believe the Earth is flat, but I do enjoy the occasional trip down that rabbit hole called YouTube. In that respect, a couple of people were the inspiration behind "Moonshot." Rob Skiba has posted numerous videos on Flat Earth, and I would be less than honest if I didn't say that they're very thought-provoking. Much of Matteo Pasquale's presentation in "Moonshot" is based on Rob's videos. I also need to acknowledge Dr. Steven M. Greer, founder of The Disclosure Project. His theory of the ultimate global false flag—a hoax alien invasion to unite the world and bring all under one government—is also a very compelling conspiracy theory. Dr. Greer has created several documentaries, both online and on demand, that will make you reconsider what you've always thought to be true.

A special thanks to J. K. Kelly—for his time, advice, and encouragement! I'm looking forward to his *Found in Time* sequel.

Lastly, I'd like to thank my family, both here and departed. Ma, Dad, Skip, John, and Lynne, you have all influenced me, from my dark and warped sense of humor and strong sense of stupid chivalry to my desire to entertain others with what I hope are colorful stories. It's all *your* fault. All my love.

www.ingramcontent.com/pod-product-compliance
Lightning Source LLC
Chambersburg PA
CBHW050349190726
48284CB00007BB/2205